Spandau Ballet

John-Michael Lander

First Edition

PAGE PUBLISHING, INC.
New York, NY

First originally published by Page Publishing, Inc. 2018

ISBN 978-1-64298-042-4 (Paperback)
ISBN 978-1-64298-043-1 (Digital)

Printed in the United States of America

I would like to dedicate this work of art to Nathan, my soul mate and life partner. Thank you for keeping me grounded and showing me I can follow my dreams.

I need to also acknowledge the following people for their encouragement and support: my team from Page Publishing, especially my literary development agent, Paula Breheny, and my publication coordinator, Danny Yarnell. Editor, Institute of Children Literature and Long Ridge Writers Group.

The people who have read many drafts: Nathan Webber, April Audia, Stacy Emoff, Skip Lang, David Moyer, Stephan Joseph, and Roy Bavaro. I want to thank the following for their support: Beth Klaisner, Illa and M. T. Taylor, and Mike and Judy Webber. Thanks to the following for their influence and encouragement: Patricia Nell Warren, Robin Reardon, Leanna Renee Hiebert, Katrina Kittle, and Rick Flynn.

A special thanks to Bella, Barkley, Bailey, and Bryn for their support and unconditional love.

Chapter 1

"Again!" Professor Weinholtz paced. "You're too erratic with your left hand, Master Klein. Make the melody smooth and steady, not choppy and uneven. Make the keys sing." He emphasized in a singsong manner while twirling his hands in the air.

I repositioned my fingers on the piano's keys that were bathing in the afternoon sun. I began the exercise for the third time today, but for some reason, the musician inside had taken a hiatus.

"What's this? Stop. Stop. Stop!" Professor Weinholtz's raspy voice echoed above the chords emitting from the belly of the black Wurlitzer grand piano. He leaned down next to my ear and whispered harshly, "Where's your mind today? You're not concentrating. Where's your focus?"

I stared at the keys.

"Speak!"

His voice caused me to snap my head to face him. His hair upon his head was tousled, bushy brows hid half of his pale blue eyes, and his chin blotched with patches of white hairs proving his inability to shave properly. He resembled a menacing old gray fox. A mixture of sweetness and stale cigarettes emitted from his breath as he stared and waited for an explanation.

Students' laughter floated in through the opened window. Josef Stork was down on the lawn, shirtless and tossing a ball to another lad. His chocolate ringlets bounced upon his head as he leaped to catch a high lob. His arms were fully extended, exposing the square swatches of dark hair. He caught the ball with ease and gracefully landed on the green grass. He smiled brightly, twisted his torso, and unleashed the ball high into the sky, sending the other student running for the catch.

"Is this where your mind is?" demanded the professor as he stepped into my field of vision, blocking Josef's image. His arms pressed firmly against his chest. "Why do you waste my time with this frivolous meandering?"

I couldn't speak, so I looked down at the keyboard.

"Do you know how lucky you are?" He untied the curtains and closed them, causing the room to dim. "Someone of your caliber and talent cannot become sidetracked with meaningless activities. You're a musician, Hans. You have potential to become an excellent pianist and perform all over the world. You're special, and yet you sit here half-heartedly attempting to practice your études, and the whole time you're thinking about tossing a ball with a half naked boy."

I chuckled.

"This isn't funny," he chided.

He walked to the center of the room and stood there silently until I looked up at him.

"I'll not continue until you remove that grin off your face," he calmly instructed in a deep voice. His hands rested on his hips.

I mechanically relinquished my grin and tried to appear as innocent as possible.

He ignored my feeble attempt to lighten the moment. "You've been displaying a lackadaisical attitude for some time now. You're not practicing the way you should. You're always coming in here late and not prepared. I'm at my wits' ends trying to figure you out. What's the meaning of all this?"

"I'm sorry, Professor Weinholtz." I lengthened my spine while sitting on the edge of the piano bench.

"That's not going to get the job done, my boy. You've got to want to be a musician. It just doesn't come easily. Yes, you have natural talent, and you are blessed. But that'll only get you so far. You've got to want it with all your heart and soul. You've got to eat, sleep, and breathe music in every moment of the day. It must consume you for you to become the best that you can be. Or otherwise, you'll only be mediocre. You could always find a job playing in a two-bit sleazy club for your bar tab or entertain your family on the holidays. If that's what you want to settle for, then fine. I can't make you want to become the best. That's all up to you. And if you aren't interested in achieving that goal, I'm sure I can fill your slot with someone who has less talent and more drive."

"No, sir," I automatically responded. We played this game every Monday. "It's just that it has been difficult lately with exams, and I'm feeling somewhat exhausted."

"That's understandable." His shoulders softened a bit as he rolled his head along the axis of his neck. "Yes, but that's when we need to buckle down and concentrate even harder so that we can achieve all that we can. Please play the piece that we've been working on." He retired to the overstuffed winged-back chair in the corner.

"Yes, sir." I opened the sheet music.

He smacked his lips with disdain, causing me to glance over at him. He was slouching against the back of the chair with his hands anchored across his chest, his lips pursed, and his eyes narrowed.

"Do we not have the music memorized by now?" his voice droned.

"It's almost memorized," I defended myself.

"Interesting." He ran a hand through his silver hair and cocked his head to the side, sending a very accusatory exhalation into the room. "When were you going to have it completely memorized?"

"I'll have it memorized. It's the last movement that I'm still having trouble."

"You have only a few days to have it completely memorized. You do realize that, don't you?"

"Yes, sir. I'll have it completely memorized, I promise."

"Fine." He shook his head to rid himself of any unpleasant thoughts. "Whenever you're ready and put a little more effort into it," he pleaded and fanned himself with a flare, as if trying to keep from fainting from the heat.

I positioned my foot on the bass peddle and rested my fingertips on the keys.

"Play it softly at first. Let the music gradually crescendo." He directed with one hand in the air while the other rested on his Adam's apple. "And a one, two, and three …"

I responded with my fingers pressing down on selected keys, causing harmonic tones to resound from the struck chords. The tones conformed into a melody, which filled the interior chamber and seeped out through the open window and down onto the surrounding yard. As the crescendo built and seeped out the confines of the studio, its musicality silenced the ball players, causing them to stop and listen to the free concert.

Professor Weinholtz smiled with pleasure, hugging himself as he stood and swayed to the rhythm, uttering a hushed "Yes." He closed his eyes and seemed to be floating on a musical carpet to a faraway land. His hands drifted into the thick air as he began to conduct an imaginary orchestra. "Yes, that is it, Hans. Feel it … Let it take you … Continue to connect the emotions. That's it … build it right here … A little more … Don't back away from it." He pantomimed playing the keys himself. "Yes, that's right, easy now … A little slower here … Let it seep through … gentle now." He whirled in front of the window, pulled back the curtain, and saw the boys standing still, listening. "That's just fine, my lad. Now let it play out. Don't push it here," he instructed.

I softly pressed the final chord as the piano's resonance retired to a deafening silence. I pulled my hands away from the keyboard, laid them gently on my thighs, released my held breath, lengthened my neck, and stared straight in front of me. I waited for the verdict to be summoned from my persistent critic. Nothing came. The only movement came from the curtains, slightly billowing from a gentle breeze.

I glanced over to find Professor Weinholtz had returned to the winged-back chair, lounging and fanning himself more vigorously than before. His hand blurred in the warm air, in front of his gaping mouth and closed eyes.

"Oh my, boy," he attempted to speak as his eyes fluttered open. "Now that's the way to play. Why don't you do that all the time?" He pulled his slumped body up and reached for a silver case that was waiting for him on the end table and flipped it open. "Please excuse me." He removed a thin cigarette rolled in peril paper and tipped with gold and placed it between his lips. "That'll be all for today." He waved me from the room, anticipating the lighting of the tobacco. "I want you to perform like that on Friday at the piano competition."

I gathered my satchel, slung its strap over my shoulder, and headed for the door.

"Leave the door open. It'll allow a breeze to come in." As I turned the crystal doorknob, he stopped me. "Master Klein?"

I looked back at him.

He lifted the match and lit the end of the wrapped paper. "That was superb." He expelled the words along with the blue smoke from his lungs.

"Thank you, Professor Wienholtz."

Chapter 2

I darted out, scaled down the stairs, and flung open the door to the outside world. A wall of heat welcomed me, and the sun's rays blinded me.

"Hey, Hans," a voice called from across the lawn.

I shielded my eyes from the brightness as Josef bounded toward me with glistening skin and the ball firmly held in one hand.

"Were you playing the piano?" He smiled brightly.

I glanced up at the opened window and saw the professor masking himself as he inhaled on the cigarette, causing the end to sizzle red.

"You mean up there?" I questioned.

"Yes, we could hear it out here."

The other lad appeared over Josef's right shoulder. His cropped hair burned copper and gold in the sun's rays, accentuating his square jaw. His large green eyes flashed behind the flutter of reddish-tinted eyelashes.

"You could?" I asked with embarrassment.

"It was good," responded Josef's friend.

"It was quite good," corrected Josef.

"Thank you." I started to walk off.

"Hey, we're going to the lake for a swim. Do you want to come?" invited Josef.

"I can't, Josef," the friend apologized. "I have to study for that Latin test tomorrow."

"Too bad for you then," Josef joked.

There was an awkward moment of silence as I tried to figure out who was this friend. I have never seen him on the school's grounds before, let alone with Josef. I was aware that Josef was very famous being the school's swimming champion and the best hope for next year's Olympic gold medal. He was a celebrity of sorts and always surrounded by people, usually other members of the swim team, housemates of Marcus Hall, or the fans who went to every swim meet to cheer him.

"Oh, I'm sorry." Josef broke the silence. "Hans, this is Karl Mastenburg. Karl, Hans Klein, the virtuoso." He smiled broadly at me.

Karl extended his hand over Josef's bare shoulder. "It's a pleasure. You sounded great."

I accepted his hand.

Josef inspected the connection happening above his shoulder.

"Thank you. It's nothing." I couldn't help but think that this was the closest I've ever been to Josef. I was in disbelief that he even spoke to me, let alone know that I existed. We've never uttered a word to each other since we started school, even though we had several classes together. I always managed to get a seat behind him or just off to the side, so I could glance over in his direction without being conspicuous. I found myself fascinated with his sideburns and how they seemed to be perfectly placed strains of dark thread that set off his perfectly shaped ears. Here he was, talking to me in the flesh, calling me by my whole name. I felt his breath and the heat from his sweating skin on my wrist. I smelled him as I inhaled deeply, a rich earthy musk.

As Karl's and my hand unclasped, I accidentally—but purposely—brushed against Josef's bare shoulder. The connection sent a jolt of electricity through my being. A thrill that only surpassed the many times my roommate, Stefan, and I witnessed Josef winning many swimming matches.

*****

"Which one is he?" Stefan strained his neck to see around the tall man with the large brimmed hat sitting in front of him.

We were among hundreds of people who came to witness the finals of the swimming championships at our school's outdoor

Olympic-size natatorium. The attendance was at maximum capacity, and tickets were near impossible. But since Professor Wienholtz was on the board of directors for the school, he was always provided with two tickets for the reserved seating.

Unfortunately, or rather fortunately for me, the professor didn't like to sit in the sun and felt that athletics was a waste of time and filled with animalistic qualities of competition. He was always qualifying this ideology with "If there were no competition, then young men wouldn't have the need to try and outdo each other, and the world would be a better place filled with peace and tranquility. I blame the Greeks for this barbarian display of inhumanity, encouraging naked young men to participate in sports for fame, for what, a laurel wreath of olive vines placed on their heads and a momentary and yet fleeting glimmer of glory? What a waste of a young man's mind."

So he always presented the tickets to me, knowing that I enjoyed such exhibitions. I gratefully accepted them every time and always dragged my roommate with me. I believe Stefan and I witnessed every race that Josef competed in, and yet we never officially met the Olympic prodigy.

"He's in lane 4 in the middle." I pointed toward the far end of the pool.

"The one that's just about to take his robe off?"

I silently nodded.

Josef slid the navy terry cloth robe from his shoulders to reveal his wool one-piece swimsuit with the school's crest embroidered on the chest. His dark hair was damp and pulled back from his face. His eyes were focused on the water as he stepped to the edge of the pool. He kneeled to test the temperature of the water with the tips of his fingers. As he reached the surface of the clear water, his back muscles rippled under the suit's straps, and his small waist bent further over, tilting his round firm buttocks into the air.

"May I have your attention please," the announcer's voice boomed over the loudspeakers. "This is the finals of the hundred-meter freestyle event. Swimmers, take your marks."

All six swimmers walked to the edge of the pool where there were numbers marked on the deck for each lane.

Josef rose from his kneeling position and sauntered to the number 4 mark, shaking out each leg as he went.

The audience hushed and held their breath.

The swimmers curled their toes over the edge of the pool and crouched down in the starting position.

Josef chose to use a runner's start, extending his left leg behind and the right leg in front with his toes gripping the pool's lip.

"On your mark. Get set."

The swimmers lowered their hips further down into the crouching position to provide the recoil needed from their legs to propel them forward.

"*Go!*"

The audience stood and erupted into a deafening roar as the competitors sprung forward in unison, flattening their bodies as much as possible to sail out over the pool before plunging into the water and stroking as fast and as hard as they could to complete the two laps of the fifty-meter pool.

Josef's strategy of the runner's start gave him an early advantage as he reached the farthest out across the water. While the others started their strokes, Josef was still gliding under the water's surface like a missile streamlining out in front. As his back broke the surface, he started kicking his legs and propelling his arms like paddles, which furthered his lead. His strokes were fast and even, reaching as far out in front of himself as permitted, and then pulling the cupped hands down along his body to push the water behind him and surge himself forward. His rhythm was precise and efficient. His strokes were smooth and seamless. He was not exerting any excess energy, and yet he pulled farther ahead.

He reached the wall of the fifty meters first, turned, and headed back to the starting place. As he retraced the same path, he passed the others still trying to reach the wall. The distance between him and the others was widening with every stroke. He kicked harder and rotated his arms faster as he approached the finish line. He slammed his hand on the wall, accentuating his victory.

The crowd rejoiced with thunderous applause and chants as Josef waved victoriously.

*****

"I hate to say it, but I'm going to have to leave you two," confessed Karl, "because if I don't get back to the dorm to study, Proctor Jacobs is going to have my ass." He laughed at his joke and patted Josef on the back. "Oh, pal, you're sweaty." He wiped his palm on the seat of Josef's trousers. "It was nice meeting you, Hans, and I'll catch up with you later at dinner, Josef." He darted off across the lawn toward Marcus Hall, the dormitory that housed the swim team and other athletes.

"Well, that leaves you and me. Would you like to go swimming and cool off?" Josef asked with barely parting his lips.

Another jolt of energy flooded my insides, sending a flushing wave of warmth throughout my body and emitting out through my cheeks. "I don't have a swimsuit," I coyly responded, trying to hide my reddening blush.

"Who cares?" With that, he whipped around and started jogging toward the direction of the lake, leaving me steadfast in my oxford shoes. Halfway across the lawn, he tossed his chocolate-curled head around to glance over his shoulder and called, "Come on. What are you waiting for?"

Without thinking, I started after him. But midway across the greens, I halted and looked back at Professor Weinholtz's window. He flicked the cigarette butt out the window, shook his head slowly, and closed his eyes. He motioned me on with a wave of his hand before disappearing back into the shadow of the room.

"Come on, Klein," Josef called from the other side of the road.

I ran, and my tie flagged over my shoulder. I paused at the curb as an old brown truck, stuffed with students in the cab, was speeding. One student leaned out of the passenger's window, shouting, "Hans, we're going to town. What to come?" Stefan Joffe, my roommate, was sitting on the frame of the open window, his hair tossing in the wind. Walter was driving with Petre beside him, and Ian was holding on to Stefan to keep him from tumbling out. Before I could answer, Ian pulled Stefan back into the cab, and they whizzed by without stopping.

I waved as a cloud of dust bathed me.

As the swirling brownness cleared, Josef waited at the edge of the woods that led to the lake. He motioned for me to follow before he disappeared down the path concealed by the thickness of trees.

Chapter 3

"Hurry up, we don't have all day," Josef called.

I made my way along the worn and winding path toward the lake and turned right by the big old oak tree. A single shoe was helplessly on its side next to the tree's twisted roots. I stopped, picked it up, and slipped it into my satchel.

Ahead, the path ascended a sharp hill where the clearing spanned out to the lake. At the top of the hill, I discovered the other abandoned shoe. I gathered it as well and stuffed it alongside its mate.

I made my way through the clearing of tall wheat grass. Giant green grasshoppers sprang high in the late afternoon sky as I forged through. Birds squawked above as they swooped down, attempting to grab the flying insects before darting back up into the bright blueness. I came across a single sock, suspended atop the blades of tall grass. I rescued it and continued.

"Bombs away!" Josef yelled, followed by the sound of splashing water.

Heated excitement exploded inside me, encouraging me toward the splashing echo. I quickly made my way through the uneven terrain and came upon the embankment where Josef's wadded pants with one leg turned inside out and a pair of carelessly discarded white cotton undergarment. I retrieved the balled-up warm undergarment and inhaled an intoxicating, earthy musk transcending from the cotton fibers. My mind spun in a kaleidoscope of senses causing my knees to buckle.

"Hey, Hans, this is great."

Across the lake on a towering jagged rock that extended high over the murky blue water was Josef. All he wore was a huge grin with shiny stars glistening from the sun's reflection off the water dripping down his naked body. He giggled and projected himself off the rock, sailing over the calm water, curling his knees to his chest into a tight ball before crashing through the surface, sending a tall and narrow eruption into the air. The upsurge panned out like a mushroom and showered the surrounding area with rain. A breeze carried a mist across the lake and refreshed my face with its coolness.

"Ah, this is great!" He confirmed again as he bobbed in the water. "Hurry up!" He floated on his back like an otter.

I removed my satchel from my shoulder, dropping it along with Josef's undergarment next to his tangled pants on the ground. I removed my black and white oxford shoes that had gotten splattered with mud on my travels. My heart was beating fast and uneven, and I was having trouble catching my breath. The more I removed my clothing, the more I felt my pulse race. Sweat started beading on my forehead and other areas of my body, adding to my clamminess.

I pulled my jacket off, looking out at Josef laughing and paddling in circles on his back. His tanned skin merged and submerged from beneath the liquid's crest. He rolled over and dove down, lifting his hips and exposing his pale buttock as his sun-kissed legs extend into the air before being swallowed by the lake.

I fumbled with unbuttoning my shirt, freeing it from behind the waist of my pants. I tugged it off over my head and dropped it on top of my satchel. The golden cross necklace adhered to my damp skin directly over my pulsating heart. I unbuckled my belt, pulling both my pants and undergarment off in one quick move. The warm breeze caressed my nakedness.

I darted toward the rock from where Josef had plunged, jogging around the parameter of the lake and skipping over rocks, twigs, and plants. Mud squished between my toes as my feet pounded along the shore, sending brown and gritty droplets upward to speckle my naked skin.

I didn't hesitate when I reached the base of the huge rock, but scaled the jagged edges to its peak. It only took me a few seconds before I was standing on the edge, with my toes curled over the rock's lip. I was on top of the world looking out over trees dressed in lush green leaves and isolating the lake. Various varieties of flowering plants brought bright colors to accent the rippling surface along the embankment. Josef gleefully frolicked in the waters below.

My mind swirled, legs became unstable, and hands reached out to the sides for balance. My vision retracted, sending the lake to appear like a small puddle of water.

"All right, Hans. Go for it," encouraged Josef.

Without thinking, I leaped from the rock. My projection sent me high above the water, and Josef screamed his encouragements. During my flight, which seemed to proceed in slow motion, my heart stopped beating, lungs stopped breathing, and blood was no longer pumping. The golden cross suspended before my eyes, frozen in time by defying gravity. I wasn't aware of my descent or any sense of falling. Suddenly, the water swallowed me with its shocking coldness, immediately turning my body numb. My limbs lost their ability to move, and I sank into the murky darkness like a ton of bricks.

The golden cross and its chain drifted past my limited field of vision. I reached for its glittering form as it spiraled up and way and blended amid the halos of light rippling above me. I defied the odds and grasped in the general area that the cross was last seen, hoping that I could retrieve it. To my surprise, I felt the metal embed into the fleshiness of my palm.

My knees sank into the muddiness of the bottom. I lingered there with my arms floating, watching the dancing lights above, and breathing in lake water as if it was oxygen. For a slight moment, I was free. I could live and breathe on the bottom of the lake. I felt at peace, and then complete darkness.

Chapter 4

Amid a darkened fog, a spark of fire ignited in the depths of my lungs, culminating in a convulsive cough and releasing a mouthful of lake water. I pried open my eyes and saw Josef looking down at me.

"Welcome back, kiddo. I think you drank half the lake," Josef jokingly said. I tried to sit up, but he kept my shoulders down. "Calm down, Hans."

"What hap—" Another rush of water welled, churned, and violently erupted upward, forcing me to vomit between my legs. Josef held me as I spat and sputtered, tasting the metallic remnants of my afternoon libation. My lungs burned and muscles ached. I inhaled deeply when another surge percolated in my stomach and purged again. My face contorted and reddened from trying to deter another mouth full of foul and dirty liquid. But to my dismay, the pressure spewed up and out, projecting a dry heave of nothingness.

Josef maneuvered behind me, extending his legs alongside mine, compressing his hips and chest against my back. He reached one arm over my shoulder and held my head while wrapping the other arm around my torso. He rested his chin on my shoulder, and his warm breath caressed alongside my neck. Tension crippled every muscle as I realized that a man was holding me.

"It's all right, just take easy breaths," he instructed.

I attempted another deep breath, feeling the abdominals twisting and knotting, which momentarily caused me to forget about the rapture of my religious teachings. I grasped his ankles for support as I lurched forward, projecting another bout of nothingness.

"That's it. You're going to be fine. You got it all out."

The nausea subsided. The birds' familiar chirping became audible again, as did the soothing sounds of a distant waterfall. Josef's warmth blanketed my backside while the sun bathed the front.

"Everything's going to be all right," he whispered. "Just relax."

A deep cough caused me to grab my throat. A moment of complete desperation overtook me as I felt for my golden cross necklace. My spine stiffened, and I stopped breathing; it was missing.

"What is it?" questioned Josef.

"My … my …" was all I could get out. I started swinging my head from side to side to see if it was lying on the ground somewhere.

"What's wrong?"

"I don't have—" I pointed toward my neck, trying to pantomime the necklace.

"What?"

"My … golden cross," I finally blurted out.

"You must mean this?" He opened his hand, and there nested against his palm was my cross necklace.

"Thank God!" I took and kissed it before sliding it over my head and positioning the cross against my chest.

"That must be valuable."

"My mother gave it to me."

He reached up and examined the golden cross, twirling it between his thumb and forefinger. He turned it around and saw the inscription on the back side. "What does this say?" He leaned in closer and read, "Remember from where you came/ Dance on." He glanced up with a quizzical expression.

"My mother was a dancer," I explained.

"I see." He released the cross to twirl back against my chest.

I placed a hand over it to cease the motion.

"Now, will you relax?"

I nodded and relinquished back against his chest. I instantly felt, at that moment, everything was all right. There was nothing wrong with a "friend" holding you completely naked while you vomit up ingested lake water. Then it dawned on me; we were both naked.

"What if someone sees us?" I asked.

He tightened his hold. "No one's going to see us. We're all alone."

My muscles eased a moment and then quickly riddled with another anxious attack. "What if someone finds out?"

"How?" he uttered softly in my ear.

I tried to pull away. "I don't know, but what if someone finds out somehow?"

"Relax, no one's going to know—unless you tell them. And if you do that, I may just have to kill you myself," Josef joked.

I quickly turned toward him. "Why would I tell anyone?"

"So then we don't have a problem. If you aren't going to tell anyone and I'm not going to tell anyone, then how can anyone find out?"

"But what if they do somehow?"

"They're not going to."

"Are you sure?"

"Trust me. There's no one here but us and those pair of eyes in the brush over there."

I jerked around. "Where?"

"Over there!"

I quickly glanced, and he tightened his wrap around me. "Where?"

"There!"

A rabbit hopped out from behind the brush and scampered off into the woods.

Josef let out a whale of a laugh that echoed throughout the lake. "You worry too much. Relax. We aren't doing anything wrong."

I gave in, knowing he was correct, and leaned my head against his cheek while his chin rested on my shoulder. His lips grazed my earlobe as they gently parted with every breath. His diaphragm expanded against the small of my back with each inhalation. The hairs lacing around his ankles were soft where my hands encased for support. I didn't want to move. I closed my eyes so I could remember this feeling and never forget the sounds of the lake, the warmth of the sun, and the comfort of being held by Josef.

"What's that smell?" I asked while remaining in my utopia.

"What?" he responded, giving evidence that he didn't want to move either.

"That stench, it smells like rotting eggs."

"Oh, that." His cheeks pulled back to form a grin. "That would be your vomit."

"Vomit?" I opened my eyes. There in front of me, in a splattered display of ugliness and occupying the ground between my legs, were the remnants of my afternoon lunch diluted with the mixture of murky lake water, exposed for all to see. On an even closer inspection, I found chunks of chewed particles clinging to my stomach, crotch, and thighs.

"Oh, shit." I tried to get up.

"It's all right." He tightened his arms and legs to keep me in place.

"But it's all over me," I muttered.

"Just sit here a moment longer, and we'll get it cleaned up." He nuzzled the nape of my neck with his chin like a puppy.

I gave in to his plea and settled back into the human blanket.

He whispered, "You smell good."

"That's it. I can't take this any longer. I stink. I'm revolting!" I snaked out from his enwrapped appendages and crawled away on my hands and knees.

He sat still in the same position as if I never left. The sun reflected strands of auburn and red in his chocolate curls that accentuate his cheekbones. His large doe eyes sparkled from under the chestnut lashes and thick brows. His thin, straight nose traveled down the center of his face and came to rest above a full mouth. His fleshy lips were permanently presenting a contagious smile, revealing straight white teeth. His sharp jaw circled down symmetrically into a gentle curve to form his chin. Broad shoulders sprouted out from his thick neck and tapered down into a small waist. A sprout of fuzz fingered his flat stomach and spanned downward as it gathered into a mesh of dark curls, accentuating a flaccid and thick penis. Tiny hairs laced his defined legs, circled his thighs, and snuck into the dark cavern between his buttocks. He sat there innocently with the glow of the afternoon sun all around him.

I attempted to stand, but my legs were unsteady, and my knees buckled, sending me to the earth again. He extended his hand toward me. I took a hold as he gave me leverage to stand. We became frozen as we considered each other's eyes.

"You know, you're right," he confessed as he didn't break eye contact. "You do smell."

"Oh yeah?"

"Unfortunately, you do."

"Thank you."

"Not a problem."

Without any indication, I wrapped my arms around his wide shoulders, pinning his arms underneath mine and pulling him into my body. "Now we both stink." I pressed my hips and thighs against him.

"You didn't." He attempted to wiggle away.

I restrained him.

He broke my hold, hoisted me off my feet, and scooped me over his shoulder. "There's only one way to take care of this." He slapped my bare butt and carried me to the water's edge.

"No." I squirmed.

He continued making his way to the lake.

"Stop, okay. Put me down."

He kept walking.

"No. I'm serious." I kicked my legs.

"Don't worry. I'm not going to throw you in." He lowered me into ankle-deep water.

The muddy bottom squished between my toes.

Josef cupped a handful of lake water and gently poured it onto my stomach to wash the vomit away, causing me to retreat from its coldness. He gathered another handful and rinsed my blondish bush, carefully not contacting my genitals. He smiled up at me and presented his hands as if he had created magic, making it all disappear.

As he stood, his legs darkened from the water weighing the hairs against his flesh. My eyes became fixated upon the tubular thickness of his penis sprouting from the drenched triangular patch of curls. I felt his gaze.

He flashed a grin and said, "Come on, let's get out of here. You're shivering." He jogged out of the water, lifting his legs high like a deer prancing through the snow. He plopped himself onto a grassy area directly under the sun.

I carefully waded out, fearing that I might slip on algae or the muddy bottom. As I made my way to the grassy area, I was in awe with how beautiful he looked absorbing the sun's warmth. He was uninhibited and vulnerable, using one arm to prop his head up while the other rested on his stomach. One leg was bent, so his ankle tucked under the knee of the other stretched-out leg. He reminded me of a combination of the Greek mythological warriors, as if the courage from Achilles, the might of Heracles, and the endurance of Marathon have all come together to create him. His face was calm and serene with his eyes closed. He looked so peaceful as if death had overtaken his youth and was preserving it forever in my mind.

I lowered myself next to him and pretended that I wasn't affected by his apparent beauty. But I couldn't help but gaze at his lips, which were tempting, full, tinted crimson, and surrounded by the flecks of emerging dark stubble. I immediately closed my eyes so I wouldn't be tempted to stare at his firm and sculpted nakedness.

"This is so much more relaxing than sitting in a classroom. I could stay here forever."

"Yes." I tried not to think about him.

"How are you feeling?" The grass rustled as if he repositioned himself.

I kept my eyes closed.

"Are you all right?" he asked.

"I'm all right." I was refusing to open my eyes.

"That was something else. The way you flew up to the top of that rock. The way you leaped off as if you've been doing it for years. I had no idea that—then you cannonballed and made a huge splash, and then you didn't come up. I kept waiting and waiting. But there was nothing. I thought you were playing a trick. I thought you were swimming around under the water and were going to ambush me from behind."

"I know, I know. I don't know what was going on in my head." I pinched my eyes tighter and rolled away from him.

"So what happened?" he timidly asked.

"I can't swim." I simply and quickly blurted out my confession. I buried my face behind the palms of my hands.

"Seriously?"

"Seriously, I can't swim," I announced with defeat.

Josef grabbed my shoulder and guided me onto my back. He lifted my protective shield from my face, took hold of my right hand, and examined the palm. "That makes us even because I can't play the piano," he stated as a matter of fact.

I peered from under my squinting eyes as he turned my hand over and traced the veins with his thumb, traveling to the nail of each finger. He pressed his palm against mine, intertwined our fingers, and folded our hands together. "Your hands are amazing."

"Why do you say that?"

"It's amazing that these fingers can push on selected keys on a piano and make incredible music." His thumb rubbed against the belly of my palm. "What do you want to do with your talent?"

"I don't know. Play all over the world, I guess."

"You're certainly good enough."

"What about you?" I rolled onto my side, facing him. "What do you want to do?"

"Well ..." He reclined on his back again, placed my hand on his warm chest, and anchored his fingers around my thumb. "After winning a gold medal in swimming at the next Olympics, I want to maybe go into politics or the military or something like that."

The vibrations of his voice rumbled through his chest cavity.

"That sounds impressive."

"The military?" he boasted.

"No, the Olympics," I corrected him.

"That's my dream."

"You're definitely good enough to win a gold medal, with all the races you have been winning." I wanted to boast that I've been witness to every one of his victories for the past several years, but I thought it might seem too desperate.

"Have you seen me race?" He propped up his head with interest.

"I've had the fortune to see you swim a couple of times," I modestly responded.

"Did you see the finals of the one hundred meters freestyle?"

"Yes, I did."

"What'd you think?"

"It was a nice swim."

"Nice?" He sat up, letting go of my hand, causing it to flop onto his thigh.

"Yes, it was nice that you won," I ambivalently tossed off.

"Are you serious?"

"I'm teasing." I sat up next to him. "It was one of the most amazing things I've ever seen. The way you flew out over the water at the start and how you defeated the competition without any trouble. There was no one even near you when you hit the wall." I imitated the way he hit the wall when he won by forcing my hand against his thigh. My face flushed with excitement.

"You were there?"

"I was there. I wouldn't have missed it."

He looked at me before grinning and plopping himself back down on the ground. He grabbed my hand again and replaced it on his chest. "That's something," he muttered.

We lay there in silence as a ladybug landed on his shoulder. He didn't even feel the insect as it circled on itself with its little black legs before parting the red shell wings adorned with two black dots and lifted itself off into the air.

I watched his chest rise and fall with each inhalation. What did all this mean? There was this strange and new feeling of comfort lying here naked next to Josef, out in the open, and with my hand on his chest. It felt right that he had his fingers holding my thumb. It felt so good that we were alone. This feeling reached deeper within me, causing me to want to be next to him. Was this wrong? I didn't even know this lad. What would the others think of this? We weren't doing anything wrong. We were just soaking up the sun. I'd never felt this close to anyone before except for Inga. Even though Inga and I developed our closeness from spending hours upon hours sharing our beliefs and future dreams, this was something deeper, richer—more intoxicating.

*****

I was in the middle of the final movement of Mozart's Ninth Symphony when something caught my eye from behind the doorway leading to the billiard room. As I quickly glanced over, Inga held up a basket and mouthed something to me. I squinted and mouthed back, "What?" I couldn't wait for her response. I had to look back and scanned the bottom of the sheet music to relocate my place within the staff of dancing notes. I recognized the ascending sixteenth notes just in time to turn the page. Once the page flipped, I glimpsed back over to where Inga was prancing in a circle. This time she moved her lips slower, overemphasizing each word. "Come … with … me." I responded with acknowledgment by gently nodding my head and smirking. She flashed a huge smile and disappeared behind the framing of the door.

The guests' eyes were on my back, anticipating the final chord, and the sound lofted high up among the beams of the ceiling.

I stood and turned to a warm and polite applause from the gathering of friends and family.

Mr. Rhoden walked to the front of the stage and placed his large hand on my shoulder. "Wasn't that amazing?" The gathering politely responded with more applause.

I took a slight bow and was about to exit toward the door that led to the billiard room when Mr. Rhoden tightened his grip.

"Every time I hear Hans play, I'm in utter amazement that someone of this caliber could have been living under my roof these past few years. It's truly a blessing to have him become part of our family. I've loved him like a son. I want to thank Father Michael and Sister Margot for bringing this child into our lives—if it weren't for your continuous hard work, we wouldn't be here today listening to this talented child." Mr. Rhoden extended his free hand toward Father Michael and Sister Margot, who were sitting amid the gathered guests and nodded back with respect.

"And I'm also so honored to have Professor Weinholtz, the man who has been tutoring Hans this summer and will be his mentor at the academy for the next four years with us here today as well. Thank you so much for taking time out of your busy schedule to come here and be a part of this celebration."

"I wouldn't have missed it for the world," Professor Weinholtz remarked as he cooled himself with a makeshift paper fan and smiled toward me.

I nodded back and started for the door again when Mr. Rhoden's hand squeezed tighter, impeding my second attempt at exiting.

"There's a lot of food, so please make yourselves comfortable. I'm so pleased that Mr. Quackenhurst has given us the run of the clubhouse. I don't think we could have fit in our bungalow. And to all the other residences of the Lake View Cottage Community who have provided the food and goodies that are awaiting you, I thank you all."

His grasp eased, and I slipped out the side doorway, leaving the guests as they rose from their seats and started milling around, talking to one another.

When I turned the corner, Inga was nowhere to be found. I hurried through the billiard room, rounding the large billiard tables covered with protective plastic. I headed for the back screened door and pushed it open, feeling the late summer's humidity push against me and steal my breath.

I leaped from the wooden porch and landed on the grassy lawn, frozen with the confusion of which way to head since I couldn't locate Inga.

She was leaning against a wooden post on the porch, giggling. "You flew out of the house so fast, you didn't even see me standing here," she stated mockingly.

"I was trying to catch up with you," I defended.

"Well, here I am," she said with her full cherry lips barely parting. She gently slinked down the two steps onto the lawn and walked right up to me. Lilac perfume emitted from her. She gently pressed her chest against mine, leaning in close that I thought she was going to kiss me, but she whispered, "I want to show you something."

She grabbed my hand and yanked me so hard that I stumbled to keep upright. She led us into a trot across the backyard and toward the winding path through the woods toward the lake.

"Hans!" a deep rich voice called from the clubhouse.

"Don't stop," pleaded Inga as she tugged on my arm.

"But it's Father Michael."

"Let's pretend we didn't hear him," she uttered. She kept focused on the winding path canopied with green leaves.

"He's already seen us and is waving me back."

"You stay then. I'm going on," she threatened.

I tightened my hand, which stopped her.

"Don't give me those puppy eyes."

I continued to portray the sympathy card until she rolled her eyes and whispered, "All right, meet me at the boathouse. But don't take too long, I'm not going to wait all day." She waved and politely said, "Hello, Father Michael. It was wonderful that you could come today."

"It was my pleasure, Inga. Thank you for the invitation." He smiled with graciousness.

"We couldn't have had a celebration without inviting you. It was you who arranged for Hans to come and live with us, and we're so ever grateful." She flashed me a crooked smile and batted her eyelashes. "If you would excuse me, Father, there are some things that I need to gather before Hans's trip tomorrow."

"Oh, don't let me hold you up. I just wanted to say goodbye. Sister Martha and I have to start our way back to the city." His eyes glistened with kindness.

"I'll see you again soon." Inga kissed him politely on the cheek while glancing at me from the corner of her eye.

Father Michael's face reddened. "Bless you, child." He returned a gentle kiss to her cheek.

Inga took a moment to look at both the Father and myself before she turned and started along the winding path and disappeared behind the foliage and brush of the woods.

"You two have become close, it appears," the Father said.

"Yes, we have," I replied.

Father Michael stood there for a long while without saying a word. His wavering hazel eyes couldn't remain focused on any one thing for very long before darting to focus on something new for a flighty moment. Finally, he took a deep breath and concentrated on the bench that was just to the right of the pathway, resting in the shade of a large elm tree.

"Could we sit for a moment?" he asked.

"Of course, Father."

"Thank you." He moved with determination toward the bench and stood to the side of it, offering for me to sit first.

His entire black outerwear—pants, shirt, jacket, and the accent of the white collar—were hiding a well-shaped man of about thirty-five years old. His temples began to edge with a touch of grayness against the waves of brunette hair that accentuated his sun-kissed cheeks. It dawned on me at that moment that he must've been young when I first met him. He and Sister Margot took me in under my mother's instructions for a while until they could place me with the Rhoden family.

Father Michael's large hand offering the seat was exposing his palm against the weather-beaten bench. This exposure reminded me of the fleshiness of Christ's palms affixed to the wooden cross. I wanted to touch the underbelly of his offered hand but knew that I never could.

I lowered myself on the bench.

He cautiously sat beside me, properly aligning himself with his feet flat on the ground, knees tightly together and hands positioned on his lap with fingers interlaced as if he was about to pray. The shape of his legs seemed confined beneath the clasped hands and black fabric as they tapered downward, expanding the material as they curved to exhibit the kneecaps, and then disappearing beneath the pleat of the pants. His back was rigid, and his eyes were focused on the clubhouse. He began speaking in a soft voice that was almost inaudible against the screeching and the calling from the birds in the woods.

"It has almost been twelve years since I first met you. You had just turned three years old when you came to St. Emmanuel's. You were so little, scared, and confused after all that you had experienced.

You were such a good child, like a little angel, never giving us any trouble." He glanced at me with a warm smile and nodded his head. "Tomorrow you begin a new chapter in your young life, going off to the academy. How impressive. You do realize how important this is?"

I nodded.

"You've turned into an outstanding young man, Hans. Your mother would've been proud, extremely proud. It saddens me that she's not able to be here today. I know how much she would." His eyes filled with sadness, and I automatically reached over and placed my hand on his knee. He stiffened and glanced down at the placement. He said nothing about the contact and didn't try to deter it. He placed his hand on top of mine. Warmth emitted from his palm and sunk into my knuckles. I looked at his hand and followed the blue veins that looked like little curving roads traveling from beneath the cuff of his jacket and spanning out to each finger. A rush of wind swirled around our ankles and blew up the trunk of the tree, rustling the leaves above us.

He removed his hand, reached into his jacket pocket, and pulled out a small wrapped package. The box seemed to weigh a ton. "Upon your mother's instructions, she wanted you to have this when it seemed to be a significant time." He placed the wrapped box into my palm. "I see nothing more important than the fact that you're going to the academy tomorrow and beginning to follow your dream of becoming a concert pianist."

He took a deep breath and slowly allowed it to expel through his tense lips that made a slight whistling sound. "I remember when we first found out that you were interested in music. You were about five, it was after morning mass, and we couldn't locate you because you had slipped away. Sister Margot and I were in the office, and we began to hear this strange form of music coming from the apse. It filled the rafters and was so sweet. When we rushed out to see who was creating such music, we discovered you. You were sitting on the organ's bench, your feet couldn't touch the pedals, yet you were creating chords that were simply beautiful. I don't think you were quite aware of what you were doing or the magnitude of that moment. It was like you were in another world, playing and content." He chuckled at the recreation of the image inside his mind. "I asked you what you were doing, and you said that you were playing music. You didn't say that you were making or creating music. You were just playing music. That's when we knew you needed to be somewhere where you could explore your hidden talents. And from that day forward, you were constantly 'playing' music. We couldn't have stopped you, which we didn't want to stop you—we encouraged you."

I just stared at the wrapped box in my hand, half listening to Father Michael, not knowing what I should do or how I should react.

"It's all right, go ahead," encouraged the Father.

"What is it?" I asked hesitantly.

"Open it and find out," he instructed.

I untied the ribbon and unwrapped the light blue decorative paper, putting it aside without ripping it. The box was brown and no larger than a ring box, and the lid easily slid off to the side. Inside was a puff of white cotton stuffing, protecting the most beautiful golden cross that I had ever seen. As I lifted the gold chain, the finely polished cross twirled in midair and sent shards of golden sparks across the lawn.

"Here, let me put it on for you," instructed Father Michael.

I swiveled my back to him. He reached around and lowered the cross in front of my face, past my chin, and allowed it to come to rest on my chest. He interlocked the clasp behind my neck and placed his palms on my shoulders. "There, that should do it."

"It's beautiful." I lightly touched the gold.

A voice rang from the porch of the clubhouse. "Father Michael, we must be going soon." Sister Margot, dressed in her habit and aglow from the warm light producing from inside the clubhouse, stood holding her palms together.

I rushed to her side and threw my arms around her short rounded body. She smelled of musk that she dabbed on her neck every morning. She hugged me back as tight as her stubby arms could reach and kissed my cheek. "We're surely going to miss you."

"We are," said Father Michael. He placed his hand on my shoulder.

I wrapped him in my arms with an intensity of not wanting to let go.

"Now, it's going to be all right. We'll see each other again." He encouraged, "You'll be coming home for holidays, and maybe Sister Margot and I can come up to the school when you have a concert or something."

"You will?" I asked like a child who wanted an ice cream cone.

"Of course we will," promised Sister Margot. "But it's now time for us to get back so that we can get prepared for mass."

Father Michael tightened his arms one last time before releasing me. "We'll be in touch. You must do well in your classes and write to us," said Father Michael.

"I will."

"Promise," he demanded.

I smiled sadly and crossed my heart. "I promise."

"Until next time, son," he said. He kissed my cheek and immediately walked through the door.

"Take care of yourself, Hans. And if you ever need anything, contact us," said Sister Margot. She patted my hand and kissed it. Her hand slipped away, and she went inside.

I was alone on the porch of the clubhouse, wanting to cry and maybe needing to cry, but not allowing myself to express it. I quickly looked toward the path leading into the woods, to the boathouse, and to Inga waiting there for me.

I was winding along the path embellished with marigolds on both sides, wild berries of red and blue, and trees arching high above me, creating a natural ceiling of green. Evidence of the summer's end displayed a single leaf on the path with red hues spanning out from its core and pushing the greenness to its tips. I wanted to keep it to remind me of this day of change. As I bent down to pick it up, the golden cross dangled from around my neck and twirled in midair. An unexpected gust of wind whipped along the path, lifted the leaf, and carried it off into the thick brush. Another threatening burst of air streamed past, gathering bits of dirt, leaves, and twigs, and sent them spiraling upward in a vortex that reached the top of the trees and released the materials to rain back down onto the earth.

As I reached the clearing to the lake, the distinguished honks of ducks as they flew overhead in a perfect V-shaped pattern cast moving shadows on the ground. They dipped down toward the lake's crest, extending their webbed feet for a splashy landing. The birds skimmed the surface of the water and then veered upward, lifting themselves toward the ominous gray clouds that were rolling in from the south and blanketing the blue sky.

A damp and mildew aroma greeted me as I pushed the boathouse door open.

"It's about time," Inga stated as she sat by the window that was bleeding with late afternoon rays. "I almost gave up on you."

"No, you didn't. You knew I was going to be here." I closed the door behind me.

"No, I didn't," she continued to play. "How would I know that?"

"Because I always do what you say."

She smiled coyly. "Maybe you got scared." She motioned me to come to her.

I followed the command like a puppy, wanting to make her happy.

The grayness of the clouds started to darken the outside world, sending a moving shadow across the window. I stopped and wondered, what was this game we were playing this time? I've spent nearly my whole life in the same house with Inga, and she was always the oldest and wisest. We've always been inseparable. We hid under the blankets when it stormed outside, told scary stories late at night, and we climbed into each other's bed when we couldn't sleep. We talked about everything: our futures, dreams, and what we wanted to be when we grew up. We created a secret world and a secret language between us. Nothing was ever going to tear us apart.

This day was different. There was a different feeling in the air. I felt a nervousness that I had never experienced and was not sure of how to handle.

"It's all right. I'm not going to bite you," Inga teased.

Gravity took hold of my feet, not allowing me to move any farther. Uncertainty, fear, and strangeness draped themselves around me. My heart pulsed harder and faster, sweat speckled my forehead and neck, and my mouth became parched.

The wind outside the window picked up, stripping the trees of their leaves and sending them scattering across the lake. A twig slammed against the window pane, causing me to jump.

"Relax," she uttered. She came nearer to me.

"What's going on?" I stammered.

"Nothing." She dropped her head to the side and curled her red lips.

"Why are you acting like this?" I could hardly get the words out of my dry mouth.

"Do you like it?" she asked. She allowed the thin strap of her dress to fall from her shoulder.

"What?"

"This." She ran her fingers down her neck and over her collarbone. She didn't wait for an answer when I felt her lean against my chest.

"Yeah, I guess so." I took a step back.

"You guess so?" She laughed and pressed harder against me. Her hand brushed against my thigh. "Hans, I like you."

"I like you too." I took another step back and ran into a pillar.

"You do?"

"Sure. But what if someone comes in?"

"No one will," she assured me.

"But what if someone does?"

"Everyone's busy at the party." She moved in and nestled against my neck with her chin. "So, you like me?"

"Sure."

"Good." She pressed her hips, chest, and forehead against me. The lilac scent made me dizzy. She tilted her head, closed her eyes, and placed her moist lips on mine.

I froze.

"What's this?" She cupped the golden cross in her palm.

I retrieved the gift and twirled it between my thumb and finger. "Father Michael gave it to me. It's from my mom."

"How sweet," she whispered. She rested her head on my shoulder and took my hand. She leaned in again and lightly kissed the cross and then glanced up at me from under her brows. She lifted my hand and placed it on her breast, cupping my fingers around her swollenness. She felt full beneath the firmness of the material and the wired bra.

Could this be my first "real" kiss? I never imaged it like this. It was supposed to be like in the movies with a young starlet, not someone who was older than me and from someone whom I thought of like my sister. I've always imagined it to be when I was rich and famous, and it'd take place in Paris or Rome, not in a boathouse at the Lake View Cottage Community.

"Mmmm, that's nice." Her lips continued to caress mine. "Do you like that?"

"I guess—" I tried to say, but she stifled my words with her lips again.

The wind picked up, and the clouds thickened, snuffing out the streams of light. Inga softly moaned. My mind raced, and I started to panic. What should I do? Then it came to me: do like they do in the movies. I reached up and grabbed her head and pressed my mouth hard against hers. Her lips parted, so I parted my lips. Her tongue darted into my open mouth. I was shocked and pulled away. She grabbed my head and invaded my mouth again with her thin tongue as she tried to suck all the life out of me.

I pulled back from her, my mouth stinging and covered with spit.

Inga looked at me, her mouth smeared with lipstick, and she was so close that she appeared cross-eyed. I almost laughed—but I managed to contain it when I saw the seriousness in her face.

"Don't you like this?" She sounded hurt and disgruntled.

I became defensive. "No, it's fine."

"Just fine?" Her head darted back away from mine.

"No, it's good." I licked my lip to see if it was bleeding.

She cocked her head to the side. "Really?"

A clap of thunder sounded in the far side of the lake and caused me to glance out the window.

She whipped her head to see what I was looking at and then back at me and announced accusingly, "You aren't into this."

"What?"

"You aren't into this, are you?"

"What do you mean?"

"This isn't getting you going, is it?"

"Going where?" I stupidly asked.

"Oh my … How could I've been so stupid?" She started to pull away, but I prevented her escape.

"What are you talking about?"

"You're not into kissing girls," she said with much discovery.

"No, what? No, it's not like that."

"Then how can you explain it?"

Outside the clouds began to shower the land.

"I was nervous … I wasn't sure what you wanted me to do. I was simply not ready."

She walked to the window and watched the rain.

I walked up behind her. My palms were wet. I needed to redeem myself for some reason, and I had to do it now. "May I try again, now that I know what you want?"

She looked over her shoulder, her eyes sparkled against the dark sky, and she smiled. She rose and draped her arms around my neck. "Ready whenever you are." She threw her head back, exposing her long neck, and closed her eyes with much anticipation.

I surprised myself. Without thinking, I guided my tongue up the side of her neck to the base of her ear.

She gently moaned.

I wrapped my lips around her earlobe, causing her to whip her head and send locks of auburn curls across my face. She intensely stared at me with her piercing eyes, quivering lips, and flushed cheeks.

I tentatively placed my lips on hers. I felt the oddness of the moment as I tried to copy the maneuvers I had witnessed on the silver screen. I tilted my head from side to side to allow my lips to change positions. Her lips were too small, her tongue aimlessly darted without direction, and there was too much saliva. I couldn't focus as my mind drifted. *An A minor triad chord has the root note A, the minor third of C, and the perfect fifth, which is E. A C major triad is the root note C, a major third is E, and a perfect fifth above the C is G. Are we going to have to walk back in the rain?*

Inga grabbed my belt and slid her hand down behind the fly of my pants.

Lightning lit the interior of the boathouse, followed with a deafening crash, causing us both to jump. We laughed from being suddenly startled, yet we remained within each other's clutches.

I stood there with her hand on my crotch. Her face flattened. Another crash of thunder deafened our ears, and she pulled her hand away and stood by the crying window.

"You're lucky," she said. The storm raged on the lake. "Tomorrow you get to go the academy and begin a new life. I have to stay at home and continue to live the life I already have."

"You'll be going back to school too."

"Yes." She smiled. "It isn't like going to a new school. A place where no one knows you, and you get to start all over."

"Why'd you want to start all over?"

She looked out at the lake that was being pelted by the rain. "Someday you'll understand what I'm talking about."

Rain beating the tin roof filled the boathouse.

I stepped toward her with trepidation. "I'm sorry about—"

She didn't even glance back at me; she just leaned her forehead on the windowpane. "It's all right. I understand."

"I don't think you do," I stammered.

"Really?" I could tell she smiled by the way she spoke.

"You're like a sister to me."

"But I'm not your sister."

"I know, but you're like a sister. I think of you as my sister. I love you as a sister."

"I know, but you can't blame a girl for trying," she joked.

I couldn't laugh with her; there was this unexplained discovery that I wasn't willing to accept. *What if she was right? What if I don't like kissing girls?*

"Are you all right?" she asked.

I was on the verge of hyperventilating.

"Hans," her voice rang with a warning. She rushed to me.

My knees buckled, and I crumpled to the floor.

"Hans!" she screamed and cradled me in her arms. She continued to rock me back and forth until my heart returned to normal. She brushed back my hair from my forehead and hummed a familiar tune that I couldn't name. I looked up at her, and she smiled. "There you are. Feeling better?"

"What happened?" I sat up and looked around.

"Nothing, nothing happened. It's all all right now. You know, we need to make a promise."

"What's that?"

"One, we never mention this again to anyone, not even to each other," she instructed with certainty.

"Fine," I agreed. I pressed the heel of my hand against my brow.

"Two, if neither of us has a date for the school dances, we'll go with each other. No one can have as much fun as we do with each other. And three, if we never find the right person to marry, we marry each other."

"That sounds like a great deal."

A loud boom of thunder caused me to shriek and jump as the interior illuminated glowed blue.

I laughed so hard, I curled up into a fetal position.

Inga watched with her mouth wide-open, commanding herself not to laugh and holding steadfast to the pillar. "Do pull yourself together. Do I always have to be the one wearing the pants?"

Her statement sent me roaring with more laughter, and I started rolling from side to side. My childish display broke her steely exterior, and although she didn't want to, she began to laugh as well. It was a slow and low rumble deep from within her, and it grew until her whole body began to shake and convulse from an onset of uncontrollable giggles.

"What a pair," I tried to catch my breath in between each word. I sat up and added, "We make."

*****

What an odd pair we made—the sports star and the pianist. Who'd ever think that the two of us would have anything in common? Yet there was this unexplainable ease about Josef.

"What part of the military?" I asked.

"Have you heard of the Movement?" He kept his eyes closed.

"You mean the Youth Movement?"

"Yes, that's the one."

"I've heard about it, but I don't know anything about it."

He turned his head toward me and smiled. "Then I'll have to tell you all about it. What are you doing tonight after dinner?"

"Not a thing that I can recall. I'll most likely be studying. What else does one have to do here?"

"We're having a meeting in the Marcus Hall Auditorium." He released my hand and sat up. "What time it is?"

The sun snuck behind the trees, the clouds were aging brown, and the blue sky was paling to a soft rose.

"Hey, we've better be getting back. It's going to be dinner soon." Josef got up and brushed grass from his lower back. He offered me his hand, which I accepted, and pulled me up next to him. Our bodies were only inches away from each other. He looked longingly into my eyes, bit his lower lip, and sheepishly grinned. "Race you back to campus." With that he darted off, leaping over a pile of rocks to our discarded clothing.

I quickly followed.

I watched as he bent over and snatched up his pants. The vulnerability of the position sent a hot flash streaming through my blood. I noted how his smooth buttocks curved and connected with his hairy and powerful hamstrings.

As he struggled to straighten out his pants, he added, "So you'll come to the meeting?"

I took his trousers and redirected the inverted leg to the proper side. "I'll be there." I handed back his pants. "What time?"

"Seven p.m. sharp." He pulled on his trousers.

"Seven o'clock it is."

"Hurry, we're going to be late." He grabbed other articles of clothing and started scanning the ground for lost items.

I reached into my satchel and pulled out his socks and shoes and handed them to him.

He sighed with relief.

"I didn't want you to lose anything, so I picked them up on my way," I explained.

"Thanks, now let's get going!" He pranced off into the wooded area as a graceful gazelle, lofting over the brush and rocks as if he was flying.

I gathered my clothes and silently slipped them on as the music from the waterfall and the birds performed their "rite of spring" for me. I paused for a moment to soak in the beauty.

Chapter 5

After dinner, I returned to my dorm room with just enough time to change my shirt and tie before heading over to meet Josef at Marcus Hall Auditorium.

The one-room occupancy contained a set of identical items: twin beds, side tables, small bookshelves, oak wardrobes, and desks. A Star of David, which hung freely in front of the window and filled the room with a spectrum of colors when the sun reflected off it, was the only unduplicated item.

A letter was on my pillow. I recognized the looping script and knew that it was from Inga. I inhaled the lilac aroma emitting from the envelope, ripped it open, and unfolded the letter:

Dear Hans, Darling,

I hope this finds you well and prepared for the competition on Friday. I'm so looking forward to coming to hear you play. I just feel that you're going to take top honors as expected.

I'm writing to share some news of my own. Mom and Dad have been using the spare room to help some people, the Stein family, which consists of a mother, father, and son. They're extremely polite. I wasn't so sure I wanted them to use your room, but it seems like it is the least we could do for them since they lost their home. They've been a great help to Father and the shop, working late into the evening and getting everything organized. Mother and Mrs. Stein are very creative in the kitchen (I help when

I'm not doing homework) in making recipes stretch to feed six instead of three. The rations only allow us to receive the portions for Father, Mother, and me—since the Steins "are only visiting." I shouldn't even be telling you this since it's supposed to be a secret, but I had to let you know. I'm advised to introduce the Steins as my aunt, uncle, and cousin.

I find this somewhat funny since I think I'm falling in love with the son, a handsome young man of twenty-two, named Ely—short for Elijah. We've become very close, and when I say "very close," you know what I mean. I can see him as being a part of my life forever. Oh, Hans, darling, I've never been so happy—except when you are home. I can't wait to introduce you to him on Friday; he's escorting me to the piano contest—since he is "relations" (I use this word to mean both "kin" and "lover"), it's only proper that he watches out for his younger cousin.

Remember that awkward moment in the boathouse, which I made you promise never to mention again? Well, I was thinking about that today, and I had a good laugh. Everyone at church probably thought I was crazy—but I knew you'd appreciate it. Oh, Hans, I hope one day you too will feel what I'm feeling for Ely. It's incredible and amazing and everything we said it was—and more. Please write me soon and tell me of someone special in your life so that we can share stories.

Your loving step-sis,
Inga

I refolded the letter, slipped it into its envelope, and carefully placed it in the shoebox under my bed that housed all of Inga's letters. I had this fantasy that one day I'd put all her letters to music and create an opera entitled simply *Inga*.

I rushed to the wardrobe and started searching for the perfect shirt and tie. I retrieved a freshly pressed white cotton shirt with blue pinstripes and a high collar when the door flew open, ricocheting off the supporting wall with a bang before slamming closed. A yelp escaped me as my whole being jumped with a start, and I dropped the shirt to the bottom of the wardrobe.

Stefan, my roommate, bounded in and flopped facedown onto his bed in a heap of exhaustion. His arms dangled over each side of the bed's small frame, and his fingertips lightly grazed the wooden floor. He was motionless, except for a quick flicker of his fingers.

I retrieved the fallen shirt, noticed the wrinkles, and hung it back up. I would have to settle for the simple white oxford. I placed it carefully on my bed before removing the shirt I wore to dinner and tossed it into the hamper. I slipped my arms into the sleeves of the fresh and crisp shirt and fastened the cuffs and buttons when I heard a dull thump.

A discarded shoe rested on the floor at the foot of Stefan's bed. The comatose roommate proceeded to kick off his other shoe with the ample dexterity of his already shoeless foot by gripping his toes around the heel of the shoe and sending it crashing to the floor. Once he completed the exhaustive task, he returned to a catatonic state.

I pulled out a tie from the tie rack without looking at it, slung it over my head, and measured it around my neck before tying a Windsor knot. The image in the little square mirror inside of my wardrobe door reflected my dissatisfaction with the tie's dark brown color. I slipped the tie from under my collar, discarded it on the foot of my bed, and reached for the dark maroon one. I repeated the routine of tying a knot, glancing at myself in the mirror, and disliking what I saw.

"Where are you going?" asked Stefan with a slight lisp and hesitation before each word. His face smashed against the pillow looked like one of those dogs with a wrinkled face, where you can barely see their eyes.

"I'm going to meet up with Josef," I responded.

"Who'sss that?" He lethargically rolled onto his side.

"He's on the swimming team." I pulled the maroon tie from my neck and flung it to lie limply at the foot of my bed alongside the brown one.

"Isn't he the really good ssswimmer?"

"Yes." I went back to the wardrobe.

"Didn't he win that racsse we went to sssee?"

"I believe so," I responded slightly sarcastic. "He has won every race we've seen him in." I had a gleeful glint.

"He'sss the really good-looking one, with the dark hair?"

"That's the one."

"Wow." He flopped onto his back, staring up at the ceiling.

I pulled out another tie and immediately tossed it onto the discarded pile.

"Oh my god, Hansss, I had quite the time," he announced with such reverie. "I haven't had that much fun in a long time." He tried to sit up but collapsed back onto the mattress and reached a hand into the air as if by doing so, he could be assisted to sit up.

I wasn't interested in playing this game about how the world revolves around Stefan. I searched for another tie.

"We went everywhere." His hand collapsed in a heap across his stomach.

I pulled out a simple black tie that widened to a full triangle and draped it around myself.

"No, not that one," he confirmed my suspensions.

I tossed it onto the growing pile that was beginning to look like a mass of dead snakes.

He pulled himself up to a sitting position. His head hung heavily upon his thin neck; he crossed his legs, leaned his back against the wall for support, and cleared his throat.

I pulled out an ivory tie with specks of blue stitching.

"No, not that one either." He sputtered and slurred his words. "I can't believe that we left ssschool like that. Hey, I'm sssosssorry that we didn't ssstop to pick you up, but Ian and Walter were too much in hurry to get away from Proctor Hoffman. We barely ssstopped long enough to for Petre to jump in—we didn't even ssstop—we were ssstill in motion when he jumped into the cab. That'sss when we became aware that Proctor Hoffman wasss coming towardsss usss telling usss to ssstop. But Walter jussst kept going and hollered back that we needed the truck to go get materialsss for the musssical. Can you believe that, a musssical?"

"Is that right?" I half-heartedly said. I was on a mission to find another tie. I held a black silk tie with a white line running the length of it under my chin.

"No. Here, take thisss one." Stefan untied a red and navy striped tie from around his neck and flung it to me. "Ssso there we were in town driving around, pretending to get thisss material for the musssical. I have no idea what musssical is being done, if any. We find that Walter hasss taken a wrong turn."

I laced the tie around my neck.

"And we pull off the road at thisss little old run-down ssshack-like place."

I guided the wider end of the tie through the loop and pulled it tight, pinching the front to form a dimple.

"There you go, that'sss the one," he complimented me on the way the tie looked.

I admired myself in the mirror and agreed before I closed the wardrobe door.

"Ssso we went in. We ssspent the whole afternoon in there."

I took a cloth and polished my oxford shoes.

"Walter wasssssso funny, ordering different kindsss of drinksss."

I slid into my jacket and secured my keys into my pocket.

"We drank and drank and drank. Oh my god, I'm not sssure all the thingsss we drank."

I walked to the door and slipped out.

"Have a good time," he called to me.

I started to close the door.

"Hey, Hansss?"

"What." I leaned my head in.

"Did you get your letter?"

"Yes."

"Wasss it from your girlfriend again? It sssure smelled good."

"I'm going to be late." I closed the door again.

"Hansss?"

"What is it?" I impatiently demanded.

"Leave that open. I think I'm going to be—" He rushed out of the room, with a green face, and staggered toward the bathroom using the wall as his guidance and support.

"Are you all right?" I called after out of obligation, hoping that he wouldn't need any assistance.

"Nope." He winced and covered his mouth as his cheeks puffed out like a blowfish, causing his eyes to bulge as well. He paused at the bathroom door and waved me on. "I'll be all right," he said and rushed in.

I propped our dorm door open and made my way to the exit. I anticipated seeing Josef's bright smile again. As I opened the door to walk outside, Stefan resounded with retching noises followed by a desperate affirmation of "I'm all right," followed by an animalistic groan.

*****

The balmy evening was thick with the rich aroma of magnolias, and lightning bugs intermittingly flashed in hopes of finding the perfect mate. The sky was active as a cold front invaded with dark thunder clouds mixing with the day's heat, sending off flares of lightning and giving the threat of an evening shower. As I crossed the lawn to the Marcus Hall, the clock tower sounded its seventh chime, indicating my tardiness.

I entered under the Gothic arch protected by the watchful eye of a stone gargoyle and made my way through the large wooden doors adorned with copper divots and hinges. A rich baritone voice bellowed behind the closed auditorium doors located across the marbled foyer. I bypassed the grand staircase with a crimson carpet and oak railings ascending to the second floor. I passed under the enormous crystal chandelier that majestically claimed the focus of the foyer. I quietly pried open the door leading directly into the back of the auditorium.

The cavernous space was dark except for the lights illuminating the stage. A red flag with a black swastika hung behind a long table. The table was clothed in white fabric and occupied by several distinguished gentlemen in uniforms.

Standing in front of the flag and table was Josef's friend, Karl, the one he was playing catch with earlier today. He wore a brown fitted shirt with matching pants, a dark tie neatly tucked behind the third button, and a band around his right arm. Several ornaments of shiny gold dazzled from his lapel. He stood erect with his arms down to his sides, appearing stiff and yet professional. His light brown hair was gelled down upon his scalp, giving it the illusions of being darker. The harsh lights cascaded from high above and accentuated his features to appear grotesque, emphasizing the severity of his angular bone structure. His brows cast a shadow over his eyes, causing them to seem hollow, empty, and skull-like. His rich voice carried easily throughout the auditorium.

"We must first and foremost remember the reason for the Movement and what our individual and personal involvement must be so that way can put an end to this unnatural section of classification." He paused for a moment to make his point while the room remained in complete silence. "We must unite to become the strength needed to rid our country of the insidious and pollutants of that which shall remain unspeakable." He raised his fist in the air. "There is only one immaculate and superior race, and we must do everything in our power to make sure nothing will impede our ascension. It is up to us, and us alone as an organization of this Movement, to assure that we are victorious."

Although his voice continued to fill the rafters, it became a distant and muffled murmur as Josef tapped my shoulder, smiling. He motioned for me to follow, which I eagerly obeyed.

Josef led me to an empty seat next to his. "I have been saving this for you," he whispered. He sat with perfect posture, back and hips squarely positioned in the chair, feet securely flat on the floor in front of him, and his hands on his thighs where his index fingers were about an inch from his bent knees.

Karl continued to address this mass of students and dignitaries. His mouth was continuing to move, and his hand was dramatically making points by stabbing into the air, but I could only think about how Josef looked at the lake earlier today.

I leaned into him so my knee pressed against his thigh. "I'm sorry I'm late."

He lifted a finger to his lips. "Shhh." Then he pointed toward the stage.

I swiveled back into my seat to face forward but kept my knee in contact with him. I attempted to listen to Karl's oration, but my mind consumed me with sitting next to Josef and the unexplainable desire to be with him. The image of his naked wet skin glistening and sparkling in the golden sun overwhelmed me to the point that I applied more pressure with my knee.

He glanced down to where the contact was being applied and refocused back on the speaker.

Embarrassed and dejected, I resigned to try to pay attention and listen to Karl's speech. I reluctantly broke our physical connection and repositioned myself in the chair. As I began to retune into the frequency of Karl's words, Josef's thigh pressed against mine, sending a flush of warmth throughout my body.

"So before I introduce our guest speaker tonight, I would like to extend a warm welcome to all the new recruits to the meeting. It's refreshing to see so many tonight. It's an indication that the Movement is going in the right direction and becoming the power we need it to be." He glanced to his right. "And now, before I waste any more time, let me please welcome SA Chief of Staff, Ernst Röhm."

A robust man stood amid an ocean of applause and provided a controlled smile as Karl relinquished the reign of center stage.

Röhm's extremely cropped dark hair was parted down the middle, adding to the roundness of his face marred on the left cheek with a jagged scar. His beady eyes seemed pinched at the bridge of his nose. His nose traveled a short distance before curving behind a small tuft of whiskers that only resided on the middle portion of his thin upper lip. His jacket was snug, straining the golden buttons, and on his left sleeve was a band of a smaller replica of the flag.

"Thank you, Karl." He remained poised as Karl retired to sit at the table. "On my way here tonight, I was reminded of myself when I was a young man and going to school. I thought the world was a place filled with promises and possibilities. I quickly awoke up to the realities that existed outside the iron gates of the educational institutions." He forced a laughed. "I've always been a part of the military. I was a career officer in the Bavarian Army during World War I and severely wounded in September of 1914, in Lorraine, France." He self-consciously touched his scarred face as if by doing so he could erase the evidence. "But I survived. When the war ended in 1918, I joined the Freikorps of Munich to combat Communist insurrection. In 1920, I helped organize the SA. And in 1923, after the Beer Hall Putsch failed in Munich, I was imprisoned for fifteen months. It was during these long months in prison that I became close friends with Adolf Hitler." He paused and lifted his right hand at an angle above his head. "Hail Hitler."

The sea of listeners stood, imitated the gesture, and chanted in one choreographed movement, "Hail Hitler."

I was the only one who seemed to be out of sorts and not aware of the proper steps. I quickly looked over at Josef and copied him.

"Hail Hitler, Hail Hitler."

The mass returned to their seats in unison.

Röhm continued, "After prison, I worked alongside Führer Hitler, and in 1930, he offered me the position of Chief of Staff of the entire SA. This brings me here to stand before you tonight. I only share this history to inform you of how you can move up within the Movement and make this a career." He reached for a glass of water and took a mouthful to moisten his dry throat. "The importance of the Movement is securing the superiority of the Master Race. We are looking to strengthen our centralized government under the leadership of the Führer, who is defending Germany and the German people against communism and the Jewish subversion. There is a racial, religious, and cultural hierarchy, and you are at the top as the superior race. However, this can only happen with the help from you, our youths of today and our future leaders of tomorrow. Look around you. Sitting next to you could be a person that'll be honored to serve his Führer and country. I'd like to bring this meeting to a close by showing you a film that best describes the Youth Movement, and then we can meet with you to answer any questions." He turned to Karl. "Are we ready?"

Karl swiftly stood at attention. "Yes, sir, we are." He motioned for two men to pull down the screen.

The lights on the stage darkened as the screen filled with the fluttering and flickering sepia frames of a handsome youth wearing a uniform like the one Karl and Josef had on and smiling directly into the camera. Vivaldi's *The Four Seasons—Spring* provided the musical background. A garbled and raspy voice narrated, "He is the picture of our tomorrow." Images of the happy and very fit male playing ball on a lawn with other indistinguishable young men with fair hair and eyes, working out with weights and tossing medicine balls to each other wearing nothing more than white athletic shorts, attending dances with attractive young women, and walking down a utopian street in the full Youth Movement Uniform as they nodded to people passing. The voice added, "This is our tomorrow." Then the screen returned to the image of the handsome youth, smiling directly into the camera. "And this could be you!" The final frame slipped through the projector, and the screen flashed brightly white.

The lights flickered on as the two young men guided the screen back up to it stored position. An assistant escorted Ernst Röhm from the stage to an undisclosed anteroom. Karl gathered a clipboard and returned to center stage.

"Come on with me, Hans," Josef said. "I want us to get in the front of the line."

I followed without any questions as he led me to the back of the auditorium to a table filled with pamphlets, forms, and flyers. Three similar-looking flaxen-haired members sat behind three signs with groupings of letters: A–M, N–R, and S–Z. Josef quickly guided me to the A–M line. "I wanted to get you through this as quickly as possible because I want to introduce you to Ernst Röhm before he leaves. He must meet you."

"Why?"

"He may be able to help you with your dream of playing all over the world."

Karl cleared his throat, causing us to turn and listen. He seemed smaller from way back here. "Now, we'd like all the members who have brought a guest to file to the back of the auditorium and sign in. There are three areas for you to line up, and it's according to your last name."

Josef held a pen for me to take and pointed to a line. "Just sign your name here."

I did without questioning.

He gathered a clipboard with a form attached to it and guided me to an empty side seat. "Sit here and fill this out, and we'll get everything going."

"What's this for?"

"It's protocol and gives the Youth Movement officials some background information about yourself and makes sure that you're not going to go out and start your movement," he reassured me of the meaninglessness of the form.

I filled in my name and address and scanned the questions: Have I ever been a part of any movement or protests, and if I have, what was the nature of the demonstration?

Do I have any relatives in the military, and if so, what are their positions?

It seemed rather informal and not intrusive. The next section asked to report my measurements and physical conditions.

"Don't worry about that right now." Josef was reading over my shoulder. "They'll go over all that with you. Just leave it blank." He flipped the form to page 2 as I inhaled his fresh, clean aroma. He pointed to the large box bordered by two columns that consisted of ten empty lines. "This is where you must list all the people close to you that you may suspect to be Jewish."

"Why do they want that?"

"They always ask that, something about seeing if you are trustworthy and honest enough to admit that you have had associations with them." He grinned. "It doesn't mean anything."

"But I don't know that many—that I'm aware of," I confessed.

"That's all right. Just think about it. And put the ones you know or anyone you may think is Jewish," Josef encouraged.

"Well, my roommate," I said out loud.

"Write his name down." He beamed with pleasure.

I scribed Stefan Joffe's name on one of the lines provided in the box.

"Can you think of anyone else?"

I looked up at Josef, and his eyes were bright with hope. He nodded as if saying, "You can come up with at least one more." I smiled back at him and wrote down *Professor Weinholtz*. "But I'm not sure about the professor."

"Do you think he might be?" he asked.

"I guess he could be, but I'm not certain."

"Oh, that's all right. If you think he might be, then leave his name there." He skimmed down the page with his index finger and pointed a final line. "Sign here. This indicates that you understand the form, that you're interested in participating in the Movement, and that you aren't—in any way—planning to start a movement from the confidential information you've received here tonight."

I autographed my name.

He gathered the sheets up and handed it to the attendee behind the desk. "Please inform Private Karl Mastenburg that Private Stork is here and would like to meet with SA Chief of Staff Ernst Röhm," he ordered.

"Yes, sir." The young man took one look at me and seemed to understand. He took the form and presented a number to me. "Please go to the parlor room for your physical and measurements. I'll inform Private Mastenburg of your presence." He stood and exited.

Josef started looking around in anticipation of the coming meeting. The area became crowded. "We beat the rush." He led me out into the foyer, to the grand staircase, where we ascended the crimson carpet.

"What happens now? I'm hoping that maybe we could take a long walk or go somewhere with fewer people so that we could talk," I proposed.

"They want to get your measurements, and then we'll see if you get to meet with Chief of Staff Röhm." Josef mentioned mechanically. We paused for a slight moment on the landing of the second floor. "This way." He took hold of my elbow and led me down the dim hallway, decorated with golden sconces dripping in costume crystals and attached to the pale blue walls aligned with white wainscoting. We stopped at a set of double oak doors, where a young man in uniform stood.

"We're here for his physical and measurements," Josef announced to the guard. "Give him your card, Hans," he whispered to me.

The uniform took my card and walked into the room.

Josef smiled nervously.

I cocked my head and tried to understand what was happening.

The door opened, and the uniform indicated for me to enter.

Josef gave me a slight shove to get me started. "I'll wait out here."

Chapter 6

The parlor room was complete with wall-to-wall mahogany bookshelves filled with volumes of famous writers of the past and present. The two long windows at the far end of the room were draped with rich eggplant velveteen curtains and held open with gold cords. A polished black Steinway grand piano, with the lid propped up, sat majestically in front of the windows. Three long oak tables for studying and high-back wooden chairs on each side occupied the principle part of the space.

"Name please."

A rather thin aging man in his fifties sat at the end of the first table with a jar of tongue depressors, syringes, vials, a large bottle of rubbing alcohol, cotton balls, Band-Aids, a white towel spread out covering one end of the table, and a pad of notepaper. His balding head was capped with white patches of filament stitched above each large ear. His thin face balanced a pair of bifocals on the bridge of his nose. His drawn cheeks gave him the appearance that his lips were always puckering.

"Name?" He glanced up at me from under his brows. He took a deep breath, crossed his arms in front of him, and tightened his cheeks and lips into a grin. "What's your name, darling?" he asked as his icy blue eyes twinkled.

"Hans," I responded. "Hans Klein."

"Good, splendid. I'm Dr. Falk," he said under his breath while scribbling on the notepaper. He looked back up at me and placed the pencil, ever so carefully, down on the table. He slowly elevated to six feet two inches of a 165-pound frame, bundled in a long white lab coat over his uniform. His long arms dwarfed the sleeves, causing his limited mobility. He lumbered toward me, hands deep into the pockets as his stethoscope swung freely from side to side from around his neck. He craned his head forward to look in my eyes as he pulled a small flashlight from his pocket. He clicked the light on and flashed it quickly into my pupils while prying my eyelids open with his finger and thumb. He leaned in extremely close that I could tell that he enjoyed unfiltered cigarettes. "Good dilation of the cornea. I would say your eye color is the same as a robin's egg, blue." He clicked off the light and returned it to the pocket.

The doctor circled me like a vulture getting ready to swoop down on its prey. He placed his long fingers on my shoulders and glided them down my chest to the lapels. He peeled back the jacket. "I need you to step out of your clothing, please." He meticulously folded and placed the jacket on the table and offered a hand to retrieve the next article, waiting for me to remove it.

I unknotted the borrowed tie, glided it from around my neck, and discarded it in his waiting hand.

He carefully draped the tie so it would not wrinkle on top of the jacket.

I unbuttoned my shirt.

Dr. Falk patiently watched with his hands shoved in his pockets, tugging on the coat and causing his shoulders to hunch forward.

I pulled open the shirt and bared the golden cross on my chest.

He inhaled deeply and released his breath through the puckered lips, sending a slight whistle into the air.

I presented the shirt to him.

He placed it with the other articles of clothing.

I removed my oxford shoes and slid them under the table myself. I unbuckled my belt, unfastened the waist button, and let my trousers drop to the floor. I stepped out of them.

He scooped down to gather and folded them. He positioned them next to the pile of clothes on the table. "Your stockings," he instructed.

I removed each dark argyle sock and stored them inside my shoes.

"And your undergarment," he insisted with a crooked smile.

I slipped my thumbs behind the waistband of my underwear, hesitated, and glanced up at him.

He lifted his brow high onto his forehead and dropped his chin. "We don't have all night." He smacked his lips together in disgust for the delay.

I guided the cotton garment down my thighs, past my knees, over my calves, and left them resting around my ankles. I stood there completely exposed, cupping my private section with both hands.

He shook his head and extended an open palm.

I stepped out of the garment puddled on the floor, bent over, and blindly handed them to him.

"Thank you." He put the garment with the others and then walked to the far end of the table to retrieve a pad of paper and pencil. He peered over the bifocals and jotted down some information.

A cool breeze caressed my skin as I wondered if Josef knew that I was standing here naked.

"Good," he muttered. The examiner approached while still writing notes. He held the pencil up to my nose like a painter gathering the perspectives and notated his discoveries. "Face is near perfectly symmetrical: sharp cheek bones, strong jawline, cleft chin, and full lips." He put the paper and pencil down on the table next to me so it was accessible to him to record. He reached and tucked his fingertips behind my ears and ran them down the side of my neck. "No swelling of the glands." He guided his hands over my shoulders and leaned back at arm's length. "Lift your arms out to the side."

I did so.

He slid his hands down my extended arms. "Lift your arms against the weight of my hands."

I followed instructions and pressed my arms up.

"Good tone. Do you work out?"

"Do you mean with weights?"

"Yes." He lifted my arms over my head. "Keep them extended." He examined my armpits, running his hands through my thick growth of damp blond hair.

"I don't work out with weights on a regular basis, several times a week at most," I replied.

He applied pressure and felt deeply in the hollows of my pits.

"Lymph nodes seem perfectly fine. I ask because you're well-toned and have definitions." He ran his hands over my chest but stopped, lifting the heavy cross. "You're going to have to remove this."

I reached behind my neck, unclasped it, and gathered it into my palm.

He held out his hand.

I reluctantly transported it to him.

He carefully placed it on top of the discarded clothing. He returned to his position in front of me, and his hands examined my chest and my ribs. He pressed his fingertips up under the rib cage. "No problems there." He pressed against my stomach. "It's tough to get an accurate assessment with your stomach muscles being so taut. But it seems that everything is in good condition." He ran his hand over my abdomen along the blond hairline sprouting down from my naval and pressed the area just above my right pelvic bone. "Appendix appears to be in fine condition." He tugged on my sac, feeling the almond-shaped testes and the tubing that reached up and connected at the base of my penis. He tucked his fingers alongside my scrotum. "Turn your head and cough."

I followed the request.

"That's fine, no weakness for a hernia." He lifted the head of my penis, pulled back the excess skin, and pried the slit open with his thumbs. "That's clean."

As he entered his findings on the paper, I started to swell, and I cupped myself with both hands.

He patted the table next to where the white towel was spread out. "I need you to sit on the edge of the table."

I hesitated.

He impatiently patted the table, causing each strike to become harder and louder.

I reluctantly positioned myself on the towel, with my feet dangling under me. I kept my private area hidden.

"Height is about six foot and weighs about 170, hair blond. There is body hair on legs, genitals, underarms, and a small amount on the chest. The subject is uncircumcised and well formed." He called over to me, "What's your age?"

"I just turned seventeen last week."

"Well, happy birthday." He smiled.

He walked around in front of me, parting my thighs so he could get closer. He put his hands around my waist and guided me to sit on the edge of the table. He looked up at me from under his brows as he discovered my semi-erection and licked his lips. He placed the stethoscope in his ears and positioned the circular round metal end against my chest. The coldness caused me to flinch. "Take a deep breath." He tilted his head as if to listen better. His bald scalp grazed against my chest.

I inhaled deeply.

"Now exhale slowly."

I released a slow and even breath.

Dr. Falk repositioned the device to another area of my chest. "Inhale and exhale just as before. That's good, now the back." He placed a hand on my thigh as he walked around the side of me and placed the stethoscope on my back. "Breathe in and out for me just like you did."

I obeyed.

He leaned to listen to the far lung, contorting his body and causing his hand to slide farther up on my thigh and came to rest next to the crown of my penis. "One more time, breathe in and out. Good." He let the end of the stethoscope drop, removed the earpieces, and walked back in front of me. He repositioned himself between my parted thighs and pulled the flashlight and a tongue depressor from his pocket. "Open wide." He flattened my tongue as he looked in my mouth. "Good." He tossed the depressor into a trash can, clicked the flashlight off, and returned it back into the pocket. He squeezed my thighs. "I'm going to need you to lie back and bend your knees, so your heels are on the edge of the table."

I lowered myself onto the table and looked up at the ceiling, placing my heels on the table's lip. I closed my eyes and tried to think about the afternoon when I was at the lake with Josef, but his image wouldn't appear. I tried to think of anything that would take me away from this experience. Nothing came to mind.

"This may feel a little uncomfortable at first, but just take a deep breath," he explained. He lifted my testicles.

"What are you doing?"

"Just relax." His finger probed the rim of my anus.

My stomach concaved as I clinched my opening tight.

He gently forced in his digit.

The intrusion created a pressure and a sensation I never experienced before.

The doctor continued, proceeding deeper inside.

I spread my thighs and tilted my hips forward, trying and ease the pressure.

He twisted his finger and probed the interior lining.

A moan escaped from within me. I tried to retract from the invasion.

Dr. Falk restrained me. "Relax," he coaxed. His finger landed on an area that sent an electrical current through my thighs, up my spine, and set a spark that warmed my gonads. I closed my eyes tighter as my penis swelled. I covered my face with my hands as my cheeks reddened with embarrassment.

He continued to massage the area.

I became completely erect.

He wrapped his other hand around my hardness and began to stroke.

I tried to stop him, but it was too late. I had no way of impeding the hot surging rush from deep within me. My breathing became heavy as I tried to prevent the inevitable. Every muscle strained to ward off the imminent expulsion as I clenched my fists with every fiber of strength.

"That's a good boy."

Chapter 7

The courtyard lamp's illumination seeped in through the parlor windows, casting bright ribbons and flooding the floor in glowing pools. I walked to the windows, leaned against the eggplant velveteen curtain, and bathed in the artificial blueness. Across the lawn, the blackened windows of my dorm room resembled two dark eyes hiding a secret from the world. The vacant windows expressed the alienation I felt, the splintering of the personae that I thought I knew, and the personae infringed upon without my consent.

The dorm windows blinked awake, ceding its darkness as amber filled the room. Stefan entered and made his way to his wardrobe to hang his coat. A sense of longing filled me to be in my bed trying to read as he incessantly recounted his evening's adventures to the nth detail, and his inability to keep from rambling and mixing up the order of the events that never seemed to pan out into a complete story. He crossed to the windows, looked out, and closed the curtains on the bitter world outside.

To the right, Professor Wienholtz stood at his window with a glass of golden liquid and a burning red ember pinched between his fingers. He appeared almost ethereal as he inhaled the cigarette and released two thin streams of smoke from his nostrils that spiraled above his head like a halo. He fanned the white swirl out the window and flicked the remaining burning stub into the night. He closed the curtains to seal out the oncoming storm, leaving the windows to become clouded eyes, and not wanting to be bothered by unnecessary problems from the outside world.

The courtyard prepared for the ominous cloud to unleash its fervor without permission. The wind whipped through the quad pillaging petals, leaves, and twigs from the landscape and scattered them in every direction. Intense lightning illuminated the billowing drab cloud that passionately reached toward the innocent earth and demanded attention.

Without warning, droplets precipitated onto the lawn, like foreplay, leaving collections of puddles and streaking windowpanes. The maple tree that resided in the center of the courtyard surrendered to the storm by exposing the white underbelly of each leaf, while the cloud's rain erased existing memories from the circular bench that sat around its trunk.

The intruder's stream of rain continued longer than desired. Its aggression grew as thunder moaned and rumbled like a procession of bass drums. The cloud released its baptism, hiding the view of the dorm and Professor Weinholtz's building behind sheets of a torrential downpour. The wrath exhibited its violence when a student emerged from the gray curtain of rain with his umbrella turned inside out and broken spokes looking like splintered fingers reaching for shelter. The figure stood in the downpour, disoriented and looking for which direction to take. Pellets danced all around him, ricocheting off his head, face, and shoulders; streaking his hair flat to his head and causing his eyes to squint. He moved to shelter under the awning covering the front porch of Marcus Hall.

I turned away from the window and found the room empty except for the tables and chairs, bookshelves, and the grand piano. Dr. Falk left the medical supplies while he excused himself to freshen up, advising me to wait here. The room flashed blue and rumbled from loud claps of thunder. The room shrank, closing in on me, causing me to labor for breath. My blood raced and palpitated painfully in my temples, causing my sight to pulsate and my ears to ring. The surroundings took on different hues of gray as the strobe effect of the bolts of lightning filled the room.

I wanted to rid my mind of the last few hours and return to the anticipation and wonderment that I felt earlier this evening. Everything seemed empty, lifeless, and meaningless, as if life extracted all the childlike joy from me.

I positioned myself on the bench in front of the piano and clasped my hands before my lips. I positioned my hands and lightly compressed the keys, filling the room with a resounding chord. It was a simple combination, something a beginner would play. The chord's crescendo reached its fullest resonance and faded until all I felt was the dying vibration through my fingertips.

I altered my fingering and engaged another chord. This one was more dissonant, composed with many flats, creating a darker reverberation. Before the chord resolved itself into silence, I struck another chord, causing the two voices to blend.

Slowly, I strung chords together, leading into an improvisational etude. The movement grew into a melodic tempo composing of a divergence between sharps and flats, providing a somber mood. The ascension built like the rumble of the thunder and seemed not to resolve itself before the next swell interceded it and took charge, and then another intervened, creating a musical conflict.

The cacophony continued to build as I provided the chords faster, allowing my mind the freedom to express itself without any limitations. I shut my eyes, and perspiration beaded on my forehead; my fingers moved effortlessly and quickly to beat out the disjointed tune of angst and pent-up violence. My left hand provided the constant bass attributions while my right hand bestowed upward and downward trills. The fever of the composition continued to rage, and my body participated by throbbing with the striking rhythm. My fingers and wrists burned with the turbulent expression, shoulders tensed with each compression of keys, and my head throbbed with the ever-growing intent.

As I compressed the keyboard for the final time, the notes joined to create one final raucous and disjointed chord, climaxing with the rumbling roll of thunder. The room rang as the vibrations leisurely settled into silence, allowing the room to return to the humming of the constant rain.

I felt drained and yet filled with a sense of relief. My hands collapsed onto my lap. My head drooped as I caught my breath and calmed the hammering effects from the adrenaline. I opened my eyes and looked at my hands, exhausted and trembling.

"Impressive."

There was an audience composing of Ernst Röhm, a tall blonde assistant, Dr. Falk, Karl, and Josef. They all had various expressions on their faces: Röhm was steely with the corners of his lips curled. Dr. Falk exhibited a lascivious and proud grin. Karl presented a professional manner, while the aide was vacant in expression, and Josef's bright smile caused me to turn away.

"Very impressive." Röhm continued to feign clapping and approached. His round face was etched with a forced smile, causing his small mustache to spread out over his lip, stretching the purplish scar. "What's the title of that movement?"

I lengthened my spine and rested my hands on the edge of the piano. "It doesn't have a name, sir. I made it up."

"You just improvised that piece?" He cocked his head like he couldn't understand.

"Yes, sir." I tried to stand, but my legs had no stability.

"Stay seated please." He placed his stubby fingers on my shoulder and pressed me back down onto the bench. He inhaled as his belly pressed against my shoulder blade. "That was very moving and filled with passion and drama." He demonstrated his pleasure about the music by caressing my shoulder. "Let me get a good look at you." He made his way around the bench while letting his hand remain draped on my shoulder. "Very nice, indeed." He cupped my jaw in the palm of his hand and lifted my chin up. "Yes, this will do."

Röhm's scar had a thick purple line running through the middle of the wound and paled as it reached out through the jagged edges and blended into his skin.

He glanced over to the others. "How did he measure up, Dr. Falk?"

Dr. Falk stepped forward and boasted, "He's a perfect specimen, sir."

"Excellent," responded Röhm. He gently patted my cheek before sliding his hand away. "Who's his sponsor?"

"I am," announced Josef with pride.

Röhm looked over to Josef and gave a knowing smile. "You've done very well. Please make a note of that." He nodded to his assistant. "I've seen all I need." He took out a pair of leather gloves and slapped them in the palm of his hand. "Oh, I just had an idea." He faced me with his beady eyes. "You'll be playing for Adolf Hitler's summit meeting this Friday at the Hanselbauer Hotel in Bad Wiessee near Munich. Josef, you'll make sure that he'll be there. There'll be two tickets at the train station in your name, leaving at 12:35 p.m." He kept his eyes on me.

"Yes, sir," Josef immediately accepted.

"Good, I'm looking forward to it. I must be going. It was a pleasure meeting you …?"

"Hans Klein, sir," whispered the assistant.

"Yes, of course, Klein." He walked to Josef and placed a hand on his cheek. "I'm counting on seeing you at the Hanselbauer Hotel with Master Klein."

"I'll be there, sir."

"That's my boy." He patted Josef's cheek and started to exit. "Oh, and Klein, this could be the beginning of a fruitful career for you," he added with his back to me. "Dr. Falk, I need to have your report on Klein. Can you walk with me to the car?"

"Yes." Dr. Falk and Karl followed behind.

Josef came bounding toward me. "You see, you see. I knew it. I knew it." He slid onto the bench beside me. "Are you excited?"

"I guess so." I tried to sound enthusiastic.

"You're going to play all over the world after this." He wrapped his arm around me.

I stiffened. "I just don't know what to say."

"Shout, scream, and holler. You're going to get that chance of a lifetime. Playing for Hitler could be the beginning of a new life for you. This Friday, in two days, you're going to be playing in front of the most powerful man in the world."

"Friday?"

"Yes," declared Josef. "This Friday."

"No, no. I can't. I have the piano competition this Friday."

"Forget about that. You don't need that anymore. You're going to be playing for Hitler. Your career is going to take off."

"What if he doesn't like the way I play?"

"How can he not? I'll make sure of it." He flashed his smile again, knowing the effects it had on me.

Chapter 8

A pale red-breasted bird swooped down from the cobalt sky with extended claws, arched her left wing, and veered toward the bench surrounding the maple tree's truck. She skimmed the grass blades, landed, and nabbed ahold of a fat earthworm. The struggle was only temporary as the worm stretched itself to a thin line before becoming her prey. The bird proudly tilted her head as she gulped down her winnings, glanced around to see if anyone witnessed her victory, and chirped an announcement of success. She lifted her shoulders and expanded her wings, hopped on her stick legs, and launched herself up through the limbs of the tree to a nest nestled between branches, where she fed her two chicks.

As I stepped on the soft lawn, my oxford shoes immediately sank, and brown liquid covered the white toes. *I'm going to have to clean them before entering Professor Weinholtz's studio. Why didn't I take the sidewalk?* It was too late to go back, so I continued through the wet grass to the spot where the worm relinquished its life. The bench appeared dried from the day's warmth, and I sat. The sun filtered through the branches and leaves, displaying a Picasso pattern across my face and shoulders. I rested my head, closed my eyes, and watched the dark shadows dance against a red background.

How was I going to tell the professor that I wouldn't participate in the piano contest on Friday? *This amazing opportunity fell into my lap.* No, that wouldn't work. *I have this great chance to play for Hitler.* That sounded too egotistical. How would I even know if Hitler was going to show? Or maybe I should say something like *I was playing last night during the storm, and this man heard me and invited me to play in Munich this Friday.* I could pretend I forgot about the competition. *Wait a minute. The professor dedicated himself in seeing that I would be at my best. I just can't waltz in there and tell him that I'm not going. That'd be like slapping him in the face, showing ingratitude, and would crush the professor. I can't go to Munich. I'll tell Josef that I'm not available, that I have a prior commitment.*

"Hans."

Josef stood before me, looking so prestigious in his blue jacket with the school's crest embroidered on the pocket, a crisp white shirt, and a dark royal blue tie knotted in a perfect double Windsor. A refreshingly clean aroma emitted from him.

"What're you doing?" he asked with a gentle sweetness that sent a spark of joy to replace my confliction.

Just then a massive tsunami of disgust engulfed me as the image of Dr. Falk's hands took the foreground of my mind, causing my skin to crawl.

"I'm trying to figure that out."

"I have to tell you." He enthusiastically slid onto the bench next to me, pressing his thigh firmly against mine, causing the shame to ebb for a moment. "What Röhm said about you last night is something. He's not one who quickly gives praise and offers such an invitation. He was extremely impressed with you. He told Karl when they were walking to his car that he thought you were a perfect model for the Movement."

"What does that mean?" I hesitantly pulled my thigh away from his.

He grabbed my knee with both hands. "It means that you could do many great things with the Movement. You'd be able to play all over the world if you wanted to."

"I don't understand. What about the physical?" I tried pulling away, but Josef tightened his hold on my knee.

"It means nothing. It was just a physical, and Dr. Falk said you were a perfect specimen."

I glanced away, shaking my head.

He released his hold.

I slid to the far side of the bench.

We sat in silence. I heard the red-breasted bird chirping an "I told you so, I told you so, I told you so" song from high above me.

"Hans," Josef softly said. "Hans, look at me."

"No." I stared at the ground where the worm declared defeat.

"Come on, look at me." He lifted my chin.

I jerked away. "I can't!"

"Okay." He leaned back against on the bench. "What happened?"

"Nothing." A new and strange strength overcame me. I decided that I wasn't going to tell Josef about the incident with Dr. Falk, in fear that he'd not understand and would never want to associate with me again. I looked him straight into his eyes and forced a smile. "Nothing." I was stunned to realize how easy it was to lie, to cover up an ugly truth.

"So why are you acting like this?"

"Like what?"

"Like you just did something that you regret."

"Oh, it's really … nothing." I glanced over to the professor's window. "It's just that I'm supposed to play in the piano contest this Friday, and I don't think I can go to Munich."

"But you must go to Munich. Röhm has invited you. He has reserved train tickets for us. I promised him you'd be there," Josef clearly stated.

"I realize that. I do. But Professor Wienholtz has been preparing me for this ever since I came here, and I'm not sure I can just waltz in there and say, 'Hey, Professor, I can't play for you this Friday. I have to go to Munich.' He's never going to believe that Röhm invited me to play for Hitler. I can hardly believe it myself, and I was there. The professor is going to think I'm lying and that I'm going off to do something else. And besides, my family's coming to hear me. How do I tell them not to come?"

"Tell them the truth, telephone them, and explain to them about this incredible opportunity."

"That's easier said than done."

"Listen, do you want to go to Munich?"

"Well, of course."

"Do you want to go to Munich and play for Hitler?" He stressed the words *want* and *Hitler*. His eyes were fully pleading.

Maybe if I do this, he'd be able to forgive me for what transpired last night during the physical examination, if he ever found out about it. Maybe he did like me and was willing to help me achieve my dream. I wanted to please him and answered without a second thought, "Yes, I want to play for him."

"Then that's what you should do. You can't pass up this opportunity." He paused and looked off into the distance and slowly looked back at me. "All right, I have to share something with you that I know you're not going to like hearing." He placed his hand on top of mine. "Hans, listen to me. Are you listening?"

"Yes," I said nervously.

Josef smiled slightly. "Even if you play on Friday and win the contest, which is what will probably happen, it'll not mean much. You see, by winning Friday, you'll be marked in the eyes of the Movement because the professor is Jewish, and this could hurt your chances of ever playing all over the world."

I slowly freed my hand from his. "What are you saying?"

"I'm not trying to hurt you." His eyes softened. "It's how things are."

"Are you telling me this just because Professor Wienholtz may be Jewish? I don't understand."

"It's believed that the Jews are the reason Germany is in this hardship. They're considered dangerous, vile, and impress upon young minds, brainwashing the innocents into believing that there's only one way to succeed—the Jewish's way. But they're selfish, controlling, and manipulative. The professor will ruin your career."

"But—"

Josef placed his fingertips to my lips. "Shhh. If you play for Hitler in Munich, your career could become instantaneous." He flashed his amazing smile and whispered, "It's your choice."

He stood, offered his hand, and guided me to my feet. He pulled my hand close to his lips. "Just tell the professor that this is something that you have to do. I'm sure he will understand."

The clock rang once, alerting me that I must get to the studio for my practice session.

I turned to go, but he held tight to my hand. "There'll be other competitions, but there may not ever be another invitation like this."

I extended my forefinger to brush his soft lower lip and nodded.

He kissed the pad of my finger and whispered, "Do you want me to go with you and talk with the professor? Because you know I will."

I shook my head.

"Or let's just skip today and go to the lake and relax." He playfully bit my finger.

I giggled like a girl. "No, I've to go take care of this now."

"I'll be happy to go straight in there and tell him that you aren't going to be competing this Friday because you have a bigger engagement to attend." He dropped my hand and feigned going in the direction of the studio. We both stopped and saw the professor standing in his window with his arms interlocking across his chest and looking down at us.

"Oh, there he is. I can tell him right now." He stepped toward the window and reached up as if he was going to get the professor's attention. I wrapped my arms around his back and covered his mouth. He pulled my hand away, waved, and shouted, "Hello, Professor. Isn't it a glorious day?"

The professor shook his head and disappeared behind the curtain.

"I better go." I was still wrapped around him, feeling his broad shoulders and hard chest.

He restrained my hands and begged in a childlike voice, "Let me come with you?"

I quickly let go. "Not this time, buddy." I grabbed my satchel and jogged through the damp grass toward the studio. I halted. I had this urge to kiss. I had no idea where it came from, but it was evident. I hurried back to Josef. "You sure I'm doing the right thing?"

"Yes."

I fought the strong urge to kiss him. "Thank you." I hustled across the lawn, trying to avoid the soft patches, all the time berating myself for not trusting the urge to kiss him.

"Let me know how everything goes," he called after me.

"Sure." I leaned on the door with my shoulder to open it.

Josef stood there smiling and waved.

I slipped behind the entry, took a deep breath, and ascended the stairs, anticipating the forthcoming altercation.

Chapter 9

I reached for the doorknob of the professor's studio when I remember my oxford shoes splattered with brown sludge from the lawn. I quickly try to rid the shoes of the unwanted substance by scuffing them along the welcome mat before entering, leaving long dark streaks behind. I pulled a handkerchief from my pocket, spat on it, and attempted to rub off any remaining evidence.

I regained my composure, calming my racing heart with slow and deep breaths. I turned the crystal doorknob and gingerly pushed open the door.

There was an unsettling silence. A silence interrupted by the mother bird's chirps out in the courtyard.

Professor Weinholtz sat in his winged-back chair. The sun bled across his face, spilling down the front of this shirt and tie, casting him in gold. He didn't say anything as I put my satchel down next to the piano, but continuously streamed his silk tie between his index finger and thumb and remained fixated out the window.

I stood erect with my hands clasped behind the small of my back and waited for the professor's acknowledgment. Finally, I broke the silence. "Professor Weinholtz, sir …" I fumbled to find my voice. "I'm afraid I'm not … going to be able … to play in the … uh … piano contest this Friday." I waited for him to explode with ranting and raving like a bohemian.

He sat there with a blank expression on his face, unblinking eyes, and the corners of his mouth pinched.

My voice weakened as I continued. "I've been asked to play at the Hanselbauer Hotel in Munich. I'm leaving tomorrow afternoon on the twelve thirty-five train. I'm sorry."

Still, he refused to respond.

I pulled the piano bench out to sit, causing its legs to moan against the wooden floor.

"Don't sit," he said in a deep raspy voice. He presented his palm in my direction while still looking out the window.

His focal point was on Josef sitting on the bench under the maple tree and writing in a notebook. The leaves on the maple trees gently swayed in the warm breeze, creating dancing shadows upon him.

The red-breasted mother bird perched on the edge of her nest where her two featherless chicks were poking their heads up, squawking with open beaks, and begging for more food. The mother's black eyes scanned the lawn and focused on a spot in the green ocean. She expanded her wings and launched another attack. She cleared the branches and circled several times, keeping her eyes locked in on her target. With a nod of her head, she pulled her wings in slightly and nose-dived toward the ground, gathering speed as she fell. A few inches above her targeted spot, she fully extended her arms, expanding each feather like fingers, and extended her claws out in front of her. She skimmed through the blades of green grass, clutched onto an earthworm, and swooped up into the clear sky. With a few strokes from her wings, she navigated back up through the tree branches and balanced on the edge of her nest. She gulped down the earthworm and fed her offspring.

The professor began tapping his fingers atop of a newspaper resting on the table next to his chair with a photograph of Röhm's scarred face appearing on the front. The professor continued avoiding making any eye contact with me. He sat there, watching Josef on the bench and drumming the newspaper.

I stood waiting and contemplating what I should do.

The professor's head tilted, watching Josef walk across the lawn to his class.

As Josef disappeared beyond the scope of the window, Professor Weinholtz glanced over with judgmental eyes, which burned as they scaled me up and down. He extinguished his glare, struggled to hoist himself up, and walked to the window to close the curtains. "Are you going with anyone?" he calmly asked.

"Yes, I'll not be traveling alone."

"I see."

I was relieved that he knew and that I wasn't making the trip alone. Maybe he would be proud that I thought through the situation and made a clear decision.

"This person you'll be traveling with, will it be with your friend I've seen you cavorting with?" The professor kept his back to me.

"You mean Josef?"

"Is that his name?" he drolly responded. "How well do you know him?"

"We're friends."

"How good of friends?" He slowly made his way back to the chair.

"Good friends. Why?" I asked with a little patience. "What are you implying?"

"I'm not implying anything. I'm just observing and asking questions. Why are you so defensive? Are you hiding something?" He turned with his eyes ablaze.

"We're just friends."

"If I may be so bold, it doesn't look like that." His voice slipped into a deeper register as he lowered himself back onto the seat cushion of the winged-back chair. He crossed his legs and lifted a glass of amber-colored liquid swimming in ice to his lips. He savored a sip ever so gracefully with his pinky finger extended.

I watched in silence.

He placed the glass meticulously on the knitted doily next to his silver case full of imported cigarettes, the crystal ashtray, and the accusatory news article. He elegantly flipped open the case and selected a finely wrapped stick from the center. He wedged the butt of the rolled white paper between his lips and lit the opposite end, cupping the flame from being blown out. He inhaled, causing the end to sizzle noisily, pulled the stick away from his mouth to inspect the burning ember, and extinguished the lit match with a flick of his wrist. He held his breath as he discarded the burnt match into the ashtray and then expelled a whirling blue cloud into the room that hid his face for a moment. As the thin veil dissipated, he added, "It looks to me that you're very close … extremely close. And that could create a problem for you."

"What are you implying?"

"All I'm wondering is if you're aware of the ramifications of this type of friendship you're experiencing with that young man?"

I remained silent.

"Are you aware of the policies of paragraph 175 of the German Criminal Code of 1871?" He took a deep drag on the cigarette that he balanced between his fingers before dramatically exhaling another stream of smoke, which snaked above his head.

"I'm not aware of the paragraph … whatever it is—what are you talking about?" My palms started sweating, and my chest contracted.

"Paragraph 175 is a statement that denounces the recognition of homosexual behavior. You are aware of what homosexual means?" The professor derogatorily asked while lowering his eyelids to half-mast.

"Yes, sir, I'm aware of what that means, but we aren't—"

"Say no more. I don't want to hear anything that might implicate you." He snubbed out his half-smoked cigarette by twisting it in the ashtray. "I'm not one to judge what you do with your spare time. I'm only concerned with your ability to perform and play the piano. What you do in your private life is none of my business."

"But nothing's happening or has happened between us."

He held up his palm to stop me.

I held my tongue.

He uncrossed his legs, scooted to the edge of the chair, and ran his hands over his face, pulling the skin down like a monster from a horror film. He stared at me with piercing eyes under his brows and then smacked his lips together. "Homosexuality is believed to be a contagious disease and is thought to be highly dangerous because of the effects it has on young people, like you, who are attending highly recognized and affluent boarding schools. Some can excuse these events while attending such schools as adolescent aberrations, but it's looked upon as a subdivision of a criminal act and is punishable by the German government. It's looked upon as a 'moral degeneracy.' Homosexuals are considered traitors to their people, can cause the decline and destruction of the country, and must be rooted out to face extermination."

He picked up the newspaper, unfolded it, and read the headline, "Röhm Recruits on Campus." He held up the paper so I could see the full front page and tossed it at me.

I let the newsprint crumble to the floor between us and made no motion to pick it up.

He shook an extended finger at me. "You have no idea what you're doing. You're more innocent than I could ever image." He lifted himself from the chair and approached me. "You're playing with fire, my boy, and this is a very dangerous game." He sprayed me with each consonant. "This Movement … this Youth Movement, are you aware of what they're involved in?"

"No."

"I didn't think so." The professor's eye darkened, and his face flushed red. "This youth movement is a precursor to the SA, which is a part of the Nazi Movement. The Nazis are known to believe that there is only one superior race, and every other race is secondary. They felt that the Weimer Republic, which was in power after the Versailles Treaty, was riddled with Jewish people, and that was why Germany faced such economic depression. The Youth Movement or Hitlerjugend grew by combining all the different youth organizations into one to support the National Socialist for the years to come by generating politically minded future leaders. The Movement promises these youth that this is a way to help their families, learn about music and the arts, and are slowly taught to hate gypsies, Jews, homosexuals, and political protesters. They are taught not to trust anyone that doesn't fit or support the ideals of this new movement."

The professor stood erect and pointed to the newspaper on the floor. "Yet this Ernst Röhm and his officers are noted for their philandering. Even though it is against paragraph 175 and the German laws, they act as if the edicts don't pertain to them and feel that they may do whatever they please. They recruit known homosexuals to protect them from the laws and attractive young men and naïve students by promising them a future. And now, you have become a part of all this." He threw his hands up into the air and rested his hip against the curve of the piano. "Did you sign your name to anything?"

I stood there staring blankly.

He must have read my silence as a confirmation. He shook his head and ran his hands through his hair before grabbing fistfuls at the nape. He staggered to the window and leaned against the window's curtain and framework. "This boy … this friend, you call him, is he the one that introduced you to the Movement?"

"Yes," I mumbled.

"What!" he demanded. "I couldn't quite hear you." He crept toward me.

"Yes," I repeated.

"Yes, you say? Yes, he's the one that took you to the meeting last night?"

I nodded my head.

"Yes, he's the one that's taking you to Munich tomorrow?"

I reluctantly nodded again.

"And then you have no idea who he is, do you?"

I glanced away, not wanting to hear any more of his opinions.

He continued, "Do you know what the superior race is?"

My eyes welled up. My stomach flip-flopped like a world-class gymnast. My fingers clutched along the seam of my trousers, twisting the material between my fingertips and thumb. I locked my knees as tight as I could as if by doing so, I could control my emotions.

"You're the typical Aryan race that the Movement is seeking. You. Did you know that?" He controlled his voice.

I focused on my shoes. There were still traces of the muck from the lawn, speckled in perfect droplets.

"Look at yourself," he instructed. He took hold of my head and forced me to face the mirror hanging on the wall next to the piano bench.

I shut my eyes.

"Look. Open your eyes and look in the mirror. Open them now!" The professor raised his voice with a harsh tone.

I opened my eyes and saw the image in the oval-shaped mirror. My blond hair was in disarray. My eyes were lined red, causing the blue hue of my irises to stand out. My cheeks were tear-stained, and my lips pressed into a thin line.

"This is what they're calling the superior race. You. You and your perfect blond hair and blue eyes, chiseled good looks, and clear skin. You exemplify the ideal Aryan. That's why this Josef character has befriended you. He's not the ideal with his dark hair and eyes. He needs to recruit someone like you to help elevate himself up to the next level of the pyramid within the Movement. When he located you, he honed in and wanted to befriend you. And when he discovered how sensitive you are, he started playing upon your emotions and proceeded to reel you in any way he could. He doesn't care about you or your needs, your feelings, or even who you are. He only wants one thing. And he'll go to any extreme to achieve that one goal, no matter what it takes. Has he ever asked you about your life, where you came from, or who you are?" His questions pelted me like an automatic rifle.

I gave no answer; my mind clamored with confusion.

His voice became soothing and took me off guard. "That's because he doesn't care."

I shot a glance toward him with astonishment, trying to figure out his motive. In my attempt to quickly sort out the possible angles of this form of attack, a fire ignited within me. He unknowingly pressed an emotional button that I had been trying to keep hidden and never wanted anyone to see. He crossed the line by stating that Josef didn't care. I tried to ward off the anger from erupting, but I was too weak to control it. I turned into a snake and showered him with venom. "You're wrong. You don't know what you're saying, you stinking old kike."

His face turned ashen, his mouth flew open, and his eyes widened with pain.

I quickly said, "I'm sorry, I didn't mean to say that."

He finally blinked his eyes. "Yes, you did." He backed away, fanning himself. He picked up the paper, folded it in half, and positioned himself with the piano between us. He rolled the newspaper into a tubular shape.

"No, I didn't mean it. I swear ..." I held out my arms toward him.

"Stay away from me," he ordered. "Get out."

I reached for him again. "Please."

He lifted the rolled paper above his head and swiped it through the air. "Go. Get out."

"No." Snot ran out of my nose, and tears streamed down my face.

"Leave! Now!" he shouted, making another swipe of the newspaper.

"I can't," I sobbed. "You're the only person I have in my life."

"No, I'm not. Not anymore. You've changed, and I want no part of it. Leave now."

"Please forgive me." My knees buckled, and I braced myself on the edge of the piano.

"I said leave. You revolt me." He turned his back to me.

I crumbled onto the floor, wrapping my arms around the leg of the piano and pressing my face against its rivets. I convulsed with a guttural cry. "No." I couldn't catch my breath, my shoulders concaved around my chest, and my diaphragm compressed between my ribs.

"Hans, listen to me," the professor softly said. "I'd like it for you to leave right now. There's no sense to have a practice today since you've decided to go to Munich. You have to go."

"But ... what ... about ... when I come back?"

"There's no more. You've clearly made your choice, and now you have to live with it," the professor educated with a soothing tone. "Someday you'll understand."

Fear set in, and I was completely unprepared. "What will I do?"

"You'll have to figure that out yourself. I'm not able to help you anymore." He walked to the door and opened it. "Now please, go." His voice cracked with emotion.

I wanted to run to him, wrap my arms around him and make everything better. I wanted to prove to him how truly sorry I was. But something told me not to, that I went too far this time. I unwrapped myself from the piano's leg and crawled to my satchel. I stood, walked through the exit, stopped in the foray, and turned to him.

"Don't. Just go," he spoke in a heartless tone without making any eye contact.

A wave of coldness flooded me as if winter came early and dabbed frost on all the unprepared flowers, aging their petals brown before their time. My spine stiffened, holding my head high, I walked away from my past, stunned and unprepared from the lack of any indications of the future.

As I descended the stairs, I deflated and collapsed onto the bottom step. I blinded myself with tears. Someone came down the staircase above me, and I hoped that it was the professor rushing to accept my apology and grant me with forgiveness. But the steps belonged to a student rushing to get to another class. I filled with a rage that lifted me from my disgrace and propelled myself out the building's door and into the afternoon with such a fury that I was unaware of which path I embarked on. My head thumped with echoing voices of snappish allegations and revengeful indictments.

Chapter 10

Stefan was sitting on his bed reading when I came into our room.

He looked up and smirked. "Look at what the cat dragged in. Had a late night last night, huh?"

I glared at him.

"What time did you get in?" he continued. "I tried to wake you for breakfast, but you weren't stirring."

I crashed onto my bed, facing the wall.

"What happened last night?"

"Nothing," I mumbled.

"I heard that Röhm was here recruiting. Did you know about that?" His voice filled with excitement. "This morning at breakfast, Ian and Walter were filling me in on the details. I guess they only selected one new candidate. Walter said that Petre heard that there were several others that they're going to put on a holding list, but only one went through the entire process. Petre said he thought he saw you there filling out papers and talking to your swimmer friend. He tried to get your attention, but they escorted you to another room. So, were you there?"

The late afternoon sun reflected off the Star of David, casting hues of different colors onto the wall. I watched shards of red, yellow, orange, blue, and violet twirl, merge, and separate from each other in a choreographed ballet.

"Are you listening to me?" He tossed his book at me. It landed on the bed next to the small of my back.

I moaned as I closed my eyes on the sparkles' second interruptive movement.

"Petre said that the doctor tried to touch him inappropriately during the examination, so he just got up and left. The rumors have it that whenever there's a convention or important meeting, there's always some extra business going on in one of the rooms with the officials. And they only want attractive people." His voice rose as he switched subjects. "Did you get to see the famous Ernst Röhm? Petre said that he has this ugly scar on his cheek that happened when he was in a battle and that he almost died from it."

I squeezed my eyes tight.

"Oh, by the way, Walter and Ian want to know if you'd like to go with us after the piano competition to that bar we went to the other day. You know, the place we went to when we borrowed the truck. Ian says you are for sure to win the top prize. The only person that can come close is Jan Jenkins, but he's not as good as you are, and his runs are always sloppy. Walter says that you have this air of elegance when you play. What do you think? Would you like to go?"

I buried my head under my pillow, shutting out his incessant droning and attempting to silence the babbling voices pounding in my head. *What am I going to do? What if the professor is right and Josef is only using me? Why was I the only one that got through? How am I going to make things right with the professor? What if Josef does like me? How will I ever be sure of how he feels? Why did I allow the doctor to touch me like that? Does that mean that I am a homosexual? What if I am? What would Josef think of me?*

A hand touched my shoulder, and I whipped my head from under the pillow. "What?!"

Stefan stood there with fear in his eyes and his hands covering his mouth. "I wanted to know if you were hungry." He spoke through his cupped hands, causing the sound to muffle. "I asked you, but you didn't answer, so I didn't know if you heard me."

"What? I can't understand you." I sat up, resting my back on the wall and cradling a pillow.

He timidly lowered his hands but kept them near his neck, protecting his larynx. "It's lunch. I was hoping that you'd go eat with me."

"Why?"

"We always eat together." His voice wavered.

"Haven't you eaten already?"

He looked down at the book he threw that was now resting against my thigh. He reached for it. "I was waiting for you." As he took hold of the book, his knuckles brushed against my leg.

"Hey, watch it. What are you trying to do?" I drew my leg away from him.

"I was getting my book, that's all."

"Did you have to touch my leg like that?" I challenged him.

"I didn't mean to."

"What's with you? You're always touching me." I brushed my leg where he made contact as if I could remove the possibility of any questionable tendencies from being transmitted through his touch.

"No, I was just getting my book." He sat on the edge of his bed, holding the book against his chest with crossed arms.

"Just be more careful where you're putting your hands." I rolled onto my side with my back to him.

"So, you don't want to have lunch?"

"No, just leave me alone. I'm tired, and I just want to get some sleep." I tucked my head back under the pillow.

"All right."

I heard him reposition himself onto his mattress, open his book, and turn the pages to locate where he had stopped reading last.

The voices began again to echo, ricochet, and bounce off the walls of my brain. At first, their desires for answers were soft and somewhat soothing, but as they gathered up speed and momentum, they also became louder, slicing and careening into each other and thumping heavily against my temples.

I wanted them to stop, but the swirling and pounding caused my mind to spin as if I was drifting, flying, falling. I was spinning uncontrollably. My only option was relinquishing my control and allowing my body to spiral into the unknown, like on a tire swing, and the rope was twisted so tight that you simply leaned back and let go, allowing the world to spin. You knew you were going to feel nauseous when it stopped, but you allowed it to happen anyhow.

I spiraled faster through some cosmos or some plane of existence between life and death. The velocity of the flight caused the voices to fade, as if they flung away one by one. Anger lost its reddish grip and was sucked into a vortex. Jealousy was unable to remain steadfast within its green armor and whipped off into a faraway galaxy. Fear, with its black talons, embedded deep into my ribs and whipped and whirled with me as we spun wildly through this unchartered dark maze.

The inability to rid myself of fear caused me to wonder if this was how dying felt. When you became disoriented and unable to control the functions of your body and you had no clue where you were, when riddled with this one emotion and unable to divorce yourself from its power, forcing you to make a choice. I had no choice but the acceptance of life's finality, allowing my life force to slip from me.

Just when I thought the spiral speed would accelerate, it slowed, and I saw clouds closing in on me. Fluffy clouds, like cotton candy, surrounded me in complete whiteness. I floated on a bed of clouds, drifting to some unknown destination. The clouds lowered me down, receded, and left me in a white room, on a table, under a large round lamp, which warmed my nakedness. I tried to move, but my arms and legs were strapped down to a metal table. I heard footsteps, but the light was too bright to make out the intruder.

"Can you just leave me alone?" I murmured.

The steps continued to click against the tiled floor.

An outline of a man in white clothing silhouetted against the whiteness of the lights and walls slowly made his way to the table.

"What do you want?" My voice sounded muffled, like I was screaming underwater.

The figure's long fingers caressed my thighs, slid toward my pelvis, and fondled me.

"*No!*" I screeched, struggling to break free from the bondage.

"Relax," a garbled voice encouraged.

The hand continued touching me as I began to inflate. I tried squeezing my thighs together, but the restraints weren't permitting any such movement. I lifted my hips to escape the predator's caresses, but I couldn't get away.

"Please, stop!"

He wrapped his hand around my swollenness, and a warm wetness surrounded the crown and slid down my shaft. I glanced up and saw myself inside Dr. Falk's mouth. His tongue scaled and darted up and down. I arched my back to free myself from his frenzied attack, but I couldn't rid myself from the suction. He continued to lap at me, sending shock waves after shock waves through my pelvis and up my spine to all parts of my body. My body tensed as I tried not to allow the release. I tossed my head from side to side, trying to escape. My body temperature rose. I started sweating. My breathing became heavy and laborious. I was losing control.

"No," I demanded.

He was relentless.

I arched my head back and saw Josef looking down at me with a sneer. I pleaded with my eyes for help, but he stroked my bangs away from my forehead.

"Relax and enjoy it. It'll all be over soon," Josef said in a soothing way and faded into the shadows.

"Hans," a familiar voice faintly called to me.

"*No!*"

I felt something on my shoulder. I summoned up all my strength, jerked my arms and legs free from the straps, and rolled off the table. In a fury, I shoved the culprit as hard as I could. I heard a loud thump, but my eyes pulsated with strobes of black and white. I blindly flung myself on top of the perpetrator and pummeled him with a left and followed with a quick right. I continued to alternate the hits in rapid successions without easing off, making sure that each contact accented with closed fists. A whimper resounded with each strike. Finally, I pulled myself back like a crab, exhausted, sitting on the floor against the far wall.

As my vision cleared, Stefan's bloody body lay on the floor, not moving except for the red liquid pulsating from his nose, swollen lip, and chin. The liquid was dark and thick as it seeped down around his neck and collected on his white shirt. My hands shook, knuckles swollen and splattered with painted red.

Chapter 11

The train's metal wheels jostled against the tracks, creating a soothing and melodic sound. My forehead rested on the vibrating windowpane as I watched passing images. The rolling fields reminded me of a giant quilt's patchwork of different sizes, shapes, and colors sewn together. A red barn appeared in the distance with a horse pulling a plow, sending brown dust into the cloudless cerulean sky.

I tried to understand the brutal attack on Stefan. I vividly recalled the gratification when my knuckles contacted his flesh and the degradation that filled me once I saw the damage. I was concerned with the hidden rage dwelling inside of me, which gave no warning signs before lashing its ugliness. Had this monster been dormant inside my entire life? And if it had, why appear now? Would I be able to tame it so that it never overtakes me again? From where did this rage stem? And why did I take it out on Stefan, who had never done anything to me but be my friend?

I searched through my memories to identify any events or moments from the past.

*****

It was a late fall day, and Mother was singing while drying the dishes. Her voice was beautiful and light, but it wasn't her singing that made her noted in the entertainment world. Mother was the prima ballerina for the Royal Berlin Ballet Company. Later, I'd learned the highlights of her career included notable lead roles in *Giselle*, *Romeo and Juliet*, and especially *Swan Lake*. It was the latter that made her "famous" and took her around the world. I'd listen to people talk about her performances of the dying swan as the most moving experience that they had ever witnessed on stage. There was never a dry eye in the place and a common phenomenon that she never received less than six curtain calls.

In fact, at her last performance at La Scala Theatre in Rome, the curtain call lasted for three-and-a-half hours. The audience wanted to see her perform once more so badly that they started to stamp and clap in unison, until her and her partner, Ivan Wolfgang, agreed to repeat the pas-de-deux from the last movement. She was ever so eager to oblige her audience. With a bare stage, since the stagehands had already dismantled the set during her bows, and a single piano, since the orchestra had already gone home, my mother publicly performed her last dying swan to the approval of the eager audience. What her public wasn't aware of was that she was three months pregnant.

She went into hiding in the countryside while carrying the baby to term and hoped to return to the stage. She didn't want anyone to know of the child since she wanted to keep the identity of the father a secret. Her small frame wasn't built to carry. But her determination against her doctor's wishes of an abortion caused her to be confined to bed rest for the final three months and rely on the assistance of a servant. The difficulty of the birth was too stressful on her hips, leaving them fractured and scarred. Her return to the ballet world was never to be.

Her long legs towered over me on that humid day. I looked up at her lean body, reaching. Usually, she would stop whatever she was doing to lift me into her arms, whirl me around in the air, and pull me into her small and firm breast. She'd tuck my head in the curve of her neck and stroke my flaxen hair. She always smelled of vanilla and hummed anything that came to mind.

But for some reason on this day, she paid no mind to my desires to be held. She continuously stepped around me, putting the dried dishes back into the cupboard and leaving me turning on my heels and reaching into the empty air. My face reddened with the frustration of being ignored, and my anger showed through as unintelligible and guttural wailing. She continued ignoring my cries. One time as she passed, I took hold of the hem of her skirt and held on to it all with all my might. She stumbled forward, falling to the floor with me tumbling after. She whipped around and planted the palm of her hand against the fatness of my left cheek. The stinging sensation ceased my cries. I stood there while the welt grew on my face, arms out to the side, eyes wide open, and my pants were wet.

Mother crawled on knees, reaching for me. She gently touched the welted cheek as tears streamed down her face. She enfolded me into her chest and held me so tight. I could tell she was trying to say something, but all I heard was the ringing in my ears. Then she suddenly started to convulse. Her frail body shook with such force that my head bounded back and forth. Her arms became stiff as her hands curled in clutched claws. Her mouth twisted. Her pale blue eyes went black before rolling back into her head and leaving her orbs white as a ghost's. Her body became limp as she toppled over on top of me, pinning me beneath her. The tremors finally subsided, and her breath ceased to exist. I remained there until the next day when the servant found us.

I never was informed of what had happened, and I never saw my mother after that. I began an ambiguous life of growing up in boarding schools. A life of trying to hide any emotions of that dreaded day. I learned how to pretend that it never happened. A life of avoiding the guilt and anger I felt toward her for leaving me. I vowed never to let anyone get close to me again. It wasn't until I was with Father Michael where I found solitude through the piano. It was here that I felt close to my mother and never alone. It was here that I could imagine her dancing that beautiful swan and never dying. It was here that she was young, beautiful, and smelling of vanilla. It was here that I was loved.

*****

Josef opened the door to the cabin and slid in next to me. "Cheer up. We're on our way to Munich," he said gleefully. "We're free from that prison of a school for the entire weekend. Aren't you excited?" He handed me a small cup of water.

"Of course I am. But I can't get that image of Stefan lying there ... all bloody," I said distractedly.

"It's fine, he's okay. He's going to be just fine. A little sore for the next couple of days, I'd imagine, but he'll heal."

"I don't know what came over me. I don't remember doing it," I confessed.

"It happened, let it go."

"I can't just let it go. I hit Stefan."

"No, you beat the crap out of him." He corrected with a grin. "Do you know what triggered it?"

"I was asleep, I guess, and maybe dreaming."

"Yes, that's what he said. He heard you moaning and crying out in your sleep. He thought you were having a nightmare, so he tried to wake you. What were you dreaming about?"

"That's just it. I can't remember any of it." I looked at him and realized how close he was sitting next to me. We were the only two in this compartment that can comfortably sit four adults.

His eyes were so saturated with concern as an uneven jolt from the tracks sent our shoulders together. He smiled and added, "It was the right thing to come get me."

"I didn't know what else to do," I explained. "I wasn't sure what would have happened if I went to the nurse and told her I beat him up."

"You did the right thing. That's what the Movement is for, to help our brothers in need. Now let's try and not worry about that anymore. You have to think about playing for Hitler."

"Are you sure he'll even be there?"

"I'm sure of it."

"You'll be watching, right?"

"Of course I will." He guided my head on his shoulder. "Relax, we have got a long ride." He stroked the nape of my neck.

I inhaled his scent, laced my fingers through his, and closed my eyes.

Chapter 12

Josef proudly boasted that there were no other artists on the playbill before leaving me alone in front of a mirror. Adolf Hitler, Ernst Röhm, along with other powerful militia and guests were gathered in the next room to hear me play.

The mirror's image reflected someone that I didn't entirely recognize. The young man looking back at me had aspects of my youthful quality as a naïve boy, yet hardness crept around his eyes. This coarseness caused the image to appear older. His blond hair impeccably brushed to the back, with a part traveling through the middle. His chiseled cheekbones and jaw were sharper and had lost their smooth edges and formed a clef chin. His lips pressed together into a thin pink line. The uniform's brown monochromatic shade blended with the skin's coloring, permitting the eye's blueness to be more vibrant.

"You look fantastic."

Josef's reflection appeared over my shoulder, and he placed his hands around my waist. His bright smile was evident that everything was about to happen.

"You are sure I look all right?" I asked with trepidation.

"You look perfect." He leaned his chin against my right ear. "Are you ready?" he whispered.

I hesitantly nodded while looking in his eyes via the reflective glass. We remained there, looking at each other, neither one glancing off to the side. Finally, he leaned in and grazed his soft lips against my jaw, just below my ear lobe.

"It's time," he softly expressed. "Wait for Hitler's nod."

I replayed the information provided by Karl, Josef's friend. "Dignitaries will be sitting all around you while you play the Grand

Steinway. There are no proscenium or stage curtains. You enter through the adjoining doorway and mingle through the guests to make your way to the piano. You must stand at attention until the Führer gives you the motion for when to sit, when to play, when to rise, and when to exit. Is this clear?"

I closed my eyes and inhaled deeply. I took a deep breath before lifting my curtains to discover that I stood alone in the reflective glass as if Josef was never there. For a moment, I wondered if I had imagined the quick and engaging interaction, the tenderness. Josef stood next to the door that separated us from the Gallery, which muffled the chatter and laughter. His hand rested on the knob, anticipating the moment when he would introduce me to this new world.

Josef was the replica of the Youth Movement posters: the wholesome and clean-cut lad wearing the carefully put together uniform, the charming smile that appealed to anyone, and those eyes that encouraged the youth of Germany that they could also be a part of this great movement. He epitomized the superior race, set aside his dark hair and eyes.

"Here we go," he triumphantly announced.

"Josef, wait."

He looked at me from under his brow with a crooked smile. "What?"

"What if—"

He stood erect. "No no no. We're not having any of this 'what ifs.' You're going to go in there, and you're going to perform beautifully like you always do. They're going to enjoy it."

"Will you—"

"I'll be right here by this door, waiting for you. I'm going to be the proudest person in the room." He straightened my tie's knot. "Now go in there and be brilliant." He quickly pecked my lips, grabbed my hand, and led me to the door.

I paused a moment, realizing that once I walked through that passageway, my life will be forever changed.

He turned the knob, and the door jarred open, allowing the chatter and laughter to spill into our space. He squeezed my hand tightly once more before letting go and pushed the portal completely open. He stepped into the Gallery and indicated for me to follow.

Many dark uniforms filled the room.

I stalled a moment to strategize my maneuvering through the seats and milling persons. I decided to take the most direct route displayed before me. I weaved and dodged guests as they clumped into small groups, discussing different aspects of their involvement with the Movement or their latest accomplishments. I sidestepped several decorated military officers as they flitted between groups without taking into consideration the small passageways between seats. I also had to be aware of the waiters carrying flutes of golden champagne. I felt relief once I reached the piano, placed my hand on the instrument's edge, and waited.

I glanced around the room, trying to nonchalantly get a glimpse of Hitler. Out of the corner of my eye, I saw the back of a smallish man standing next to Karl and addressing other men in uniform. His impish frame was adorned in the dark military jacket that draped down and cinched at the waist with a thick leather belt. His black riding breeches were tucked into his leather boots that reached up over his calves. His cap secured under his arm against his ribs. His cleanly cropped dark hair was slicked down to his head.

Ernst Röhm whispered to Josef and patted his cheek before giving a command to an assistant, who glanced over toward me. I quickly looked in the opposite direction. The guests seemed to be unaware of my appearance as they obliviously continue their conversations, causing the murmuring to grow in the room.

Two sharp claps silenced the room and caused everyone to focus on Röhm, who stood with his chest puffed out and a smirk on his round face. He made his way next to Hitler and Karl. Hitler's pinched face was accented with the two small square swatches of hair above his upper lip. His beady eyes darted out from under the dark hair that was parted and swooped down over his left brow. He eyes scaled up and down as I watched him evaluate me. I held my breath, waiting for him to give me the approval to begin my performance.

Hitler stepped away from Röhm without any warning and walked stiff-legged toward me. He halted by a chair while keeping his intense stare upon me. He sank onto the chair's cushion, crossed his legs, and caressed his mustache. He nodded for me to sit.

I lowered myself onto the bench, lifted the lid to the keyboard, placed my hands on my thighs, and looked back at the Führer.

Karl sat to the left of Hitler while Röhm remained standing behind them. The other guests made their way to their seat and prepared for the concert.

Röhm's assistant said something to Josef before walking out of the room.

Josef stood there alone, forcing a smile.

Hitler lifted his palms and nodded for me to start playing.

I placed my fingers on the keys and exhaled. I compressed the keys down, sending sound waves out to the far corners of the Gallery before echoing back. The amplification of the room produced a tinny effect as the newly struck chords intermingled with the returning chords, filling the Gallery with the swelling of an improvisational musical composition.

The opus became a distant voice to my ears as Röhm excused himself and made his way toward the exit. He paused for a moment in front of Josef, where he leaned in whispering something while watching Hitler out of the corner of his eye. Josef curled the corners of his lips and nodded, sending Röhm to toss his face toward the ceiling with a quiet but jovial laugh and placed his hand on Josef's chest. Josef masked Röhm's hand with his own. The two looked at each other, and Josef nodded again. Röhm walked away, glanced back at Josef, and exited through the doorway that led to the hallway. Josef glanced around the room before resting his eyes on mine, causing me to rush the next several bars. He broke the eye contact, and without looking back, he slipped out the door that Röhm previously existed.

My breath was uneven and rushed as the music became audible to me again. My left hand fumbled for the next sequences of chords, causing the meter to be unbalanced and erratic. The disjointed music resolved itself in the clear, creating an intense mood in the room. I allowed the resonance to dissipate to a silence before I composed the interlude. I glanced over to Hitler, who seemed enthralled with my improvisational etude. He leaned forward with his chin resting on his fist while his other hand wrapped around and stroked the Swastika armband.

With a pulse of my head, I instigated a new melodic movement that interrupted the sounds of the falling rain into a quiet pool. The music drifted off into the far realms, becoming a distant humming in my ears. Several other military officers left the room, pulling my attention with them as they exited through the same doorway as Josef and Röhm. My mind raced, causing my interlude to become rapid and flighty like a departure of a swarm of bees as my fingers fluttered across the keys disjointing the peaceful mood of the raindrops.

I played in a trance. My mind was blank to the complexity of the composition and the climactic moment of the movement. I was numb to the resolution and the resolve of the forthcoming final chord. I became automatic in my presentation and unable to decipher the desired combination of the final notes clearly. I pictured sheet music in my mind's eye, and the notes slipped from the staff, leaving blank paper. I scrambled to provide a cohesive finale, which seemed to take a life of its own. My fingers performed without any connection to my thoughts, as if they belonged to someone else and disconnected from my soul.

I was escorted back to reality with the solo clapping from Hitler. Slowly, his appreciation accompanied by the other guests. Hitler raised his palm to the sky and nodded to me. Karl indicated for me to stand.

As I stood, the room spun as my eyes throbbed, and I leaned against the edge of the piano for support. Josef was gone, triggering my stomach to twist and turn. I felt uncomfortable, abandoned, and nauseous. I lurched my way past the Führer to the doorway.

A hand grabbed me, stopping me from exiting. Hitler stood while retaining his hold on my wrist. He appeared smaller than what I expected as he looked up at me. His hazel eyes were intense, yet there was a sense of kindness. Without saying a word, he nodded to me and released his grip. I nodded back and headed for the nearest door, without thinking, and blindly left.

In my haste, I found myself alone in a strange hallway. I realized that I should've departed through the other door that led back to the adjoining room. I started to turn to go back into the Gallery when I froze with the fear facing Hitler again. I decided to try to find the spare room through another access.

Portraits of militia personnel dating back to early 1800s adorned the hallway. I glanced at the stern faces and rigid postures as I passed. Being lost began to creep into my psyche. I saw a door up ahead and rushed to it. I turned the handle and entered.

The room was cast in dark shadows as the lights had been turned down. I walked into the foray, and I heard strange sounds coming from deeper within the room. I approached, discovering discarded uniforms in heaps on the floor and draped over chairs. A strong musky odor filled the air. I quietly walked in farther and saw a huddle of men. They were naked and stroked themselves as they watched something performing in the center. I backed up and bumped into a desk, sending a helmet crashing to the floor and interrupting the soft moaning. The men broke the circle and looked at me. As they parted, Röhm had his hands anchored to the hip bones of a naked lad positioned in front of him.

"It's … good … of you … to … drop by," Röhm announced as he thrust his pelvis with each word and caused his blubber to ripple. "Master Klein. How do you like this performance?" Röhm drove his hips extremely hard, causing the boy's spine to arch, flinging his head back, whipping his dark hair through the air, and revealing his face contorting with pain. My stomach dropped when I recognized Josef positioned there, naked, and offering himself so readily to Röhm.

I backed out of the room and felt a hand slip under my arm and escorted me down the hall. I tried to pull away, but the grasp was too tight, and the fingers dug into my flesh.

"We have to get out of here now," the voice commanded. "Just come with me."

Karl ushered me down the hall. I tried to speak, but he interrupted.

"I'll explain everything when we get into the car."

"But, Josef—"

"Don't worry about him. We don't have time. We have to leave now."

I looked back and saw a group of soldiers with rifles drawn kick in the door and rush into the room I just left.

Karl forced me down a back staircase and out onto the driveway. The brisk evening air chilled my burning cheeks.

"We can't just leave him—"

"Trust me," he demanded. "You do not want to be in there right now."

A distant sound of dogs barked.

He opened car's door. "Get in!" he shouted.

"But—"

The darkened windows on the second floor flashed a series of white and red blasts. The sharp popping sent us crouching to the ground and covering our heads from flying glass.

"Now!" Karl shoved me into the vehicle's back seat and climbed in on top of me. He tapped on the front seat. "Franz, go!"

"Yes, sir," responded the driver.

The car pulled down the driveway and into the dark of the night. Karl's breath warmed my neck, and his racing heart pounded against my chest.

Chapter 13

"We should be all right now," Karl said once we were safely away from the hotel's ground. He pulled himself off me and looked out the windows. The darkness of the night hid half of his face. "I'm sorry for all that," he stated as he adjusted himself in the seat. "I was ordered to get you out of the building and take you back to the train as quick as possible."

"I don't understand," I replied.

Karl offered me a hand to help guide me onto the leather seat next to him. "It was a setup. This whole weekend was a secret plan." He brushed something off my shoulder.

"A setup?" I watched black tree trunks and bushes whiz by the window.

"Adolf Hitler has been having some second thoughts about Ernst Röhm's intentions within the political party," he explained.

"So what does that have to do with me?"

"Nothing. That's why Hitler ordered me to find you and get you away as soon as possible." He placed his hand on my shoulder.

I refused to acknowledge his compassion.

He removed his hand. "You exited through the wrong door. If you would've gone into the adjoining room, I would've detained you there until the whole ordeal was over. Hitler thought you were going to walk into the trap when you went out into the hallway."

"What kind of trap?"

"The 'cleanup' that Hitler ordered," he casually said.

"The cleanup?!"

"I don't have all the information and details—"

I interrupted him, "Then tell me what you know."

"It doesn't concern you."

"I was in the middle of a massacre or what surely seemed like a massacre. And now I'm trapped in a speeding vehicle with a man that I hardly know. A man that was supposed to be Josef's best friend, who left him behind. Excuse me if I seem a little confused and angry right now."

"I can understand," he softly spoke, yet his eyes remained stern.

"Do you? It doesn't seem like it to me. You sit here acting as if this is a regular event. That this happens at every big meeting."

"You're right, and let me try to explain." He positioned himself, facing front with his hands clasped in his lap. "Hitler felt that Röhm and several other military leaders of the SA had grown distant to the progression of the Nazi Regime. He felt that they were angry with him for abandoning the socialist principles. Since Röhm was associated more with the socialism than with nationalism, he was a threat to the continued support of the chancellor within in the army and the business community that helped raise Hitler to power."

"Excuse me for asking, but this was an act based on Hitler's fear of a possible coup?" I asked with sarcasm.

"It had a making of one," he explained.

"But was there any evidence that it was going to happen?" I questioned him.

"The potential was there."

"The potential?" I was beside myself. The idea that the potential was there, and there was not any evidence of a coup seemed so outlandish to me. I couldn't help but wonder, who did this Hitler believe he was? These were the people who helped put him into power and had done everything to keep him there.

"You must try and understand the background and how this was making the Führer nervous. When the stock market crashed in the United States in 1929, all the financial loans that the US was supplying to Germany after World War I was withdrawn, leaving Germany in an epidemic of layoffs and unemployment among the working class. This recession created widespread poverty."

"Thank you for the history lesson, but I don't see how this ties into tonight," I bravely said.

"I'm trying to explain it to you."

I resigned, leaned back, and tried to listen.

"So for these unemployed people, the creation of the SA brought hope back into their lives. Many of them joined the SA, which was about seven hundred thousand men, and about 85 percent were from the working class, creating a group with an active socialist lean within the SA and took the attention away from the national-socialist policy. The SA continued to grow and seemed to move more away from the Nazi leadership. The SA wanted to become the core of the new German army."

"But why would Röhm want to destroy everything he created with Hitler?" I asked.

"That's just it. Hitler didn't want to see that either."

The car swerved, causing me to fling into Karl's shoulder. Karl quickly grabbed hold of me and kept me from falling onto the floor as the wheel thumped.

"Sorry, sir, something ran out in front of the car," announced Franz, the driver.

"What was it?" asked Karl.

"I'm not sure, sir, but it seemed like some animal," he explained.

"It sounded like you ran over it."

"I believe I did. Sorry."

Karl and I looked back at something lying in the road.

"Are you all right, sir?" asked Franz.

"We're all okay back here," Karl responded.

"It just darted out of the brush."

"The poor thing," Karl said as he still looked out the back window.

I repositioned myself back onto my side of the seat. I was confused with Karl's empathy for the animal and stoic demeanor toward the massacre we just left.

The car resumed its speeding path toward the train station, and Karl faced the front again.

The hum of the engine and the wheels on the pavement filled the car.

I asked, "So the SA was becoming a threat because of its size?"

"Yes." Karl slowly nodded. "That and the fact that Hitler was feeling pressure to reduce the SA's influence. Since the SA was composed of mostly working class, the wealthy industrialist supporters were concerned about the SA's socialist leanings."

"But wasn't it the socialist rhetoric that had been useful for Hitler's rise to power and the Nazis?" I asked.

Karl looked at me as if he was impressed. "Yes, you're correct. However, many feel that the socialist ideology stands in contradiction to the Nazi's current goals. And Röhm wanted to have the German army become part of the SA."

"What if Röhm's intentions were credible? What if his intentions were for the best of the movement and the prosperity of the German people?"

Karl didn't respond but stared straight out at the road ahead.

I continued, "It doesn't seem logical to me to eliminate someone that has been so instrumental in the growth of such an influential organization such as the SA. Why couldn't that all be worked out between them?" I felt there was something more to the reasons behind this secret plan, some other reason that Hitler wanted to have Röhm removed.

We sat in silence as the driver continued to steer the vehicle through the dark back roads of Munich.

I broke the silence. "There's something else that you aren't talking about?"

Karl broke his stare and looked down at his hands.

"What is it?"

"It's only speculation," he muttered.

"What's only speculation?"

He glanced up at me and shook his head. He started to say something, but resisted and looked out his window.

I felt this rage inside that I deserved the right to know. Blood set my ears on fire. I grabbed his jacket, just below his armband. "What is it?"

"I don't know," he apologized.

"Just say it."

He looked back at me. "It's only speculation."

I held his attention with my eyes.

"Many of the officers of the Nazi Party are conservative," he added.

"So?"

"They were against Röhm and some of the other officials that he appointed because of their overtly homosexual practices. These acts are against paragraph 175."

"Are you telling me the Nazis removed Röhm because of his attraction to the same sex?"

"It's not well accepted."

"But Hitler must have known about Röhm's interests. They've known each other for a long time."

"But it was getting out of hand. Röhm didn't try to hide it. Like this evening, Hitler knew that there would've been another performance going on in the other room. He was aware of that as soon as Röhm exited the room."

"What about Josef?" My eyes stung. "How could you leave him behind like that?"

"What could I have done?" Karl asked.

"You could've warned him. You could've forced him out like you did me."

"I did warn him." He spoke with a softness that expressed his loss.

"He was aware of the secret plan?"

"Not exactly." He looked out the window and caused it to fog with his words. "He didn't believe the possibility that the plan could exist. He was confident that it'd blow over like it has done so many times before."

The world stopped spinning as I realized that this wasn't the first time that Josef was in this situation. Was the professor right when he said that Josef was only out for his advancement? "I thought you were best friends."

"I only became a friend with him recently," Karl stated.

Franz pulled into the train station and put the car in park, letting the engine idle, and handed Karl an envelope.

Karl examined the contents and forced a smile. "This is your ticket for the train. The train is loading right now. I also have this order for you to report to a new assignment. Hitler was impressed with you and wants to help you in any way that he can. He said you have promise." He handed me the envelope. "You have to go now."

I took the envelope, opened the door, and climbed out. I felt numb. My life seemed lost, and I was shuffled off, yet again, into the world that was completely disheveled. I had no idea where I was going or what I was going to do. I opened the envelope and looked at the contents, which contained a ticket, some money, and an official-looking paper.

"Hans." Karl leaned out of the open car door. "Things are going to be different from now on. There's no longer an SA organization. I'm a member of the SS, and we'll be taking over the SA assignments. I was ordered to attend your school to keep an eye on the Youth Movement and the recruitments that Röhm was conducting. I had known about Josef Stork before I met him. He has been favored by Röhm for some time now."

I started walking toward the train.

Karl rushed out from the back seat and grabbed my arm. "Your life is no longer what you think it is. You are to return to your dorm and gather what you need. Do not try to question too much. It's easier to go with the flow. The school you left this weekend is not the same school you'll find when you return. This opportunity is a second chance. Take it and make the most out of it. I'll come to pick you up tomorrow afternoon and bring you to the disclosed camp that's indicated on your orders. You're to start a new occupation immediately. Now go before the train leaves." He gently shoved me.

The car door slammed, and the tires squealed against the pavement.

I was alone. I automatically walked to the train, climbed aboard, and found my seat. The train jerked and slowly moved forward. I leaned my forehead on the vibrating windowpane.

The morning sun peered from the east, shedding its orange fingers onto the sleeping countryside. I didn't see the red barns and the farmers working in the fields like I did on my travel to Munich.

As the train followed the designed tracks, I saw an encampment of barbed wire in the distance. Long tubular shed-like structures inhabited the interior parameters and factory-like buildings with stacks spewing darkened plumes of smoke into the dewy sky. I watched the entrance to the camp as another train entered through an arch that proudly flew a giant red flag with a black swastika. I continued to view the encampment until the train tracks gently curved, sending the location out of my sight. A quilted patchwork of the landscape woke up under the sapphire sky filled my vision.

Chapter 14

Exhausted, I walked to my dorm room, longing for a restful nap with my head upon my familiar pillow and wrapped in my sheets. The desires to regain my strength and to settle my racing mind were my two primary objectives. The afternoon sun bled through the hallway, sending shards of red, orange, and yellow across the tiled floor. The splintered door to my room hung open from forced entry. Inside, the room was in shambles, like an elapsed war zone.

Both wardrobes' doors were pried off and tossed to the side, resting clumsily against the wall. The contents piled in the middle of the floor were saturated with red paint. Broken and splintered hangers scattered on the floor like twigs forgotten in the forest. In the corner, my cherished Oxford shoes lay on their sides with laces reaching for assistance and bleeding red. Neckties were scattered around like discarded snakes that were trying to find shelter beneath the protection of the beds.

The stripped mattresses appeared naked and sliced down the middle several times, exposing interior stuffing. The beds' crippled legs leaned sideways from the lack of support.

The crushed identical desks looked like toothpicks. The textbooks' pages were torn out and littered everywhere. Pencils speared into the ceiling and hung with their erasers pointing in all different directions. The enfeebled wooden chairs clung together for support as they anchored each other against the wall under the window that resides between the beds.

"Jude" and illustrations of Jewish caricatures consisting of large noses that resemble the number 6 desecrated all the walls in sloppy and dripping red paint. Other choice words such as "Die," "filth," "trash," "pigs" and large swastikas adorned the rest of the available wall space amid the small dorm room. The odor of fresh paint permeated the air, chasing the oxygen out the broken window.

The only item not marred was the Star of David, which remained peacefully hanging in front of the broken window, casting a soft stream of rainbow colors that danced upon the carnage of hatred.

A slow, mournful dirge seeped into my head as I took inventory. The dissonance combinations of flats and sharps gave the solemnity a dark soul and reflected Bach's *Toccata and Fugue*. The polyphonic composition declared the emotional journey of the past days. I braced my weight against the fragmented wardrobe as I shook with paroxysms of laughter and tears.

"They came for him, Hans."

Petre stood in the doorway cradling a box of books. His face paled with exhaustion, eyes wistful and lined red, cheeks sullen, and his lower lip swollen purplish-red with a tinge of greenish-yellow expanding down over his chin.

"What?" I asked.

"They came to take him. The Nazis. They came for all the Jews. Anyone they thought might have been Jewish. They're all gone," he stammered in a monotone that accompanied shock. "They had a list and took them. If you were on the list, they took you without any questions. If you weren't on the list, you were left behind. They took Walter and Ian away too."

"Where? Where did they take them?" I asked.

"Out … away. They were tied with their hands behind their backs and taken out like garbage. They took them out the back to an awaiting truck and loaded them in. They kept pushing them into the truck. They didn't even care if there was room. They just kept cramming them into the truck." His eyes dilated and turned black as they filled with liquid. "If they obeyed, the soldiers escorted them to the truck, but if they tried to resist, the soldiers punished them. Walter went without a struggle, nodding and smiling. He tried to convince Ian to go peacefully, but Ian resisted. Three of them hit him with their rifles until they had to carry him out. Walter walked right alongside with his head held high. He didn't even cry. Ian was bleeding badly, and Walter just kept smiling." Petre's voice quivered as his breathing labored. "Stefan fought. He barricaded the door, but they pried it open with such force, I thought the whole building was going to cave in. That didn't deter Stefan from fighting. He fought hard too. He broke away and ran out into the hall. Two of them followed. But you know how quick and agile Stefan is. He may have gotten away, I don't know. It was dark when I woke, and he was gone. Everyone was gone." His voice faded as he stared off into the room. His lips twitched as he gripped the box of books tighter against his chest. He jerked his head toward me. "It's my fault, Hans," he confessed. "Walter and Ian are gone because of me, because of my stupidity."

"What are you talking about, Petre?"

"It's my fault that the Nazis took Walter and Ian." His eyes widened. "I wrote their names down when I was filling out the forms at the Youth Movement Meeting the other night. You know, there was a section that asked if you knew of anyone who was Jewish or you thought might be Jewish. I told them that I didn't know anyone who was Jewish, but they wouldn't take my form until I wrote several names down. So I wrote Walter and Ian's names. And now they're gone." He balanced the box in one arm and reached for the wall for support. "What have I done?" His fatigued body started shaking.

I removed the box from his hand and placed it on the floor.

His abdomen concaved inwardly, and he hid his face with his hands, sobbing uncontrollably.

I wrapped my arms around him.

He buried his face against my sternum.

"Come on now, Petre. It'll be all right." I tried to sound reassuring.

He sternly looked at me. "How can it be all right? It's my fault. Where were they taken? We may never know. We may never see them again, ever. They're thought to be Jewish, and that's not a good thing. They're gone. What've I done?"

"Are you sure it's the form you filled out for the Youth Movement?" I asked.

"I'm certain. They told me," he sobbed.

"Who told you?"

His strained face was contorted and blotchy. "One of the commanders in charge informed me that they collected the names from Ernst Röhm when he was here. He held me by the throat and stated that I was a traitor for trying to help Stefan, one of the despicable breeds that got away, and that I didn't have the spine needed for the SS. He said that they were going to shoot that dirty Jew on the spot when they find him, for resistance and subordination. Then he threw me against the wall and said that I'd have to live the rest of my life knowing that I was responsible for condemning the people I listed as Jewish, even if they weren't Jewish, and that their blood was forever on my hands. Then he clobbered me with the butt of his rifle." He tenderly touched the puffiness along the side of his chin.

My mind raced to the names I listed. Maybe Stefan had gotten away. If anyone could, it'd be him. What about the professor? He was older and not in the physical condition as Stefan. The professor wouldn't be able to fight them off or outrun them. I had to find him. "Are you all right, for now?"

He nodded.

"I'll be right back. I have to go see if—"

"He's gone too," Petre interrupted.

I looked at him.

"They took the professor too," he stated as he picked up the box of books.

"Are you sure?" I grabbed his arms.

"They took him first before we knew what was happening. We had no idea what was going on. It was almost as if they came to take him to the piano contest. But there wasn't going to be any piano contest. They canceled it." He shook his head as he talked. "I was coming down from art on the floor above the professor's studio, and I heard this knocking. It was more like a rapid session of taps on his door. The professor opened the door and said, 'Hello.' Someone asked if he was Professor Weinholtz. He admitted that he was and if he could be of any assistance to them. They ordered him to go with them. He obliged, but not before he asked if he could gather a few things before his departure. They agreed because when I arrived on the landing outside the professor's door, I saw the back of three soldiers. I thought that maybe the professor did something wrong. But he appeared in the doorway with a warm smile and said that he was ready. One of the soldiers grabbed his arm to tie it, and that's when Professor Weinholtz saw me. The professor assured the commander that there was no need for the restraints, and he promised that he wasn't going to be any problem. He chuckled, looked in my direction, and said, 'What an honor to have an escort to the piano contest.' He touched my cheek and added, 'I must be paramount to have so many uniforms to accompany me to the contest.' And then he walked away with them."

"He just left?" I asked.

"Yes, but it was that look in his eyes that made me wonder. It was that look from him trying to say something to me without speaking. That's when I knew that the soldiers weren't escorting him to the contest. I ran down the stairs and saw them put him in the back of the truck. As he climbed into the truck, he looked back at me one last time, and there was fear in his eyes, although he tried to smile through it. I knew. I knew, and I ran to the dorm. Everything was in slow motion. The harder I tried to run, the slower my feet would go. When I got across the lawn to the dorm, soldiers were already storming through the halls, pounding on doors and yelling."

I darted off. I had to see for myself if the professor was gone. He couldn't be gone. I kept praying that Petre was wrong and the professor would be standing in his window, smoking a cigarette, and shaking his head with disappointment.

As I raced down the hall, Inga entered my mind.

*****

"Shhhh, Hans!" Inga hissed.

The afternoon sun beamed down from high in the sky, streaking through the branches of the trees and reflecting strands of copper and gold in her brunette hair. The fifteen-year-old and two years my senior mechanically grabbed my hand and tugged. I stumbled over a stone and almost hurled the picnic basket across the uneven field before I gathered my balance.

"Hurry!" she commanded over her shoulder. With another sharp yank, she forced me to pick up speed. "Hans Klein, you're slower than Grandma."

"I'm trying to carry the lunch!" I shouted toward her.

"Come on, Grandma," she teased. "Spring's the best time." She dropped my hand and hurried ahead. "That's when the babies hatch."

We rushed onto the bank of the lake curtained by tall fir trees. Our pace slowed as we migrated along the familiar path to the location where we have been enjoying our late afternoon lunches for the past week. Our mission was to watch the geese and the hatching of the offspring. We made sure that we had positioned our luncheons close enough, yet far enough away not to bother the mother goose or her large eggs. Two days ago, we felt proud as parents when the first of five shells quivered, cracked open, and a chick emerged drenched in mucus. We reveled in how the newborn stumbled and hopped out of the nest and staggered in circles while its downy feathers dried and fluffed up. We held our breath as the small puff ball bound to the water's edge, naturally taking to the water, and bobbed on the lake's surface.

"Hurry," she demanded. She rushed back and took the basket from me. "We can't miss this." She darted off ahead.

I rushed to keep up, staggering over rocks and foliage.

We admired the commitment the mother goose had as she sat and kept the eggs warm. We marveled at the way the father goose protected his family with vicious standoffs against any unwanted predators that wandered too close to the nest by rearing high on his webbed feet, extending his massive wingspan, thrusting his long neck out, and hissing a warning with its beak wide-open and tongue jutting out. But what we admired most about this family was the undying dedication and love between the two parents.

"They mate for life." Inga stated the facts as truth.

"I thought that was only swans and penguins." I challenged her authority on the subject.

"No, geese as well. I'm almost certain. I read that somewhere," Inga justified.

"Where'd you read that?"

"In my science book at school," she answered.

"Interesting."

"Well, it's true!" she emphatically announced. "If it's not true, it'll be true for me from now on."

Yesterday, we watched and waited, silently holding our breath, as three more eggs quivered, cracked, and freed more goslings. They staggered over the discarded shells on pencil legs and extended their tiny arms to dry their downy feathers. They formed a perfect line behind the mother and older chick and paraded to the lake. They paddled to the center of the lake to soak up the sun's warmth. The father remained behind to watch over the last egg.

I scampered up next to Inga. "What if today's not the day?"

"Shhh, don't say that. I just have a feeling that today's the day." She suddenly stopped. She looked puzzled as she turned and looked at the lake. "Something's wrong," she mumbled.

"What?"

"Shhh!"

Yesterday, we counted at least seven pairs of geese and several dozen offspring. The lake was being overrun by the invasion of a growing population this season and was creating a nuisance for the summer inhabitants of the Lake View Cottage Community. The concern of noise and disease carried by these animals were of the most importance to the homeowners. We had joked about having to watch where we walked as not to step on "goose poo land mines."

A strange stillness hung in the air, like after a terrible thunderstorm. Inga dropped the lunch basket and ran toward the nest, not caring where she stepped. Then she let out a bloodcurdling scream.

I ran to her.

She stood there, hands trembling and covering her mouth.

"What is it? What is wrong?" I asked.

"Look!" She pointed with her eyes in terror.

There displayed in ruins next to the destroyed nest were a congealed mess of a flattened shell, the remains of an unborn fetus, and a carpet of violently twisted feathers.

"Maybe it hatched."

She ignored me and ran off toward the wooden pier next to the boathouse.

I followed.

We stood on the edge of the pier that reached out over the water, bathed in the unsettling silence, and stared at the geese-less lake.

"Where are they?" I asked.

"I'm not quite sure," she said.

A majestic pair of white swans with a newly hatched cygnet paddled in circles in the far corner.

"Maybe they are on a walk," I stated.

Inga lowered herself to sit on the pier. "All of them?"

I sat down next to her.

"That'd be a very long goose parade," she tried to joke.

"I'm not sure, but maybe they'll show up while we are eating."

"I wonder where they all are."

I suddenly looked at Inga. "Do you think someone took them?"

"What do you mean?" She looked at me.

"Maybe someone came and gathered them up in a big truck and took them away."

"Where'd they take them? Why?"

I added, "I don't know. But maybe because the geese had become a nuisance."

"You might be right. Maybe someone wanted to get rid of all the geese. Maybe they came in the middle of the night while the geese were asleep and took them away." She halted and looked off at the swans. "But why not the swans?"

"The swans aren't a nuisance!" I guessed.

"Maybe swans are more attractive than geese?"

"Maybe?"

We watched the swans extend their long white necks and lovingly twist them around each other as if they were hugging.

"Where would they have taken the geese?" I wondered aloud. "They wouldn't hurt geese, would they?"

We just looked at each other.

*****

As I arrive in the courtyard, the professor's window was empty, lifeless, and dark; the building gave off a cold, gray aura, like an invisible cloud settled around its foundation and screamed a silence that caused my ears to hurt.

I ran across the lawn. As I passed the circular bench under the maple tree, I saw something on the seat that made me stop. Lying there on the bench was a contorted, featherless, and naked chick that must have fallen from a nest. Its neck twisted, giant bug eyes closed, beak slightly opened, swollen belly flanked by a gray-colored wing with a fringe of tiny feathers, and little stick legs suspended in the air, rigid. An agonizing squawk sounded from the mother robin perched on the branch with her wings spread out and looking down at her offspring. Her chirps resounded with sadness as I imagined tears streaming from her black eyes.

I made my way to the professor's building, leaving the grieving mother behind and the remains of her chick unprotected from any predator. The professor's door was wide-open. I walked in; the curtain's slight billowing gave the room the only sign of life. The professor's winged-back chair sat empty next to the little table adorned with the crocheted doily and rock's glass with a small amount of watered-down golden liquid pooling at the bottom. The ashtray with a half-burned cigarette and the opened silver case exposing the remaining tobacco sticks occupied the rest of the table. The piano was motionless in the middle of the room, and the bench pulled out, waiting for someone to sit down and play. The sheet music I was going to play at the piano contest, Mozart's *Piano Sonata No. 2 in F*, rested on the grand piano.

At any moment, the professor would be rushing in from lunch or a stroll around the campus, smiling and chatting about the way the lunch line was moving so slow or how the iris have added a hue of purple to the flowering beds and their fragrance that made his head spin. I waited for him to show up and yell at me for missing the piano contest and how I would have won if I participated. He'd then express how proud he would have been with my second movement, and he would sit at the piano and imitate my performance, emphasizing my unique characteristics. I'd allow the music to move me, taken on a musical carpet ride to a faraway location. His shoulders would round a bit, his head would start swaying to the sides with the rhythm of the music emitting from his fingers, and the whole time he'd have this incredible proud smile plastered on his face.

He'd instruct me to pull down the good scotch from the cabinet and pour us some into two rock glasses as he continued to stroke the keys. Although I didn't care for the liquor, I'd tell myself I'll enjoy this victory drink. Once I offered him his glass, he'd pause from playing and hold the glass up in the air so that the afternoon sun could illuminate the golden color. I'd do the same. He'd glamorize a meaningful toast. "To the world's next virtuoso, may you continue to impress the people everywhere and always have sold-out concerts and six encores." He'd look at me and add, "Bottoms up." He'd not drink until I finished with mine first. The liquor would burn my tongue and throat as it went down, causing warmth to expel throughout my chest and my eyes to well up. Once I finished, he'd follow up with his portion of scotch, laugh, envelop me within his arms, and crush me against his chest.

"Hans." A voice pulled me back into reality.

I turned in hopes to find the professor standing the doorway, miffed at why I'm in his studio without him being here. But it wasn't the Professor. Karl, another soldier, and Petre stood in the doorway.

"He asked me where you were," confessed Petre. "He said he has news."

Karl said, "We have a car waiting to take you."

"Where are you going, Hans?" asked Petre. "Why are you dressed like that? It's funny I didn't even notice it before."

I couldn't respond as I pressed my hand against the brown tie and shirt.

"What's going on, Hans?" Petre's eyes bounced between Karl and me.

"Petre, I need you to do something." I wrapped my arm around his shoulder and led him out to the hallway. "I need to you go back to your family and make sure that everything is fine. Make sure that you help your father with the store."

"What about school?" Petre questioned.

"School's going to be on break for a while," I said.

"Where are you going, Hans?" He looked at me with concern.

"I have to go with Karl. I promised that I'd play for a party."

"Oh, that makes sense why you are all dressed alike. What instrument does Karl play?"

"I sing," Karl interjected.

"You do?"

Karl nodded.

"Petre, I need for you to get going." I directed him toward the staircase.

"What about my things?"

"Don't worry about them. Here, take this and get some new stuff." I handed Petre the money that Karl gave to me in the envelope at the train station.

"But—"

I interrupted him and said sternly, "Petre, you need to follow my request. You need to go to your family."

He looked at me for a long moment, looked to Karl and the other officer, and back at me. His eyes filled, and he whispered, "I didn't mean to hurt anyone."

"I know, I know. You must go now, Petre," I instructed.

"Will I ever see you again?"

"You'll be in the front row of my world-tour concert." I forced a smile.

"Promise?" His eyes widened.

"I promise. Tell everyone I said hello and sent my love."

"I will." He headed down the stairs. "See you soon."

"Bye." I waved to him.

"Nicely done," stated Karl.

I forced a smile.

"Private Mastenburg, we must be going," advised the officer.

"Yes. Hans, let's go." He indicated with an open hand.

I descended the stairs.

Chapter 15

Two leather seats resided in front of a large oak desk in Commander Heiden's sparse office. A large window looked out onto a green square acre that included a ditch, electric barbed-wire fence, and a wall with seven guard stations protecting the camp from the outside world. Rising amid the green ocean was a tall tower with a 360-degree glass-encased viewing room, armed soldiers facing every direction, and a large searchlight that crowned the roof.

Trains arrived at intervals of approximately every twenty minutes during the busiest times of the day and then tapered off to every hour to every two hours. The trains arrived at the temporary depot to the left, which was a wooden platform elevated for the debarking passengers. Like clockwork, the whistle sounded to announce the arrival, followed by the rumble and vibrations as the trains slowly came to a stop, and then again when the trains pulled out of the station.

An archway welcomed the weary travelers as they piled out of the cramped cattle cars to the refreshing clean air. The platform amassed with people buzzing for information. Soldiers were ordering them to form lines and requesting them to leave their suitcases and bags in a designated area. Lines of people milled down the stairs from the platform as more soldiers corralled them into rows on the lawn, different lines for different qualifications. After being signed in and identified, the passengers were herded through a gate connected to an electric fence with barbed wire spiraling along the top. The path led to rows of barn-like structures.

An open field was across from the courtyard where workers toiled in the sun to rid the area of stones, boulders, and other debris. Soldiers were stationed tactically throughout the field. This work area led to factory-like buildings about a mile away. These gray industrial units accompanied several different sizes of stacks reaching into the sky. Some of the flues spewed thick smoke in billowing surges, while several thinner chimneys continuously stream whitish haze into the air. The intermingling clouds of smoke and smog hovered over this part of the camp and blocked out any glimmer of sun.

As I sat waiting to meet Commander Heiden, I thought of how quickly this had all transpired. Not more than a week ago, I was in the professor's studio trying to figure out what music I'd play for the competition. Listening to him calculate the stratagem of playing a Mozart piece as opposed to Brahms, Beethoven, Weber, or Wagner. He'd pace back and forth, holding on to a glass of whiskey, pinching a cigarette between his first two fingers, and waving his other hand dramatically in the air. His flamboyant jesters were his method of planning his artistic attack on the other competitors. "We need to perform something that the judges wouldn't expect, but they would expect from a student like you, and yet will show your technique and passion at the same time. It must be difficult enough, yet soothing to the ear and appear easily played. We need to make sure that you have the piece that'll distinguish you from all the other competitors."

Emptiness filled the pit of my stomach as I pictured his crazy hair, uneven whiskers, and his never-ending judgmental glares. Shame rushed in as I replayed calling him a name that I wished I never uttered.

I tried shifting my thoughts to Josef's face, but the image of him in front of Röhm became prominent, causing a shot of bile to surge up the back of my throat. I tried imagining him lying by the lake, naked and blanketed by the afternoon sun. I envisioned every detail except his face—it appeared out of focus and lacking detail. I could get a sense of his beauty and the secret man he revealed to me. I relived the tender moment on the train when he guided my head to his shoulder and reassured me that everything would be all right by holding my hand. I remembered his sweet aroma. I recalled the simple kiss he placed on my lips before presenting me to Hitler and the pride on his face when I started to perform. But that tender moment shattered as the Hanselbauer Hotel windows flashed white from flying bullets and showered the night sky with fragments of glass. I imagined Josef lying in a pool of blood with a single bullet through his beautiful head. The duality of this handsome, sensitive, and caring man that I thought I knew and the calculating, manipulative, and callous stranger that emerged and offered himself for such orgies to better his advancement in the hierarchy of the Youth Movement plagued my mind. But I'm not able to retrace the chiseled curves of his cheeks and jaw or the outline of his full lips—these images seemed to be gone forever.

My throat tightened and my shoulders tensed as I realize how quickly he altered my life and then disappeared out of it. Did he ever exist? Did I merely imagine his chiseled features, dark hair, and Greek-god like physic?

Stefan's corky face flashed into the foreground of my thoughts, with his broad smile and the urgency to tell me about his experiences for the day. His constant and, at times, annoying ability to mix details up and taking forever to tell a story. I missed him. His innocence, love for life, and positive outlook were the qualities that I held dear of him.

I imagined him escaping the Nazis and running through the wooded area, through the field of tall grass to the lake, and forging through the thickets along the river to safety in a small town somewhere. I pictured him living to a ripe old age and telling his grandchildren of the time the SS almost captured him. A sense of pleasure filled me as I thought of him growing old and grouchy, with a head full of curly hair and beard and hunched over as he struggled to walk to the post office.

My heart constricted as I thought of the beautiful Inga Rhoden, the girl whom I grew up with, the first person I felt that I was related to, my first love, my first kiss, and the first person I lied to. I remembered the last time I spoke with her. I was at the train station with Josef, waiting for the train to take us to Munich and to play for Hitler.

*****

"Hello," a voice answered.

"Inga? Is that you?" I asked.

"Hans? I can hardly hear you." I could picture her wearing her blue cotton dress and leaning against the wall. "How's everything?"

"Things are fine. How's everything there?"

"It's a mad house as usual. Something's always going on."

"How's your cousin, Elijah?" I tried to emphasize the word *cousin*.

She gave a quick little giggle. I heard her cover her mouth piece to the phone. "Ely is so beautiful and wonderful and gentle—"

"Enough, I'll have that image burned in my mind forever now." I glanced over at Josef and wished I could share the same adjectives about him with her. He flashed an inviting grin and tapped his wrist. "Hey, listen, I don't have much time to talk, but I wanted to let you know that the competition has been canceled."

"Seriously?" Inga asked, followed by silence.

"I'm not sure why, but I was just informed. I wanted to call you to let you know."

"That's a relief. I know that the professor called and talked to Dad," she said.

"What'd the professor tell him?"

"I'm not quite sure, but that there were some difficulties and that you weren't participating in the contest. Something about this tremendous opportunity—" The line crackled. "Hans, are you still there?"

"I'm still here. So you're not coming up?"

"Things here aren't good. I'm relieved to know that they canceled the contest because I don't think we would've been able to come. Things here are getting strange. Uncle and Aunt Stein aren't allowed to leave the house for any reason—" The line crackled again. " … and Ely and I—"

"Inga? Hello? Inga, are you there?"

Josef walked over to me.

I pulled the receiver from my ear. "I think the line went dead, or we were disconnected."

"Are they going to come up to school for the competition?" asked Josef.

"Hello?" I called. "Nothing." I replaced the receiver in its cradle.

"Well, what'd she say?" asked Josef.

I looked at Josef and said, "She thinks I'm doing the right thing by going with you to Munich and playing for Adolf Hitler. The possibilities of this overjoyed her."

"I told you." He hugged me hard.

*****

I wondered where Inga was and what would become of her and Ely. Would I see her climb off one of those trains? Would I ever see her again? I decided to write to her and explain that I was whisked away on a world tour and that my dream of becoming a concert pianist was a reality.

I quickly shook my head and took a deep breath to rid myself of the saddening realization that I was all alone. I focused on myself sitting here in this office, waiting for my new orders, and trying to grasp the meaning of why I was here. *I'm a musician, not a soldier.*

Karl tapped my thigh, and I immediately stood at attention. I heard the uneven footsteps of the commander as he entered the office.

"At ease," Commander Heiden commanded.

Karl and I stepped one foot out to the side and placed our hands to rest on the small of our backs.

The commander looked at me as I stood and waited for the next direction to follow. "Please, be seated." He indicated to the chairs with an opened hand.

I lowered myself back onto the seat. The commander was in the late fifties, average height, and slightly overweight. His short pallid hair highlighted with strands of blue and gray was neatly parted to the side. The bushy brows and bifocals balancing on the bridge of his nose hid hazel eyes. His full cheeks were tinted rosy and converged down to his jaw with little separation, creating a rounded head. His mouth seemed too small for the width of his face and resembled that of a boxer or bulldog, where the lower lip camouflaged the upper. There was a serious tension to his appearance.

"Well, you've come highly recommended, Klein," he stated. He flipped open a file that had my name imprinted on the front.

"Thank you, sir," I said.

He glanced up at me from under his brow and looked back down at the file. As he scanned the information, a loud popping echoed from the courtyard.

As I looked up, three newly arrived passengers fell limply to the earth.

Commander Heiden remained steadfast. "They must have been belligerent or may not have been healthy." He continued to scan my information as I watched a soldier order two other people to carry the dead to a wagon.

"You must understand that most of the people that come here are repeat criminal offenders, Communists, gypsies, homosexuals, or a-social. They're here to become rehabilitated and removed from infecting the German population." He looked up me and reassured me, "We're doing a great service for Germany and by following the instructions of our Führer." He glanced at Karl. "Private Mastenburg, does Klein have any military training?"

"No, sir. He had recently joined us last week," Karl said matter-of-factly.

Commander Heiden inhaled as he shuffled through the papers, closed the file, and leaned in with his elbows rested on the desk. "This place is a training center for the SS camp guards. You'll learn everything you need to know with us. We'll take you through the steps to become a successful SS officer. We're always bringing in recruits and training them. We're the model for all the other camp sites because of our organization and routine. Let me give you a quick idea of the layout of the site. As you can see, the Administration is located here in the gatehouse, and the main entrance is where the trains come in." He indicated with a wave of his hand. "This is the central hub of the camp. Several supporting buildings comprise of showers, laundry, areas for workshops—where you'll get most of your training—and a bunker for prisoners that need direction and rehabilitation. There are thirty-two barracks." He pointed in the general direction. "There are special barracks for special cases such as the one reserved for clergy imprisoned for opposing the Nazi regime and one reserved solely for the medical experiments."

The commander stood and looked out across the courtyard. "This used to be a munitions factory. We've torn down the old buildings that were of no use to us, and that is the area that they are clearing. We'll be constructing several new buildings that'll be very important to our work. The far building on the other side of the clearing area is restricted, and there's no need for you to venture there unless assigned to duty there." He turned back to the desk and sat, leaning back in his chair. "Any questions?"

"No," Karl piped in immediately.

I glanced over at him as he remained focused on the commander. "No, sir," I aped.

"Good." He pulled a form from the side of his desk. "I'm going to have you start on Train Patrol, which is a rather simple duty since you'll want to focus on officer training. And with your appearance, you'll be very effective there. On Train Patrol, you'll direct the incoming passengers to the proper locations and help them get to the courtyard. I'll take you out there in a moment. Please sign here." He pointed to an empty line on the bottom of the page.

I signed with a slight reservation but hid it from the commander and Karl's view.

The commander stood and offered his hand toward Karl. "Outstanding job, Private Mastenburg. I'll make sure that Master Klein is comfortable and that you get the credit you deserve."

"Thank you, sir." Karl shook the commander's hand.

"Welcome to Spandau, Klein." The commander offered me his hand.

I obediently took the offering.

Chapter 16

The sharp whistle blew, and I took the same position I had been taking for the past several months. I stood at attention, anticipating the vibrations from the tracks and preparing to direct the confused and bewildered people to the desired locations.

The sun was bearing down, defying the calendar's declaration of September and filling the mercury stick to 90 degrees. The heat rose and wavered from the wooden platform and the steel tracks and caused my feet to swell within the confines of my boots. Sweat beaded along the brim of my cap, streamed over my forehead to sting my eyes, and trailed down the back of my neck.

The number of people that had come through here was beyond anything that I ever imagined. I tried to make them faceless, phantoms of moving bodies without names or identities. I tried not to recall any features or characteristics. A technique was drilled into us during training: "Do not waste your time looking in the faces of these degenerates. You must always look just above their heads. You must keep in the power position and immune yourself from any hesitations. Remember, the utmost importance is Germany." I was successful at first, but then there were several occasions when a bright red jacket or blue shirt caught my attention, and I looked to see if I recognized the owner's face. I created the excuse that it was only the aesthetic value of the hue that caught my eye, but that was a lie. I was always looking to see if I knew anyone. I wasn't sure what I would have done if Inga, Professor Weinholtz, Stefan, Walter, or Ian climbed off the train, but there was always a sense of relief every time the crowd cleared, and they weren't among them.

The 3:00 p.m. train rolled in and stopped, sending a cloud of gray smoke into the air. The cattle doors opened, and the heat and odor from within immediately escaped and was overpowering. There wasn't any rush of people; their diminished spirits were a result from constant belittlement and beatdowns. Even with the doors opened, they waited for direction. A guard rapped the side of the car with the butt of his rifle and ordered the people to exit. Their movement was slow and cautious as their eyes adjusted to the brightness of the day, and I quickly glanced at their faces.

That was when I saw him. He was young and full of life, just a few years my junior. He had such a fresh face full of wonder and hope. He looked Polish. His eyes were large, belonging to the inquisitiveness of a college student absorbing everything in sight. There was a glow about him that separated him from the others climbing off the train. His herringbone jacket with the large lapels was neatly adorning a crisp white shirt and a tan corduroy vest that tapered to his slim waist. His ecru wool trousers accentuated his thin, long racehorse legs, and his black shoes were slightly scuffed. He trotted right up and looked directly at me, said nothing, but communicated everything with the glint in his brown eyes. He suddenly stood at attention with his right hand touching his eyebrow and clicked his heels together. He flashed a youthful grin, giggled under his breath, and flicked his hand into the air before prancing off and disappearing among the sea of milling and confused people. He was gone. His face imprinted on my mind.

Chapter 17

The late afternoon sun bled through the small lavatory window, sending hues of oranges and reds across the tile flooring as I sealed the door snugly within its framing and paused a moment to listen if anyone was coming. Once I was certain that I was alone, I made my way to a stall, torqued my shoulders to permit the door to close, and secured the latch. I maneuvered out of the full-length wool overcoat and flung it heavily over the partition, causing the golden buttons to clink against the wood. I freed myself from beneath the tight grip of the leather straps of the pistol's holster that wrapped across my chest, pulling it over my head, and positioned it atop of the overcoat. I unfasten the two top buttons of my jacket, releasing the rigidness from the uniform's stiff collar around my neck. It was several days since I had a chance to be alone.

I unbuckled my belt, unbuttoned the wool trousers, and opened the fly, allowing the grip of the waist to ease and slip down around my thighs. I peeled down the cotton drawers, exposing my damp blondish curls. A musty odor filled my nostrils as I lowered myself on the commode's seat, spreading my thighs as far as they would permit. I swelled with this freedom, arching toward the ceiling and aching for a release. I peeled back my foreskin, revealing the purplish helmet as its slit oozed a clear single droplet.

Knowing that the time was limited, I began my solo ritual by running my right hand up under my fitted-uniform shirt to pinch the tip of my erected nipple, causing a stinging sensation. Beads of sweat sprouted on my forehead and neck as I slid my hand down over the hills and valleys of my stomach, along my inner thigh, and between my legs, allowing my index finger to probe the warm, moist forbidden orifice. I tossed my head back, sending my cap banging against the wall behind me and crashing to the floor next to my boot. My other hand stroked evenly and consistently, feeling the smooth, supple foreskin sliding through my rough palm.

With my eyes closed, I imaged a beautiful young woman wearing a white negligee billowing as the wind pressed the material against her feminine form. Her long dark hair bounced in ringlets around her oval face, hiding her eyes and lips from view. She approached, ever so calculating, like a panther on the prowl. Her slender hips, small waist, and full breasts all culminated to imitate the agility and quickness of a feline's anatomy. As she neared, her flowing dark hair parted and exposed clear olive skin and full lips. The closer she came, her delicate features thickened with an angularity and sharpness that appeared masculine, causing bushier brows, a longer nose, stronger jaw, and facial skin shadowed from day-old growth of a beard. She morphed into the young Polish lad I encountered on the train station's platform several months ago and who had been haunting my dreams late at night ever since. He stared at me from behind his dark curly hair, bright skin, and full lips. His large brown eyes gazed at me with more interest than they should and revealed a desire that I should not permit.

I squeezed my eyes tighter to free my mind from this haunting image. As soon as blackness filled my visionary field, I took a deep breath and refocused on the female. She quickly refilled my internal screen with her beauty and grace as she waltzed to an imaginary tune. Her graceful hands combed through her flowing locks of curls and caressed her alluring neck. I fantasized slowly unbuttoning her negligee, and each disengaged button revealed more milky skin covering her collarbones. As I peeled back the material and exposed more of her sensuous chest, her skin became thicker, and soft dark hairs sprouted, spread, and swirled around the large pink nipples. The breasts flattened and firmed. The swirling pattern of dark hairs tapered down and raced along a hard flat stomach, forming a thick hair line that ducked behind the gathered material around the waistline. I glanced up, and the Polish lad smiled back.

Don't look in their eyes, I reminded myself of the training lessons. I pulled away from the image's alluring gaze and tried to remind myself of my secret oath of not entertaining such impure thoughts—again. I surrendered human will to the degradation several nights prior. The fact that I allowed this weakness to encompass my soul was a dangerous disease. I needed to fight its alluring power with all my might and disentangle myself from its firm hold. I summoned deep within myself the willpower to escape from its tantalizing and euphoric release. It wasn't natural. It was against the morality of the Aryan race and an abomination toward the Fürher. I needed to stand firm.

I was too weak. I gazed up into the Polish lad's brown eyes, which seemed to cast a spell over me that I couldn't combat. *Fight it!* I tried diverting the temptation and release myself from this unnaturalness. *You must fight it!* My will caved. I brushed my lips against his abdomen, inhaling his scent, thrust my hand down behind the gathering of material, feeling the thicker and courser sponge of hair. I tugged the material down over his hips to his ankles, exposing his legs covered with a forest of fur, and the fullness of his circumcision stared at me with its crimson head only inches from my lips.

Fight it!

An intense feeling of wrongness riddled me with perversion. *Am I sinning?* How could I sit here and think of pleasuring myself to the image of a male when I was male myself? How sinful was it to spill one's seed without the preconceived notion of procreation, let alone out of wedlock? Why was this lad's image so powerful over me? Who was he? I don't even know him. I may never even see him again. I swore I'd never let this sort of thing ever happen again. I allowed myself to be weak before, and I promised, with all my strength, I'd never allowed this evil back in my life. The initial perpetrator was a swimmer for the German Olympic team and was devastating to my morale and confidence. The involvement caused such heartache and pain that I'd never entertain such notions again or ever mention his name. Somehow another serpent maundered into my soul. This Polish lad's image plagued me in my nightly dreams, taunting me, and smiling at me, especially when I was at my weakest. He relinquished himself to me, offering himself by slowly nudging against my naked chest and placing his head on my shoulder. It felt so right in my dreams to hold him close to me, kiss his lips, caress his skin—but it was only safe in the dark of the night. When morning came, I realized how impossible it all was. It wasn't natural for love to be between two men. It declared so in the Bible. It was the devil's way of tempting you away from the righteousness of life. I tried so hard to prevent it from wrapping its tentacles around my soul and dragging me to the depths of perversion, degradation, and a life of unhappiness.

I promised God that I'd never entertain these notions of frolicking with this image and nameless individual again. One night, a few weeks ago, I experienced a dream that left me convulsing, short of breath, and wet from an unexpected emission. I woke at the thought that I was experiencing death. I lay there completely spent, gasping for air, and unable to move. It wasn't until later that I realized that I was lured in by this beautiful lad to commit a forbidden act. I was aware that once I tasted this forbidden fruit, I'd find it easier to return to it in the future until I would become a ruined man. I fell to the floor and prayed for forgiveness and redemption. I promised, then and there, that I'd never touch myself in that way again. But here I was again, facing the dilemma of such an evil character.

The outside door squeaked open.

"Klein? Are you in here?" a voice called. Footsteps entered the latrine.

I hunched over, covering myself with embarrassment, even though I was in an enclosed cubicle.

"I know you're in here. I can see your coat over the partitioning," the voice continued.

Black boots stopped in front of the stall's door.

"I also saw you come in."

The stall's door vibrated with several sharp raps.

"Klein?"

"Ja," I stuttered. "Is that you, Waller?"

"Who else?" He didn't wait for a reply. "Commander Heiden is looking for you. He wants you to report as soon as possible." Silence filled the bathroom. "Did you hear me?"

"Ja," I said.

"What're you doing in there?"

"Nothing," I quickly sputtered. I didn't want to look up in case Waller was trying to peer through the crack of the door.

"I understand. I see," Waller said with a chuckle. "I'd hurry it up if I were you. You don't want to keep the commander waiting." The black boots' heels clicked against the tiles and then stopped. "Oh, I almost forgot, there's a letter for you on your bunk. I think it's from a female admirer. Maybe it's the one that—"

"Thank you, I'll be right out," I said with an edge.

He refrained from saying anything else and left.

My mind raced as to why the commander wanted to see me and who sent the letter. I stood, tucking myself back in my trousers, limp and moist, relishing the minute victory against evil in the secrecy of this moment. I knew full well that the evil was always going to be lurking over my shoulder every minute of the day and trying to tempt me. I refastened the fly and buckled my belt. I shimmied myself back into the confinement of the holster over my shoulder and across my chest and pulled the overcoat from the partition and guided it over my shoulder.

I walked to the sink, turned on the faucet, and cupped my hands to gather a pool of cold water. The sparkling liquid magnified the designs in my palms. I reverently splashed my face, chasing the internal battle of pleasure, sin, and lasciviousness back deep into my memory. Quickly, the second handful revived me to the present as a dripping image stared back at me. I studied the mirror's reflection: blue eyes, chiseled nose leading to my perfectly shaped lips, a sharp jawline converging into a cleft chin and shadowed by golden razor stubbles. The cropped blond hair was perfectly parted down the middle, adding to the angularity of my face.

I glanced back down at my errant hands bathing in the crystal water, washing away the sins of my weak flesh. My once-innocent hands that diligently spent hours upon hours practicing scales at the piano and perfecting my interpretation of Mozart's *Piano Sonata No. 2 in F* were no longer caressing the ivory keys. The dream of becoming a concert pianist and playing all over the world ended when I got recruited by the Third Reich.

On my way out of the latrine and toward the commander's office, I decided to stop to get the letter. It was from Inga.

I tore the end of the letter next to the stamp and removed the interior. The paper was thin, fragile, and sprayed with lilac perfume. As I read the letter, I heard her voice:

Dearest Hans, Darling:

I'm so sorry it has taken me so long to respond to your last letter, but things here are not going very well. I'm most certain that this may be the last letter I will be able to write to you until this war has ended. God be with all of us to make it through these trying times. We're being moved again since they discovered we sheltered the Stein family, and this time I'm not sure if we'll have the privilege or freedom to converse through letters to those on the outside. Everything's being intercepted and examined before being forwarded. I'm not even sure if this will reach you.

I don't have much time to tell you everything, but they've informed us that we must meet tomorrow morning at the post office (so I thought I'd attempt to write you, I could slip the letter in the out box). They compare our numbers to the papers that they have on us, and if they don't match up, I'm not sure what will happen.

The other day, I was offered a position to work for the central office that would take me out of the guarded ghetto grounds, but I couldn't leave the others. I'd have had to exit the grounds without returning to the apartment. I wouldn't have had the chance to say goodbye to anyone. I couldn't do that; I'm not sure why, but I feel that I have this responsibility to the others.

Hans, I'm pregnant …

"Klien," Waller called. "Commander Heiden is waiting."

"Ja, I'm on my way," I responded without thinking. I looked back at the words "Hans, I'm pregnant." A rush of excitement and confusion caused me to lose all sense of coordination. I temporarily forgot how to walk; I wasn't sure I could walk if I wanted since my knees became so wobbly. I could no longer read the words on the paper since they took on some form of hieroglyphic writing, consisting of sacred symbols of ancient Egypt.

"Klein! Now!" Waller's distant voice rang.

Chapter 18

Upon entering Commander Heiden's sparse office, I bumped into a startled creature. I nearly knocked him off his feet. He fell against the cluttered desk, sending a pile of papers and files crashing to the floor. He nimbly regained his balance, scooped up the discarded paperwork, and replaced it as if it was never jarred. He whirled around and froze, facing me, eyeing me like a trapped animal. His thin two-toned cotton garment engulfed his frame like a worn dirty tent cinched at the waist with a knotted rope.

His almond eyes were surrounded by long thick lashes and seemed to hold a sense of familiarity for me. I reached out and took his hand in mine. It was a thin and fragile hand, small boned compared to mine. It was callused and dry with an iciness that tingled from each finger, and yet there was an intense energy emitting from his palm that kissed mine.

He darkened his eyes to almost ebony and tried to pull his hand away with a quick yank.

I didn't release but tightened my grasp. I reached over, felt the softness of the hairs on the inmate's arm, and I rolled his forearm to expose the paper-thin skin inked with numbers on the underside. I pulled the tattooed area closer for inspection.

He whimpered, jerked away, and successfully hid his arm against the crevice of his chest. He turned to exit directly into the path of Commander Heiden and quickly maneuvered around him without so much as brushing the commander's sleeve.

Commander Heiden looked a little perplexed as his eyes followed the wounded animal scurrying off. He halted momentarily before making his way to the oak desk, lowering himself onto the wooden chair with a heaviness that sent a whiff of cologne into the air. He flipped open the file that he had carried in. "Klein?"

"Ja." I snapped to attention. My mind lingered on the young man, his oval face and pallid skin speckled with day-old growth of beard, his chocolate curly hair neatly tucked behind his largish ears, his sweet mouth wanting to speak but finding no words to utter, and his expressive eyes revealing more than he wished. This feeling of familiarity was bothersome to me since I was almost sure that I have never met this inmate before. My mind lingered longer on the length of his unshaved hair, which was unlike the other prisoners. Maybe this was a privilege since he was the commander's aide, and this helped distinguish him amid the other detainees. Whatever the reason, it was one of the characteristics about him that caught my attention, besides his eyes and lips.

"I have orders to move you over to barracks patrol," Commander Heiden announced. His piercing hazel eyes glanced over the rim of his bifocals and under his thick bushy gray brows. "My instructions are to have you on duty by 1700 hours. You'll continue the platform duties as well. You have a welcoming appearance …"

As the commander continued to give me my new orders, the commonality and sense of sharing a prior moment with the startled creatures grew ever stronger. Could it be? I tried to dissuade myself from making such connections, but could the inmate be the same young Polish lad who haunted my dreams? I recalled the first moment I saw him. The way he trotted like a colt right up to me, not skittish at all, and saluted. Without saying a word, he communicated clearly with his large brown eyes. Time stopped while we gazed at each other. Then he broke the spell by galloping away and disappearing amid the sea of people.

"Klein … Klein?" The commander was displaying papers for me to sign.

I did so on the dotted line where his thick finger pointed.

He signed on the line below my signature and handed me a copy.

I thanked him, turned on my heels, and walked out wondering if I would ever bump into "my" Polish lad again.

I adjusted my cap as I exited into the brisk world outside. The late-afternoon sun threw long shadows across the snow-covered campgrounds. I walked to the edge of the wooden stoop where the sunshine settled on my face and glanced down at the order. All I had to do was report to barrack #265L, stand watch, and dictate on daily activities. I folded the signed promotional paper into fourths and squinted up at the sun sneaking behind the silos to the west, painting the evening sky with strokes of orange, red, and yellow. As I slipped the paper into my coat pocket, I felt another envelope and remembered that it was Inga's letter, the one that I didn't finish reading. I took it out and contemplated opening it when a rush of arctic air almost stole it away from me. I decided that it could wait till later and safely returned it to the pocket.

I stepped onto the snow-trotted pathway and made my way to the mess hall for a hot meal to celebrate my new promotion before reporting to my new post.

Chapter 19

Reveling in receiving the promotion and seeing the Polish lad again caused a spring in my spirit as I approached the mess hall entrance. What were the chances that I would see his brown eyes again? Could our paths cross again?

"Evening, sir."

Private Hemple, a young and ambitious recruit and recently assigned to me, stood at the door as if he had been waiting for me.

"Private Hemple," I said as I reached for the door.

Hemple's thick brows arched high on his forehead like umbrellas over each sunken eye, causing his forehead to wrinkle. A forced smile added length to his oblong face as he eagerly opened the door and allowed me to enter.

"Thank you."

The hall was abuzz with clanging and scraping of utensils against plates, an orchestra of chatter, and the aroma of vegetables and beef stew.

Private Hemple guided my overcoat off my shoulders and extended his hand toward me.

I looked at his offered hand and then saw that he glanced up at my cap. "Oh." I removed it and placed it in his palm.

He hung the coat and cap on hooks by the door. Then he removed his jacket and hat and hung them next to mine. He slipped his hand under my elbow and escorted me to the stack of metal trays, in which he retrieved two and positioned them on the shelf that ran the length of the counter displaying the limited food options. He nodded his head and afforded for me to proceed as he guided both trays behind me.

The first stop was in front of a rather large man dressed in a white jacket, a hairnet, and serving the stew. I watched as the server dug the ladle deep into the concoction, scooped up a sizable portion, and dumped the steaming suffusion into a metal bowl. The serving appeared to be mostly liquid and sloshed over the rim of the bowl as he handed it over toward me.

Hemple intercepted the offering and placed it on a tray before receiving his own. The metal bowls were hot, causing Hemple to nurse his fingers with his tongue and lips. He guided the trays along, paying close attention to try not to spill any more of the stew, and paused long enough to request two hard rolls by extending his first two fingers. He placed each roll on our trays respectfully.

At the end of the service area, Hemple gathered silverware and napkins. He hoisted both trays simultaneously, balancing them like a performer spinning plates on the end of a pole, carefully carried them as if he was walking a tight rope in midair, and gracefully placed them down at an empty table with ease of a troubadour. He pulled out a chair and presented it to me with the flair of a jester by nodding his head.

I accepted the offered seat.

He graciously scooted the chair in for me, leaned over my shoulder, and formally asked, "Would you like some coffee?"

"Sure," I responded. "But you don't have to do that."

"It's not a problem. I'd like to do it." He went toward the coffee urns.

His bowed legs performed an uneven gait as if one leg was longer than the other, which caused his hips to sway with each forced and manipulated step. The downward motion weighed heavier on the left side.

I eagerly slipped my spoon into the ecru stew, ladling up a clump of potato and stringy beef, and blew on the hot mixture before tasting it. The blandness was in dire need of salt, but it didn't bother me for some reason. I scooped another spoonful of mostly brown liquid and relished in its simplicity.

"Here we go." Hemple placed a cup of hot coffee in front of me and one in front of his tray.

The aroma of burned coffee grounds filled my head and turned my stomach. My mind raced to estimate how much sugar was going to be needed to mask the burnt flavoring. My estimation was interrupted by the distinct feeling that Hemple remained standing next to my chair. I glanced up at him grinning so proud of his accomplishment and seemed to be waiting to for praise. I allowed the moment to pass without providing the intended plea and refocused on my dinner by slipping the spoon back into the stew.

He slid into the seat next to me, bumping his knee against mine. His contact lingered a second too long as he smiled before adjusting in his chair, breaking the connection.

I looked at his deep-set eyes and wondered if there was any intention behind the accidental contact.

"How's the stew?" he asked as he turned to look at me, sending my attention back to my bowl of muddy water.

"Bland. It could use some salt."

He started to pull away from the table when I grabbed his wrist. "I don't need any salt."

"But it's not a problem," he replied.

"Thank you, but I don't need any."

He eased back into his seat.

I released my grasp.

We ate in silence as the orchestrated noise around us continued to ring, clink, and clamor.

Hemple's beady eyes darted back and forth from sneaking glances at me, to his stew, back at me, to the other soldiers eating, and back at me.

"How long have you been with the Movement?" I asked, thinking that I might be able to shrug off this uneasiness if I was able to learn more about him.

"Oh, I've been, uh, involved since I was … Well, I had just officially become a member about six months ago." He bashfully fluttered his eyelids, shrugged his shoulders in uneven intervals, and ticked his head several times before landing his focus on his spoon that was skimming the surface of the stew.

"What were you doing before that?" I asked.

He hesitated a moment before taking a quick snort through his crooked nose. "I was living with my grandparents and working on their dairy farm." His eyes glazed over as the spoon sank to the bottom of the bowl. His face turned more ashen as he bit on the far side of his lower lip. After a slight moment, he jerked his head toward me and lifted his brows to widen his eyes, crinkling his forehead, and gaped at me with much intensity. "My parents left me with my grandparents when I was quite young. My mom and dad were in no position to raise me. So, I went to live with Grandpa Wilham and Grandma Sophie, on my father's side." He leaned in closer and whispered, "They didn't want me either—you know, the typical unwanted child syndrome." He forced a laugh, curling the corners of his mouth. "My parents weren't married." He broke his polished table manners and dropped his head into his hands, running his fingers through and clutching a handful of the thick reddish hair. He cocked his head to the side, peered from under the tousled hair, and pursed his lips. "So once Grandma Sophie died, I had no ally or no one to provide a buffer for me and no one to talk with about anything. Grandpa Wilham wasn't the communicative type. I had to constantly take care of myself, keep an eye out for Grandpa Wilham, and make sure to feed the dog. Grandpa Wilham was never the same after Grandma Sophie's death, and the farm fell on hard times and disrepair. One day, while we were in town, Grandpa Wilham was doing some talking with the bank. I was bored and went wandering around outside. That's when I saw the advertisement poster for the Youth Movement. I liked the way the uniform looked." He reran his hands through his hair and pushed the strands back into place and sat erect.

"You liked the way the uniform looked?" I asked with reservation.

"Yes. I know that it seems shallow, but the youth on the poster seemed so happy and full of possibility, and the uniform made him look so together and noble, in a way," he stated.

"But you are aware of the importance of the movement? It isn't to look 'together' and 'noble,'" I administratively said.

"Oh, I'm aware of the importance. That's what I've been doing the last six months, learning the importance." He raised an extended arm. "I swear to God to give my unconditional obedience to Adolf Hitler, Führer of the Reich, and its people, Supreme Commander of the Armed Forces, and I pledge my word as a brave soldier to observe this oath always, even at the risk of my life." He smiled proudly and playfully added, "But the uniform looks sharp." His face became serious. "It's the first time in my life that I feel necessary. The way I feel when wearing this uniform is beyond anything I can imagine. I feel proud promoting a cause that I believe in and can be a part of. I'm tired of not fitting in anywhere, and I know that I can make a difference here."

"That's very impressive. I'm sure you'll do extremely well," I offhandedly responded. "How'd you get assigned here?"

"I requested it. I mean, not exactly this location, but I asked that I wanted to be where I could do the most good," Hemple said with confidence.

"Wouldn't recruiting be more your motif? I mean that way you'd be seen in your uniform."

"That's what I thought at first as well. But when I went through training, I discovered that I could handle more involved things," Hemple boasted. "And when it came time to be assigned, I had the best score in the class and was given options. I vied for a position like this, a position to work alongside someone with an excellent reputation and respect." He looked me directly in the eyes. "Look how lucky I am to have been appointed here. I couldn't have asked for anything more."

"I'm no one special."

"Everyone knows about you," he proudly stated.

"What do you mean?"

"That you played for Hitler right before the SA was dethroned and the beginning of the Night of the Long Knives," he boasted.

"That's not something to be proud of."

"But it is. You see, you were there, a part of history. You experienced it firsthand." His words rushed together as his face reddened with his excitement.

"I did nothing."

"Don't be so modest." He reached under the table and placed his hand on my thigh, causing me to stiffen. He pulled the corners of his mouth back in a crooked smile, exposing uneven teeth. "You see, you're someone extraordinary." He slightly squeezed my thigh.

I reached under the table, seized his hand, and deliberately placed it back in his lap.

He looked at me from behind his brows with a feeble expression.

I glared back at him.

He simpered before placing both hands on the lip of the table. He focused down on his tray and took a deliberate breath before exhaling it between clenched teeth. He picked up the hard roll, tore it apart, and drowned it in his stew.

"Klein?" a voice rang over my shoulder.

"Gunter Waller," I pleasantly announced, pushing my chair back. I stood to greet him with an extended hand. After shaking hands, I automatically offered my hand to the other.

"This is Private Max Schnell, a recruit. Schnell, this is Officer Hans Klein." Officer Waller introduced us.

"Nice to meet you. I've heard so much about you," Private Schnell said politely. He took hold of my offered hand.

"It's a pleasure to meet you as well." Our hands cordially shook before the young soldier permitted its release.

Officer Waller looked over to Private Hemple, who was still sitting and brooding over his stew.

"Excuse me, Officer Waller, this is Private Jan Hemple. He's a recruit as well and has been assigned to me," I explained.

Hemple tried to stand but bumped into the table, causing the stew and coffee to spill. He grabbed a napkin to sop it up before offering a hand.

"No need, son," Waller stated. They acknowledged each other from a distance.

Hemple slowly lowered himself on to his seat.

"What'd Heiden want?" Waller asked quietly.

"A new posting, which starts tonight," I explained.

"Congratulations." A sly smirk crawled over Waller's face. "I wasn't sure you were going to get there this morning. You were in the latrine for quite some time. Did you get all your business handled?"

Hemple curiously looked up at me.

My face heated up. "I swear, Waller, you've only one thing on your mind."

"Do you blame me? What else am I supposed to think when you keep getting these letters with fancy cursive writing and smelling so delicate of lilac?" His smile grew wider across his boxy face like a Boston Terrier. "What'd she want this time, more money? Or is she missing you with all her heart?" He swooned and placed the back of his hand against his forehead. He looked over to Private Schnell and added, "Can you blame her? If I were a woman, I wouldn't let this man out of my sight." He turned back to me. "I've said it once, and I'll repeat it. Klein, you're too pretty to be a man."

"That's enough," I uncomfortably stated.

"I could turn over a new leaf for you for one night if that lady friend of yours doesn't work out." Waller preened and curtsied. "Just woo me with lilacs, be gentle, and call me Anya."

"Don't hold your breath. It's never going to happen." I shot back at him.

"Why? Is it because I'm not pretty enough?" He feigned being rejected and forced his eyes to tear up. He tried to hold a serious face but broke into a laughing fit.

Schnell joined in with the laughter.

Hemple only lifted an eyebrow.

"If it was only that easy," I teased back.

"Oh, it is!" Waller smiled. "If you only knew how easy?" He lowered his voice. "You're an officer. You can get whatever you want, whenever you want." He pulled me away from the others and leaned closer to my ear. "Take it from me, I know. The inmates will do whatever you need." He patted me on the back. "Just let me know, and I can fix it up for you." He stated loudly, "Enjoy your dinner, beautiful." He released a deep moan and motioned for Private Schnell to follow. The two headed toward the door.

I sat back down next to Hemple, who stared at me.

Chapter 20

A silence filled barrack #265L as I posted my orders on the board that resided just inside the door. The cavernous space occupied rows of scaffolding-like bunk beds, stacked four tiers high, with two or more persons sharing each bed with a thin cotton blanket and one small square piece of foam as a pillow. The smell of body odor, urine, and mildew filled the rafters, and the floor was an exposed slab of cement. The windows were composed of small squares of thin panes of glass with some cracked or missing and allowing a cold draft to haunt the inhabitants.

Each inmate exemplified varying degrees of physical and mental stability, with different levels of emasculation. The attempts to erase their dignity were evident in the shaving of their heads and titivating them in unconventional and ill-fitting and thread-barren garments. The luxuries of undergarment and socks were rare, leaving several exposed to the elements. Their appearances were in different stages of health, some emaciated while others seemed well built and sturdy. The sense of witnessing the deterioration of their fellow barrack mates was apparent in their eyes as they appeared dark, lifeless, and swollen with hopelessness.

Today was the first time since arriving that I had a chance to see the inmates in their environment and the effects the camp had on them. I never imagined this degree of devastation and depravity. My initial post, platform duty, was to greet the incoming and separate the men, women, and children. I completed my assignment once I cleared the platform, and I prepared for the next arrivals. Even during the daily routine of walking from the officers' quarters, to the train platform, to the mess hall, to the showers, and back to the officers' quarters, I was rarely in the presence of the inmates. Except maybe the occasional appearance of aides who assisted Commander Heiden or one of the other higher officials. These chosen few carried a rather ordinary façade, set aside the cotton-thin clothing. Their heads were not shaved, and the awarded more food rations gave them an air of health. This initial discovery was overwhelming. I was amazed at how protected the soldiers were from the actual evidence of the neglect and punishment these humans were put through.

My mind replayed the propaganda imprinted since the day I arrived. *These creatures are dangerous criminals and advocators to keep the "chosen" race from reaching the pinnacle of superiority and attempting to ruin the country. They are degenerates and epitomize the lower echelon. They are highly treacherous and vile. They are representatives of Jews, political protesters, gypsies, and homosexuals—all the worst products of the human beings. It's our duty, to the Führer, to rid the world of these pestilential predators, especially the Jews since they're the cause of the fatal epidemic of the financial depression that's destroying this great nation. The homosexuals are guilty of conducting sinful acts and traitorously preventing the procreation of the superior race.*

Even with these premeditated proclamations proclaiming superiority and honor that I must hold for my country, all I saw were humans struggling to survive. This feeling immediately ate at my stomach lining like acid and inundated me with an ever-growing flood of remorse. I realized that I was going to have to convince myself that all I was doing was taking notes about the lives of these prisoners and reporting the results back to the commander. What happened in the trenches, the laboratories, or the far side of the camp had nothing to do with me, and I was innocent of any wrongdoings. Besides, what choice did I have? I couldn't simply walk away from my assignments.

After I tacked the official order to the board, I turned around to find the Polish lad standing there, beaming. The mere appearance of him caused a flutter deep inside me. He appeared angelic and unadulterated. We exchanged no words, and yet we were communicating, like we did on the platform.

He lowered his eyes to the floor, turned, and walked toward the back of the long cavern. As he passed inmates lying in various bunks, some stared, some hissed, and one large man stepped in his path and spat onto his face. My young lad held his spine like a cat, and without flinching, he smiled at the confronter and continued making his way to the back, never wiping the sputum from his face. He disappeared in the shadows.

I notated the conditions and actions of the inmates.

Chapter 21

It had been two weeks since I bumped into the doe-eyed Polish boy in Commander Heiden's office. Two weeks since I first entered barrack #265L and found him standing there with his coquettish smile. Two weeks of sharing our secret language and longing to touch his hand again. Two weeks of his image invading my dreams and stirring the undesirable emotions from deep within. Two weeks of losing the battle not to violate myself to the likeness of his image and sinking deeper into the horrible sin.

Tonight, I found myself full of contempt and rage. There was a sense of vulnerability and fragileness that was unable to ward itself against these dark desires unleashed. A wild man-beast, covered with fire-red hair, was awakened, lurking at the bottom of an unexplored and bottomless lake, waiting for something to set it free or waiting when I was unable to suppress it any longer.

I managed its presence by alleviating the pressure with the violations of myself late at night to the lad's image, forgoing the promises to God and the ideals of morality. These torturous past weeks gave the wild beast the strength to push off the muddy bottom and swim toward the surface of the murky lake. As it broke the water's crest, it released an unfathomable wail that echoed throughout my being. Spiraling threads of liquid sprayed from its long and tangled mane as it whipped its massive head from side to side, adhering strands to its burnt and rusty beard. Animalistic eyes sat deep within its compacted cranium, hidden by the untamed flames of brows. Its feral black pupils rapidly darted from side to side, trying to locate and focus on my exposed soul. Its thick stump of a neck spread out to form large shoulders as it spanned out its robust arms and anchored its enormous hands to the inner lining of my stomach. Its hunger was boundless and its strength unconstrained, and I was too weak to defend myself against its growing desires any longer.

I tried reasoning with this creature's ego with every unsteady step I took toward the barrack. Its intentions were apparently clear, and there seemed to be little to no room for negotiating. Its demands, at first, appeared to be invasive and boisterous as it growled, "Take the boy and have your way with him! You know he wants it. He has been asking for it. No one will know, just make it quick. Everyone's doing it!"

But my negotiations seemed frivolous and ineffective until I discovered a reasonable and sound resolution: do not look in the Polish lad's eyes. This simple gesture caused the wild man to resort to drastic measures to avoid going back to the bottom of the murky lake.

The onset between man and beast began when the wild animal ambushed and advanced to the front line by scaling up my rib cage and wrapping its thick claws around my neck. It took no mercy in its attempt to fulfill its desires. The powerful redheaded creature wouldn't be satisfied with just a simple smile from the innocent lad tonight; it needed to touch, to pillage, and to release the pent-up passion.

As I neared the barrack's door, the invader provided creative and strategic plans of taking the dark-haired Pole against his will to places where I could make him pleasure me. The beast continued to infiltrate me with information of how other officers had their ways with these types—the types that toyed and played with an officer's emotions, leading the officer to think that the prisoner was interested so that the prisoner can be spared hardships and expect special treatment and privileges in return. These types were asking for it.

My counterattack mantra was ever so important, simple, convincing, and plausible: don't look in his eyes.

I ascended the steps feeling the burning in my stomach that sent hot flashes up through my body and throbbed in my temples. My eyes pulsed with a redness that caused my head to pound. I flung open the door, sending it sailing against the wall and causing shrieks throughout the dank barrack.

My eyes adjusted to the darkness to find the Polish lad standing in the usual spot as expected. *Don't look in his eyes.* I murmured my mantra within my head. But the chant was drowned out by the monster's thunderous and guttural rumble of disdain. His talons enclosed tightly around my wind pipe and vocal cords, restraining them from producing any sound. In the attempts to avoid the Polish boy's eyes, I glanced at the back of the barrack. I felt the Pole's stare burn through my armor.

"Look into his eyes," ordered the red-haired beast.

Don't look. I retorted by focusing down on the cement flooring.

"Look in his eyes, I said!" the monster roared, applying pressure that could crush my larynx.

Don't look. I reputed, trying to regain my control over the intruder. I was too weak.

I glanced and saw the Polish boy looking at me with his big brown eyes. He wasn't smiling. His eyes were narrow and burned into mine as if they consisted of a hundred torches.

A strange occurrence came over me; the actual act of looking in this lad's eyes had the opposite effect. A cold downpour of rain washed over me, bathed me in refreshing solution, quenched my fever for the moment, causing the man-beast to slip, lose its grip, and sail back into the murky abyss. A freedom of breath filled me before I imbued with the wake of foamy black water from the wild-man's descent, bathing me with embarrassment and shame. I deflated in front of the dark-haired lad.

I rushed out of the barrack into the snowy night, walked in circles, not knowing which way to go, felt the pellets of ice stinging my heated face. I walked toward the empty mess hall, gathering speed as I attempted to escape the clutches of the beast.

I stepped inside and was alone except for the chairs, the long tables, and this inner wild creature that was gathering strength to forge another attack. A stream of brightness traveled through the room as the searchlight hit the rectangular windows, projecting an eerie effect along the quiet walls. I crumbled to the floor and convulsed. I couldn't believe the violence that had grown inside of me. I had to destroy this monster to free myself from its degrading images and desires. I tried to summon up the courage to reach for the creature floating the dark and murky depths. Now was the time to overpower him since it was least expecting me to have the strength and the will power for another confrontation.

A hand touched my shoulder.

I retracted, not wanting to be disturbed or distracted by my defensive attack on the internal beast, no matter who it was. *Let it be the commander; let him demote me.*

The hand didn't release but began to knead my knotting shoulder. Another hand touched my other shoulder. Both hands gently worked, compressing, squeezing the thick sinews along my neck, and causing me to abort my revenge as the wild beast escaped farther out of reach.

The Polish lad stood there as the searchlight made another pass, illuminating his stained face before sending him into darkness again.

He took my face between his palms and whispered, "Paulik." He placed his lips ever so gently on mine as his dark curls cascaded down around my face. He explored my mouth with his darting warm tongue.

The lad's peaceful willingness to share himself uncovered the craving that I sowed for him. This desire was different from the wild beast's desperation. It was a need that presented itself more gently and kindly. A craving that germinated on that hot day on the train platform and sprouted its roots inside my being when I ran into him in Commander Heiden's office. Its stalk grew strong as we shared our secret language in the barracks and every time we passed each other in silence. Tonight, its tender buds bloomed with pink and orange petals, topped with a tinge of yellow as we embraced.

But even though I was filling up with this gentler craving, I still possessed the dark desires of the beast who wanted to express wild eagerness and dominance. Something caused me to pull his lips from mine. Looking deep in his eyes, I lifted my finger to his face and caressed his soft, moist lips and rest my forehead on his. We both knew that our exploration wouldn't venture any further on this night, but our unique oneness was united.

I lifted him to his feet and led him to the door, pulling him from the entrance as the searchlight swept past, hiding him along the wall until the darkness engulfed us again. I pressed my hips against him to provide evidence of my hardening desire for him. He responded by pressing back. We remained face-to-face until the light swept past again. I pecked his lips and guided him out.

I watched him walk off toward the barrack. His figure became a shadow amid the night sky and silvery snowflakes. A flood of light engulfed him as he opened the flimsy barrack door and disappeared behind it. I headed the opposite direction to my quarters.

As I turned the corner, I was startled by a figure leaning against the building, inhaling on a cigarette and emitting a red glow from the burning ember. He exhaled a billow of smoke and mumbled, "Klein."

I tried not to show any surprise as I casually glanced back over my shoulder to make sure that Paulik was nowhere in sight. Squinting my eyes, I asked, "Hemple? Is that you?"

"Ja." He took another puff and flicked the burning stub into the air, arching a red line through the black night. He leaned in toward me, reeking of scotch, and exhaled a white cloud into my face as the searchlight briefly illuminated the area. He pried his eyes wide, trying to see past the bridge of his brow, and crumbled against my chest.

I caught him from falling.

He leered at me and placed his dry lips on mine.

I pulled away.

Stunned, he studied me with his blurry, beady eyes, causing his brows to become one as his mouth turned downward. He grabbed my face and pulled my mouth to his. He kissed hard, biting my lower lip.

I tasted a mixture of tobacco, scotch, and blood.

The searchlight made another pass as I whipped him around and pinned him to the wall with such force that his head banged against the bricks.

He started crying, squeezing his eyes tight and clinching his bloodstained lips.

I released my hold, and he scaled down the wall until he rested on the snow-trotted ground.

I lifted him up over my right shoulder, carried him to the recruiters' dorm, and unloaded him onto his cot.

I guided him out of his overcoat and tossed it onto his trunk. Unhooked his holster, hung it on the hook next to the head of the cot, unknotted his tie, and slipped it from around his thin neck.

He opened his eyes and reached for my face, caressing it with the back of his hand, grazing my lips with his rough knuckles. He reached with the other hand behind my neck and pulled my face to his.

I stood, letting him flop down against the mattress.

He remained there staring, scared, and yearning for something I wasn't willing to give. He reached up weakly and whimpered before collapsing the arm to his side. He tried to sit up and unbutton his shirt, but he swayed to the left and almost fell off the cot.

I caught him, replaced him, and unbuttoned his shirt.

He batted at my hands.

I pulled the shirt off, tossed it to the floor, and pushed him down on the cot to unbuckle his belt.

He giggled.

I unfastened his waist and fly and started unlacing his boots.

He kicked his feet like a child.

I tugged the boots off and placed each one under his cot. I tugged his pants off, exposing milky white smooth skin. I discarded the trousers on top of the wadded shirt and tucked him under the blanket.

He grabbed my hand and guided it to his swollen crotch.

I pulled away.

He grabbed my hand again and shoved it beneath his cotton undergarment.

I felt the soft flesh of his penis and the matted hair surrounding it. I jerked back my hand again.

He took a hold of my wrist, digging his nails into me and pleading with his strained eyes.

I broke his hold with my other hand and shoved him back onto the cot.

He recoiled to the edge, curling into a fetal position and burrowing his face under the pillow. Sleep overtook him with an occasional twitch of a shoulder or foot.

I leaned against the window and realized there was something in my pocket: Inga's letter that I had forgotten. I took it out, smelling the slight hint of lilac. I tilted the paper so that the outside light would allow me to read it.

Dearest Hans, Darling:

I'm so sorry it has taken me so long to respond to your last letter, but things here aren't going very well. I'm almost certain that this may be the last letter I may be able to write to you until the war has ended.

I skimmed through it.

The other day I was offered a position to work for the main office that would take me out of the ghetto, but I couldn't leave the others. I would have had to exit the grounds without returning to the apartment. I wouldn't have had the chance to say goodbye to anyone. I couldn't do that. I'm not sure why, but I feel that I have this responsibility to the others.

Hans, I'm with child, and it is Ely's. I couldn't leave him behind. I'm his wife and will soon be a mother. How could I walk away? It was so tempting, Suzette, the other secretary who helped get the order together, kept telling me that I wasn't Jewish. Why should I suffer? I don't know what to say, but I made a commitment, and I'll follow it through no matter where it takes me. I can't believe that my parents and I have hidden Ely and his parents for nearly two years before being discovered. A stupid mistake. I wanted to show Ely our picnic area where we watched the geese hatch—someone saw us.

Since we were harboring Jews, Mom and Dad were taken away. I've no idea where, but I fear for them. I was sent to the ghetto with Ely and his parents. It isn't a very nice place—people are dying every day from starvation and neglect. I've never thought humans could be so heartless.

I'm on the bus to the post office. There they'll decide what to do with us, either send us back to the ghetto or shuttle us to the train station, and where we go after that isn't clear.

I love you, darling, take care. I'm so proud of you. Please make beautiful music and play all over the world.

Love,
Inga Rhoden-Stein

I turned the letter over, hoping that there was more on the back, but it was blank. I lifted the paper to my nose and enjoyed the lilac aroma.

"Keeping watch, Klein?"

Officer Waller stood in the glow of the moonlight at the foot of Hemple's cot.

"What?"

"What are you going in the recruits' lodging?"

"Oh, I was making sure Private Hemple found his way back." I refolded Inga's letter and slipped it into its envelope.

"He tied on another one, did he? How bad this time?"

"Let's say I don't think he's going to remember too much in the morning." I placed Inga's letter into my breast pocket.

"This seems to be becoming a habit, the third time in two weeks," he commented.

"He's adjusting to the surroundings."

"Well, I can understand that. It took me several weeks to get an understanding of this place." Waller nodded his head.

"What brings you around at this hour?"

"I'm on night watch, and it's part of the sweep to check in on the privates. Everyone seems accounted for—I was missing Hemple on my earlier pass and thought I would just take one more check before having to make a report. But since I know that he was with you, there's no need to write it up." He grinned. "I like to bend the rules occasionally."

I nodded and forced a grin.

He started to giggle like a schoolboy about to burst forth with a secret. He broke his erect stance and folded over at the waist to suppress his triumphant joy. He covered his mouth with one hand and supported his weight with the other hand braced on his thigh. His enthusiasm was so overpowering for him that he snorted, sending him into a convulsive laughing fit.

"Shhhh!" I grabbed his shoulders to stand him upright.

Waller stifled his outburst. He grabbed my lapel, guiding me out into the cold and snowy night air. Once outside, he released a deep, rich laugh that filled the night sky. "I'm so sorry. I just couldn't help it." He leaned his shoulder against the door, catching his breath.

I looked toward the main camp where the barracks and buildings were silhouetted black against the main watchtower in the center of the courtyard. The flood of yellowish light shrouded downward from underneath the main platform that circled the outer perimeters of the watchtower. Two armed guards rotated with precision and timing that kept them on opposite sides. Two other guards were located inside the enclosure, keeping constant vigil of the surrounding areas. The calculating sweep of the searchlight revolved from the top of the tower, streaming a harsh white tunnel of light across the terrain. A purple-black plumb cloud lifted in the distance over the far end of camp where the factories were located.

"I have to tell you, Klein"—Waller joyously slapped my shoulder—"I had the time of it tonight."

I politely smiled, hiding that I wasn't interested.

"I can't begin to tell you what these inmates are willing to do for absolutely nothing. You promise them that you'll get them a slice of bread, and they are on their knees and willing to please."

I started walking away.

"What? Did I say something wrong?" He rushed to catch up with me. "What's wrong?"

"Nothing's wrong, Waller. It's late, and I need some shut-eye." I quickened my pace to the officers' quarters.

"Wait up and I'll walk with you."

I paused in my tracks, allowing him to catch up, before resuming long strides to try and deter him from sharing further details of his nightly rituals and escapades. The pace did nothing to impede his pride of sharing.

"All I have to do is walk in and click my heels together, and the prisoners line up in rows. I simply walk down and look them all over. When I come to someone that catches my eye …" He leaned in and whispered, "Or just someone that I want to worship me for the night, I stop and nod. The chosen one reports to the anteroom and waits for me to arrive. I sometimes make them wait a long time."

I quickened my pace.

Waller kept up. "Tonight, I had two young ones waiting for me, cute in their animalistic way—you know with the long hooked nose, eyes set too close together, and stringy black hair. They must have just arrived because their heads weren't shaven yet." He poked his forefinger against my shoulder. "That's when you want to get them, as soon as they come off the train, because they're still clean and not riddled with lice. You must be extra careful about the ones with lice—sometimes they beg for you to choose them so they can give you lice or crabs or whatever else those dirty animals carry. It's some sort of silent victory for them. But if you can find the fresh ones, you don't have to worry about all that. Well, tonight, they were fresh and young. They may have been related, I've no way of knowing, they all look the same to me. So, I made them wait for me. When I got to the anteroom's door, I could hear one that of them crying and the other one, probably the older one, telling the younger one, 'Don't cry, and do whatever he says. That way we'll be spared.' Let me tell you, I didn't spare either of them."

I stopped dead still in my tracks and glared at him. I inhaled and calmly said, "Officer Waller, I'm glad for your successes tonight, for the fact that they were young, still had their hair, and appeared to be lice-free. But it's extremely late, and I'm sorry, but I'm not interested in hearing any more tonight about what you may have done or what you had them do."

"That's it, that's what I wanted to tell you. I did nothing to them. I just stood there, and I had them do each other."

"That's terrific, I'm so relieved. Good for you, but I'm not in the mood to thoroughly appreciate this story the way you would want me to. I'm simply too tired."

"Sure, sure. I understand. I'll catch up with you later and fill in the blanks," he assured me with a glint in his eyes, the corners of his mouth curling upward.

"I look forward to it." I continued to the quarters, and he remained silently next to me.

Snow began to fall as I held the door for him to enter, but he remained steadfast. He glanced over his shoulder into the night.

"Officer Waller, I'm letting the heat out."

He glanced back at me and smirked. "The night's still young. I should make another rotation before turning in. Would you like to join me?"

"I appreciate the offer, but I'm tired."

"Come on, I show you how it works. It'll be worth it." His eyes widened, and his face filled with anticipation like a child preparing to open a Christmas present.

"Not tonight."

"All right, it's your loss." He grinned.

"Good night, Officer Waller." I started closing the door.

"Night, Klein." He went toward the barracks and disappeared into the snow-filled night.

Chapter 22

Far off in the mist, a dark and obtuse form approached me. It mutated two thinner oblong orbs extending downward from the main shape, two more extending from the sides, and another formed at the top. It continued shifting through the thick mist, taking on human qualities with two legs, a body, two arms, and a head. The thick fog hid the identity, but it was taking on the form of a woman. The figure approached with arms stretching out toward me. Her gait was smooth and steady, as if she was gliding, not walking. Maybe she was floating on a cloud.

The coolness of the mist kissed me, but I wasn't uncomfortable. The brightness of the light that followed the figure, like a rising sun, warmed me. The light continued to grow, changing the color of the mist from a drab grayish-white to a soft canary yellow and then to bright gold. The golden color bled through the woman's thin clothing, exhibiting her feminine body and radiating out from between her stretched fingers. She emitted a sense of peace.

She floated right through me as if she hadn't noticed me standing there. A gust of warm air trailed her, bathing me and blowing back my hair. In her wake, a sense of love, protection, and guidance transcended a feeling of complete understanding. She circled and swooped up behind me; her breath tickled the back of my neck. She reached around and took hold of my head, turned me to face her, and kissed my lips. The heat from the golden light burned my face as she sucked my breath and deflated my lungs. She gathered strength as she filled her lungs with my air.

Fear rushed in as I realize she was robbing me of my life. I tried to pull away, but her strength was too much. Panic to disconnect myself filled my being. I pushed against her shoulders, but our lips infused as if we mutated into one being. I knew the pain was going to be unbearable to rip our lips apart, but I knew I had no other choice except to accept her invitation to death.

I mustered enough power, pulled, and ripped my lips from her hungry mouth. Pain riddled through my nerves and penetrated the synapses in my brain. I grabbed my head to keep it from exploding.

Quickly, I grew accustomed to the pain. I regained my senses and stood back at a safe distance, looking at her. At first, she appeared to be Inga with her hair swirling around her like a halo, then she shimmered into Paulik with his brilliant smile, and then transmuted into Hemple with his leering eyes daring me to escape his wrath. I rushed and pushed with all my might against the image's chest, sending the figure back into the depths of the mist.

I woke with a jolt as if I free-fell from the atmosphere onto my bed. I sat, trying to understand what just happened. Was it a dream? Was it a nightmare? Was it telling me something? Was it warning me of something? I sat there staring into the darkness of the room, wondering what the time was. It must be early morning since it was still dark.

Resolving that it was just a stupid dream, I replaced my head on my pillow. Paulik's lips filled my mind, the way they sweetly parted when he said his name and how soft they felt when he pressed them against mine. The way he wanted to share with me and how natural it all seemed, nothing perverted or deviant. We were two people connecting on another level. Private Hemple's image rushed in with his clumsy display of affection, which seemed depraved and dirty, laden with distorted desires. How could they both be so different, and yet both be considered the same wrongful and sinful act?

I wasn't going to be able to return to sleep, so I decided to go to the mess hall to have coffee, revise my report for Commander Heiden, and write a letter to Inga. It had been weeks since I received her last letter, and I wondered where she was and how she was doing. Although we have always been close, we always had to decode each other's actual truth.

*****

"There! That formation looks like a lion roaring." I pointed toward the blue sky filled with fluffy white clouds.

Inga and I had just finished one of our traditional summer lunches out on the clearing next to the lake. The grass was lush and soft to the touch.

Every year during the summer months, the Rhoden family moved to their lake house at the Lake View Cottage Community so we could enjoy the cool breeze, the lake, and the boathouse, and to escape the hustle of the city. Inga and I created a secret society, the Summer Tans, that consisted just the two of us since we were the only two near the same age. Everyone else was ancient. She was president while I was vice president, secretary, business manager, and event coordinator.

We conducted our secret meetings by spreading out a blue-and-white checkerboard blanket and unpacking our picnic basket of avocado sandwiches, sliced apples, cheese, and whole wheat crackers. Inga called the meeting to order by holding our cups of chamomile tea high in the air to acknowledge our society's mascots, the geese that inhabited the lake.

Today, for some reason, was a special day. We were pretending to be members of the truly elite society. So we indulged in a bottle of wine that Inga confiscated from the wine cellar.

Holding her wineglass up to the sky, Inga began her toast to the geese. "To our feathered friends, with whom we spend our summers, we raise our glasses with much appreciation and love. Continue to bring your honking, careless and splashy landings to our community, for you represent our freedom to life." She always altered the speech to fit the way she was feeling at the moment.

"Your honking, careless and splashy landings?" I questioned.

"Shut up and clink," she stated.

We clinked the edges of the glasses and drank.

"Oh, my goodness, that's terrible." I gagged.

Inga made a face and proceeded to spit the liquid on the ground. "It must be an acquired taste."

"But why would you want to acquire a taste for dry sour grapes?"

"It's what the elite do." She took another sip and forced herself to swallow. "It's not so bad the second time."

"If you say so." I took another sip, and it went down smoother. "I think you may be right."

We continued to acquire a taste for the pinot noir until we had almost finished the bottle.

With our heads spinning and feeling tired from the heat of the day, we stretched out on the blanket and watched the clouds form shapes as they streamed across the late afternoon sky.

"That looks like a hand waving," I stated.

"It does. See how the little finger is staying up, just like the rich people do when they are drinking their tea." Inga pantomimed holding a delicate teacup with her pinky finger extended. "Cloud formations are like reading tea leaves, but on a much bigger scale."

"What are you talking about?"

"What if we were able to predict our futures by reading the shapes of the clouds?" she questioned enthusiastically.

"What would a waving hand be?"

"Someone is saying goodbye," she stated.

"Who would be leaving?"

"Maybe you'll be leaving to go somewhere. Maybe the image is predicting that you're going to be going on a long trip."

"Why me?" I questioned.

"Because you saw it first, which means it's your future."

"I don't like this." I started to sit up.

Inga grabbed my arm and sternly looked at me. "Come on, give it a try. It's just like reading tea leaves. But it'll be easier because you can see the shapes. It's not like straining your eyes at the tiny leaves on the bottom of a tea cup and never being sure what the shapes are."

"I guess so." I repositioned myself next to her.

We watched the sky in silence.

"This takes an artistic eye. You need to be creative. You'll need a persuasive description to support your discovery and prediction, or the other person may counter and give their interpretation on the cloud's shape."

"Are these the rules?"

"Yes, they make the most sense. The more detailed the description, the closer we can predict the truth of our future."

We examined the sky.

"There's a roaring lion." I pointed to the clouds over the lake.

"Are you sure it's a lion roaring?" she questioned.

"Of course it's a lion roaring," I stated defensively. "Can you see the mane surrounding the two big eyes and the way the cloud becomes darker near the center? That looks like a lion's mouth, and it's open like it's roaring." I used my hands as if they were an artist's brushes.

"I'm not sure, Hans. I can't quite see the lion's mouth roaring. I know what you think is the lion's mane if I squint hard, but as for the mouth roaring—I just don't see it."

I impatiently sat up and started to raise my voice. "How can you not see the lion roaring? It's right there in front of your face as plain as day." I looked down at her and continued to jab my finger toward the slow-moving clouds.

"It's only your interpretation. I'm having a difficult time seeing a lion roaring." She used her hand as a visor to shade her eyes.

"Well then, what do you see?" I asked.

"You want to know what I see?"

"I asked, didn't I?" I was about to explode with frustration.

"Okay, let me see." She sat up, drew her knees to her chest, and tucked them under her skirt. She rested her chin on her arms that she wrapped around her folded knees. She cocked her head, furrowed her brow, and squinted her eyes. "Yes, of course. I see, now let me make sure I say this just right. See how the upper part of the cloud arcs?"

I quickly glanced up.

"That reminds me of the top of a head. Can you see how the cloud rounds on both sides and feathers out?"

I nodded.

"That's Jesus's hair being blown by the wind. You can see his eyes looking down at us, and that darkened area that you think is the lion's mouth roaring is Jesus's beard—and see, he's smiling at us?"

I took a moment and contemplated this notion. My mind couldn't grasp the image of the holy man amid the clouds. Could she be fooling and trying to manipulate me? But maybe she was correct. Maybe if I tilted my head at just the same angle as she had her head, I'd be able to get a sense of what she saw. No matter what the image was, I always changed my mind to match her. So I convinced myself that I could see the Savior. "Oh, there he is. You're right! It does look like Jesus smiling down on us."

She laughed.

"What?"

Her impish grin indicated that she was joking with me. "Are you sure you see Jesus smiling down on us?"

"Yes!" I implied confidently. "Right there as plain as the nose on my face."

"But can you see the nose on your face right now?"

"What do you mean?" I demonstrated my ability to see my nose by crossing my eyes inward. "I see it."

Inga let out a belly laugh and rolled on her side. "You should see yourself right now! That's the funniest thing I think I've ever seen."

"Ever seen in your whole life?" I challenged her declaration.

"Ever, up to this point of my life," she qualified. "The way you crossed your eyes to see your nose was funny."

"So you're telling me that you don't see Jesus up in that cloud?"

"No, I don't, but I do see a lion roaring."

"Then why did you say you didn't?"

"I wanted to see if you would change your mind, and you did." She giggled again.

I became silent and looked at the lake.

"What is it?" She tried to stifle her laughter.

"Nothing," I disinterestedly responded.

Silence fell upon us like an unwelcome wool blanket on a hot, muggy day.

"I was only playing around," she said. She poked my ribs with her finger.

I moved out of her reach.

She stared at me for a long moment.

I pretended not to notice.

She slapped her hands down against the blanketed earth, adjusted herself rigidly next to me by elongating her spine, and released a long-drawn-out sigh. "I'm sorry if I upset you."

I looked farther off by turning my shoulders away from her.

"You're so sensitive. I said I was sorry."

I was enjoying the attention and decided to milk it for all that it was worth. I inched myself to the edge of the blanket.

"Okay, forgive me?"

I folded my arms across my chest.

"What do you want me to do, beg for you to accept my apology?" she announced in an almost desperate voice.

I held this perfect act of martyrdom. I extended my hand behind me and offered it to Inga, while still focusing on the far-off landscape.

"What?" She gasped with astonishment.

I simply wiggled my fingers.

"Are you kidding me? No, I won't. I can't," she announced defiantly and crossed her arms.

I kept wiggling my fingers.

"Oh, for God's sake. No! I'm not doing it. You're going to have to suffer."

I lowered my head and continued wiggling my fingers.

"No, stop it. Come on, don't do this!"

I didn't stop.

Finally, she morosely stated, "Just this once." She took my hand. "If you tell anyone about this, I'll flatly deny it and beat the crap out of you." She kissed my knuckles lightly. She overdramatically pleaded, "Please forgive me."

I smiled.

She realized my pretense, grabbed my hand, and twisted it behind my back, causing me to lumber onto the blanket. She pounced on top of me, straddling me with her thighs and pinning me helplessly against the ground.

I tried to buck her off.

She was too agile and rode my hips like a bronco rider.

I tried myself out and relinquished my attack.

"Are you finished?" she questioned. She leaned over my face with her hair canopying my head.

Without a word, I mustered up strength and thrust my hips again.

She was ready and tightened the grip of her thighs and rode with my rising hips and remained in contact as my hips returned to the ground. The descent landed with a thud, and I was left winded and gasping for air.

"Are you quite finished now?"

I couldn't speak and nodded my head.

"I can't hear you. Are you going to be good?"

I nodded harder and faster.

"Say it."

"I … can't …" I tried to explain. "You're cutting … off … my … air …"

"What?"

"You're sitting on my diaphragm," I struggled to explain. "And I can't breathe."

"Is the baby having a difficult time breathing?" she said as she leaned closer to my face.

I recognized the opportunity and bucked my hips one last, quick, hard thrust.

She was bucked off and flipped over my head with an animalistic yelp. She flew a couple of feet and landed on her back with a deafening thud onto the ocean of soft green grass.

I rolled over and faced her.

She remained stunned and motionless, with her arms and legs sprawled out in all different directions. Her hair masked her face, and she appeared dead.

I was on my hands and knees, panting and watching her.

Finally, she flicked her fingers then her wrist and rolled her head from side to side. She let out a moan that originated from the small of her back and resonated from her throat. The noise reverbed in quick short spurts that sounded like a machine gun. Her diaphragm oscillated, and the hair that was covering her face lifted into the air with the exhalation of each moan.

I thought she was dying. I quickly crawled to her to see if I could help. When I arrived at her side, I recognized that she was not dying but laughing.

"Where the hell did that come from?" she asked with glee. "I didn't know you had that in you."

"I have lots of surprises," I said with relief that she was going to live. I lowered myself onto my back and positioned my head next to her collarbone and cheek, so our feet were pointing in opposite directions. Our cheeks pressed against each other's as we resumed watching the formation of clouds in silence and listened to the call of the sparrows diving through air currents above us.

I finally broke the silence. "What's going on, Inga?"

"What do you mean?" She shielded her eyes from the sun with a flat palm of her hand.

"I can tell there's something that you aren't talking about."

Tension wrapped around us.

"No, there's nothing," she flatly said.

"Are you sure?"

"Why would you ask?

"I can just tell."

Silence filled the ocean of green grass again as I felt that she was mustering up the courage to share with me what was on her mind.

"I don't know actually," she began, and then she halted.

I patiently waited, knowing that she was about to express the one thing that was weighing on her mind. I could smell the fresh lilac perfume, being so close to where she dabbed it behind her ears.

She was a combination of a tomboy and a girly girl, and you were never sure which person you were going to encounter until you were amid being tackled to the ground or witnessing a tearful and passionate display of emotions. On this day, I was privy to both, having been pinned beneath her and now a shoulder on which to cry.

"Do you want to talk about it?"

"I'm not sure."

I was in a fragile place and needed to proceed with extra care not to frighten her. It was like sneaking up on a wild rabbit hiding in the brush. If I was patient and proceeded with caution, I could get the animal to eat the carrot that I was holding, but if I rushed too quickly, I'd spook it, and it'd hop away.

"I'm all ears." I attempted to be funny.

"You're too sweet. Look there." She changed the subject by pointing toward the sky. "There's that hand waving goodbye again."

"Why are you changing the subject?"

"Because I think if I don't talk about it, it'll go away." Her voice faded.

I lifted my hand and stroked her hair.

She sniffed. "I do not know what to do."

"What do you mean?"

"It wasn't supposed to happen like this."

"What wasn't?"

She quickly shifted her weight and rolled onto her stomach to face me. Her eyes were red and swollen. "I can tell you anything, right?"

"Of course. Why would you even ask?"

"All right. But you can't tell anyone."

"Who am I going to tell?"

She suddenly blurted, "I'm late!"

"Late for what?" I tried to understand this game, but the rules always changed.

"You know."

I shook my head.

"You're dense sometimes." She sat with her shoulders slumped, knees drawn to her chest, and encased with her arms. "I'm late with my period."

I still couldn't figure out the ramifications of her situation. I remained there staring up at the clouds, waiting for the explanation that was never going to come. I pulled a blade of grass and positioned it between my lips, tasting the sweet bitterness.

"You don't know what I'm talking about, do you?"

I glanced over at her and shrugged my shoulders.

"Oh my!" She quickly darted her focus off to the distance and then blurted out without hesitation, as if by doing so she could get all the information out without any problems. “I have not had my period yet.”

“Is that a bad thing?” I asked.

“It could be.”

“Why?”

“Because Mom and Dad will kill me if they find out.”

I was completely not able to follow, but I didn’t want her to think that I didn’t comprehend her situation. “No they won’t. They’ll understand.”

“Hans, they won’t!” she exploded with disbelief. “Missing my period could mean that I’m pregnant.”

“You don’t mean—?” I quickly sat up. “But how? I mean, I know how, but you’re only fifteen. Can you have a baby at fifteen?”

“A girl can have a baby whenever she has had a period,” she explained like a teacher to a twelve-year-old boy.

“I don’t follow. When did this happen?” I asked as if she was on the verge of a death sentence.

“Remember I asked you to cover for me when I snuck out of the house?”

I nodded my head, even though I’ve been covering for her ever since I moved into the Rhoden house.

“I didn’t go over to Greta’s. I snuck out to see Helmut, the soldier. We’ve been seeing each other for some time now.”

“You mean the German soldier? I thought you were forbidden to see him. He’s too old for you.”

“I couldn’t help myself, and besides, when did that ever stop me?” Her face became strained. “One thing led to another, and now I’m sitting in this field telling you about it, and I’m not sure what to do.” Her eyes welled, and a single teardrop inched down her cheek.

I reached over and pulled her to me. “We’ll get through this. I promise.”

She buried her face into my shoulder and released her pent-up angst, causing my shirt to become wet.

I held her for what seemed to be a long time, rocking side to side as if I were the older sibling. The whole time I wondered how I could make this right again. I watched a cloud float by that resembled a dancing ballerina, but I choose not to share it with Inga.

*****

I walked into the mess hall, and I realized how different it seemed now from last night when Paulik gently kissed me. How the harsh lights shed a reality to the interior. I paused on the exact spot and tried to relive the moment in my mind, but it had slipped away as if it never happened. I sat at a table next to the window, which put distance from last night's encounter.

"Morning, Klein, sleep well?" Officer Waller was smiling at me.

"All right, I guess," I responded.

"Mind if I join you?" he asked politely. He held a cup of coffee in each of his hands.

I nodded my head and indicated for him to sit. "Please do."

He placed a cup in front of me. "I saw you come in, and I thought to myself that it's too early to be getting ready for the day, so you must not have gone to bed yet." He sat and leaned into me. "Tell me all about it."

"About what?"

"What you did last night and why you're getting in so late?" He grinned devilishly.

I shook my head and shrugged my shoulders. "I couldn't sleep, so I decided to get up and prepare my notes for the commander."

"You mean to tell me that you're getting ready for the day?" He looked off with disappointment.

"That's what I'm saying."

"You didn't take my suggestion and seek out some fun?"

I shook my head.

He leaned back in the chair and let out a full-belly laugh that echoed throughout the hall. "I'm sorry, I just assumed."

"Sorry to disappoint you."

"You aren't disappointing me. You're only depriving yourself. Last night, after you went to bed, I went and had my fill." He leaned in and whispered, "I mean my fill." He slapped me on the back, lifted two fingers and rotated them, and then brushed them under his nose with pride. He stood. "Don't work too hard, Hans."

"Waller."

He stopped in his tracks and glanced back with a hopeful expression.

"I'm just curious. You mentioned that the inmates were young girls. I didn't know that this camp housed females. Aren't they transported to Bergen-Belsen or Birkenau for incarceration?"

He cocked his head as if to hear me correctly, his eyes twinkled as a lascivious smile stretched across his face, and his attention diverted. "Rupert," he called to a soldier who was placing a cup of coffee onto a table across the room. "Rupert Abrams, what have you been up to lately?" He proudly strutted to accompany Officer Abrams, a large square man with an incessant snarl embedded on his face. They sat, and Waller proceeded to elaborate his conquests to an eager listener.

I tasted a sip of bitter coffee and began to write to Inga.

Dear Inga,

I hope this letter finds you and you are well. I'm worried about you and all that you are experiencing. I wish that I could be there to help. But I've been swamped.

The concert tour is more than I could have imagined. It's everything you said it would be and more. I'm visiting many different cities and countries. One night we are at La Scala in Milan and then at the Amphitheatre in Athens. It is never-ending. I find myself sometimes feeling guilty for having this opportunity, but it would never have happened if it wasn't for you encouraging me. I'm here because of you.

You were in my dream last night, and I'm still trying to figure it out. You floated in on a cloud and kissed me like the time at the lake house. Interesting, huh? Then you just faded away like the morning mist. Could interpreting dreams predict the future like clouds? If so, I'm a bit nervous about this one.

For some reason, I even remembered that time near the lake when you confided in me about Helmut. Everything worked out just fine. A close call, but we got through that together. We'll get through this as well. Have faith.

I'm so excited about your little one on the way. Do you know what sex it is yet? I think it's going to be a boy. I just have this feeling. If it's a boy, I think you should name him Paulik.

Well, I must get going. We're leaving for Paris today. Give my love to everyone. Let me know when the baby comes.

Love,
Your Hans

Chapter 23

I made my way into Commander Heiden's office, hoping to get a glimpse of Paulik delivering files. Unfortunately, he wasn't anywhere in sight. I slipped Inga's letter into the outbox on his receptionist's desk. I removed my overcoat and hung it on the standing rack next to the door.

Private Schwartz, the receptionist, rushed into the waiting room.

"Is Commander Heiden in?" I ask with authority.

The receptionist halted and saluted. "Commander Heiden had to step out for a moment, but he's expecting you, Officer Klein."

"Is it all right to wait for him in his office?"

"Please do." Private Schwartz motioned me to follow, and he opened the commander's office door.

"Thank you, Private Schwartz."

"My pleasure, Officer Klein. Please make yourself comfortable." Private Schwartz returned to his desk in the reception area.

I sat in a chair and watched the early morning sun peek over the horizon, shedding a pinkish light on the delicate flakes wafting down onto the camp's yard.

A young man walked in, intently focused on placing an armful of files onto the commander's desk and didn't notice me. He wore a thin wrinkled cotton pullover, matching pants, a pair of worn and weathered boots, and his black curls seem disheveled and greasy. As he turned, it was Paulik.

My heart stopped beating.

He retracted with a startled gasp upon realizing that someone else was in the room. He recoiled against the commander's desk, bracing himself, and diverted his attention toward the exit. He quickly redirected his focus onto me and paused. He exhaled his held breath, releasing the tension in his shoulders, replacing the color to his ashen cheeks, and wrinkling the corners of his eyes and mouth as he recognized me.

I tried to stand.

Paulik rushed me and placed his lips on mine, forcing me into the curve of the chair and sending it tilting on its two back legs. He put his hands on my thighs to swiftly guide the seat back down with a thud on all four legs. His childish grin widened as he giggled, covering his mouth with his hand.

I caressed his sharp cheekbone and stared into his chestnut eyes.

He pulled my palm to his lips and kissed it.

In one quick move, I stood and whirled him around so that I had him in a vise grip with his back sealed against my chest. I tightened my grip over his mouth as if I was about to snuff the life out of him.

His body went rigid.

We remained motionless as we both watched snowflakes flutter down outside the window.

I leaned in so my lips were next to his ear, and I nipped at his lobe.

He pressed into the stinging sensations and melted into my body.

I whisked him around, restraining him against the wall behind the office's opened door. He whimpered.

I pinned my chest against his, looked deep into his fear-filled eyes. I glanced out the crack, just below the door's upper hinge, to observe the reception room on the other side of the wall. Private Schwartz cradled the phone receiver between his ear and shoulder while typing a letter. I looked back at Paulik and removed my hand from over his mouth and replaced it with my lips, tasting the salty sweat lingering above his upper lip. I forced his lips apart and invaded the warmth of his cavern.

Paulik responded by sucking on my tongue. He pulled his lips away and slid down along the wall to his knees while looking up under his eyebrows. I heard the outer door open and voices emitting from down the hallway. I pulled him to his feet.

He stood before Commander Heiden and Private Hemple entered. Paulik swiftly and tactically slipped out from behind me and exited the room without trying to attract any attention.

I stood at attention.

Commander Heiden obliviously and deliberately walked to his desk as Private Hemple glanced at me then out the door and then back at me, before extinguishing a cigarette butt into the ashtray on the commander's desk.

"Klein, at ease," Commander Heiden announced. He lowered himself onto his chair and leaned back with his arm behind his head. "What do you have to report?"

Hemple moved in behind the commander, leaning against the window that exhibited the dawn's glow and snow falling heavier.

I handed my observations file to the commander and stepped back, anticipating his approval of my commentary.

The commander flipped the file open and glanced over the report.

Hemple continued eyeing me with furrowed brows, tense lips, and clenched jaw. His eyes were lined red from his overindulgence last night as he tried communicating something to me.

I deliberately looked away from him, sending him to stand erect.

"This looks adequate, Klien." Commander Heiden gave his off-handed compliment. "Was there anything unusual?" He signed the bottom of my report.

I glanced over at Hemple as he pleaded in silence.

"Private Hemple has informed me that he thought there was some subversion last evening." The commander looked up.

"No, sir, there was nothing unusual," I stated. I focused on the commander.

"I thought you were escorting a prisoner back to the barracks," added Hemple with an edge to his voice.

"No, sir, there were no problems," I retorted. I looked to Hemple, wondering what he had witnessed. My palms began to sweat. "What you saw was no subversion, Private Hemple." I stressed the fact that he should back off as nicely as I could. We locked stares.

"Well, what was the situation, Klein? Is it something that should be reported or not?" proceeded the Commander.

"No, sir. What Private Hemple is referring to is that I had dropped my pen when I was leaving the barrack, and a prisoner rushed it out to me. It was nothing more than that, sir. I then proceeded to make sure the prisoner was able to return to the barracks without any implications of wrongdoing from any other officers." I broke eye contact with Hemple and looked toward the commander with a sense of purpose.

"Well, you must be more careful. What if it was a part of the report that you had dropped? We don't want to have anything tainted by the exposure of our observations." He flipped the folder closed and placed it on the desk. "That'll be all for now, Klein. Keep up the good work." He removed his glasses and pinched the bridge of his nose before rubbing his tired eyes.

"Thank you, sir," I said. I saluted him, clicked my heels together, and started for the door. I paused for a moment as I look at the place where Paulik and I huddled in the corner. A smile crawled across my face as I passed through the doorway.

"I'll walk you out," called Hemple.

I retrieved my overcoat from the rack and slid it over my shoulders. Paulik passed by in the hallway. The receptionist carried files to a cabinet.

"Thank you, Private Schwartz."

"Have a good morning, Officer Klein." The young receptionist returned to his desk and sat. "It looks like we are in for another day of snow."

Someone grabbed my elbow. "I want to talk to you," Hemple demanded.

"Not here." I deflected and smiled to Private Schwartz, who was watching.

"Why not?"

"This isn't the place to talk about what I think you want to talk about," I explained. I nodded toward Private Schwartz. "Is there any additional snow accumulation reported for today, Private Schwartz?"

"An additional inch or so by this afternoon," said the receptionist.

"So when and where?" Hemple whispered.

"There's no need to ever talk about it." I started to walk out of the office.

"I saw you," Hemple blurted out loud enough for the receptionist to hear.

Private Schwartz glanced at us over his shoulder. "Is everything all right?"

"Everything is excellent, Private Schwartz," I assured him.

"Schwartz," Commander Heiden called for within his office. "Can you bring me the latest transport report?"

"Yes, sir." Private Schwartz grabbed the file and disappeared into the commander's office.

I moved toward Private Hemple and calmly asked, "You saw what?"

He stepped back. "I saw you talking to that prisoner."

I chuckled and glanced around to see if Private Schwartz was still in with the commander. "What's wrong with that? We all talk to prisoners. What's your point?"

Private Schwartz returned to his desk. "Is there anything else I can do for you two?"

"No, we were just catching up." I smiled and walked into the hallway.

Hemple rushed after me. "You aren't supposed to be fraternizing with the prisoners after lights out."

I halted. "Who was fraternizing?"

"You know what I mean." He cowered and dropped his head to the side as if to see if anyone was listening.

"No one's listening to us now," I emphatically announced. "Which prisoner are you talking about?"

"I saw you," he repeated. He obviously couldn't think fast enough.

"You saw me talking to someone? Can you describe who it was?"

"No, but I know it was a prisoner."

"How can you be so sure? You were intoxicated. You couldn't even stand. I had to carry you back to the recruits' lodging." I leaned into his face.

"I know," he sheepishly whispered.

"It's you who should be brought up on charges. I could inform the commander of your inebriation and advances you made toward me last night, and you would be on the next train out of here or confined into the blockade. But I decided not to report you as of right now."

Hemple softly confessed, "And I appreciate that and want to thank you."

"You have a fine way of showing it, by throwing suspicions out loud to the commander so he thinks that I infringed the regulations and some subversion had taken place."

"I know." He paused. "You aren't going to inform on me, are you?" His voice quivered.

"What do you think?" I diverted attention to two officers walking past us. "Good morning, Officer Luntz and Officer Krosigk."

"You too, Officer Klein," Officer Krosigk parroted.

Officer Luntz responded, "Good day."

I headed for the exit.

Hemple stopped me. He looked at me for a moment, and then his shoulders slumped in relief. He clasped his hands to his mouth as if he was praying. "Thank you. I was afraid you were going to say something to the commander during your report."

"Is that why you were in his office this morning?"

"Yes," he confessed. "I wasn't sure what to think."

"Why did you tell him that some subversion happened?"

He shuffled from foot to foot. "I panicked. I was desperate. I needed to have some reason to be addressing him this morning."

"You could've gotten me into a lot of trouble." I glared at him.

He shrunk to a little boy. "I know. I know. I can't explain it. I'm sorry."

"Let's remember this." I encouraged him to create an unspoken alliance with me.

"I will, I will," he agreed. He grabbed my hand with gratefulness.

"All right, but that's enough of that." I freed my hand from his clasp as two other officers passed.

He waited until the two officers entered Commander Heiden's reception room. "Right, you are right. I'm sorry. Someone might see us."

I walked away. As I sauntered down the hall, I passed Paulik. I glanced at him, and he barely glanced back, pretending not to know me as he was also aware of Hemple watching.

Chapter 24

The siren rang throughout the camp.

"Lights out."

The extinguished lights sent the cavernous barrack into total darkness, except for the sweep of the searchlight's bright beam sneaking through the windows and temporarily exposing bunk beds and occupants.

I glanced toward the back for Paulik before retiring for the evening. The roving beam revealed him standing in the aisle between the stacked beds. He smirked and lowered his eyes before disappearing into the darkness.

I waited for the roving light to bathe him once more. As my wish came true, he appeared closer. During the wake of the beam's travel, he crept toward me. My body trembled as a flame entered through my boots, ambushed my bloodstream, and scuttled to my pounding heart. His lips were ever so inviting as the light caressed his face for the third time. In the darkness, he brushed past my arm and exited through the door like a cat without anyone noticing. I waited for the peremptory light to confirm his vanishing act and present myself to the other prisoners in case someone did happen to see his departure. I counted to twenty before exiting into the snowy night, wondering where he escaped.

The latrine door slammed. Could Paulik have meant for me to follow him? My pounding heart caused pulsating vision as I stepped through the searchlight's beam, the blindness of darkness, and reached for the door. But as the light swerved back around, I was confronted by Hemple standing between me and the latrine.

"How was your watch?" he asked nonchalantly.

"Fine."

"Aren't you going the wrong way?" The searchlight grotesquely exaggerated his face, causing his nose to protrude farther out, his left eye appeared eliminated, and only half his mouth was visible.

"I need to use the latrine."

He glanced over his shoulder to the shack-like structure. "Why not use the officer's quarters?"

"I can't wait." I abruptly ended the conversation by grabbing my stomach and stepping around him.

"Is there anything I can get for you?"

"No, I think I'll be fine if I can get in there." I pushed open the door, nodded, and shut him out.

My eyes adjusted to the darkness and abstruseness of the latrine. The stalls lurked amid the multitude shades of gray. I extended my hands and forged carefully. The pungent smell of urine stole my breath away. A rattle came from the far side of what I determined was the last stall. As I felt my way toward the back, I fumbled onto a person, feeling his cheeks and curly hair. I knew it was Paulik when I inhaled his familiar scent.

He hesitated as he made certain that it was me. He traced his fingertips over my eyes and lips and leaned in, sniffing my neck.

I whispered, "Paulik?"

He placed his mouth on mine and hungrily proved his passion.

I returned the kiss, forcing him back against the wall. I pulled off his cotton shirt, pinning his arms temporarily over his head. I ran my fingers through the hairs covering his chest, found a nipple, and enclosed my lips over a tender orb, biting the sensitive tip until it hardened. He whimpered, arched his back, and directed his chin toward the ceiling.

Our bodies radiated heat. My senses spun with Paulik's aroma and my fervor to release him of his pent-up ardor.

"Klein?" The door flew open.

I froze.

"Klein, is everything all right?"

I carefully turned my head and saw Hemple standing in the inflow of light at the doorway.

"Are you all right?" he asked again.

I covered Paulik's mouth. "I'll be fine."

"You've been in here a long time." He stepped into the room and allowed the door to slam closed. "It sure is dark in here. How can you see what you are doing?"

"I'm fine."

"It sure does smell. Is there anything I can do?"

"Yes, just leave me be," I begged.

"I don't think that's a good idea. If you're not feeling well, I want to make sure that you can make it back." He came closer as his heels clicked against the flooring.

"I'll be out in a minute. Let me finish up here, and I'll see you back at the quarters."

"I'll wait outside for you," he gallantly offered.

"Fine," I hurriedly replied.

His steps took him to the exit. The door opened, delineating the outside world covered in snow. Hemple leisurely left.

I released my muzzle over Paulik's mouth, cupped his face, and kissed him hard and long.

He pulled away and replaced his shirt. He guided my shoulders toward the door and gently shoved me.

I halted, spun haphazardly in his direction, and blindly felt for him in the sea of darkness.

He somehow sensed my earnest attempt to find him and easily stopped my flailing hands. He redirected me toward the exit.

I dug my heels into the floor, not wanting to leave.

He leaned against my back with all his strength.

I whipped around and wrapped my arms around his shoulders, smothering his face with kisses.

Loud pounding rattled the door. "Let's go, it's freezing out here," Hemple called.

Paulik placed his fingertips to my brazen lips, ending my display of affection, and turned me toward the door and nudged me away from him.

I reluctantly conceded and adversely trudged to the door, feeling depleted and exhausted from the bafflement of the situation and

Hemple's inconsiderate intrusion. As I opened the door, the crisp air chilled my feverishness.

"You look terrible," Hemple stated. He offered his hand to help me.

I ignored the offer, leaving Hemple's hand dangling in the cold night air. I glanced back into the latrine, hoping to see Paulik. But all I saw was blackness. A moment of relief filled my head, realizing that Hemple couldn't see Paulik and myself in the depths of the latrine. I allowed the door to slam.

A gust of arctic air whipped around and pressed harshly against our faces. Hemple quickly turned his head and protected his face with his hands. I welcomed the iciness and barely batted my eyelashes, allowing my eyes to stream with salty liquid. The coldness didn't seem to penetrate my skin. My mind was warmed by the image of Paulik.

"Halt!" A loud voice peeled out of the darkness ahead, causing us to stop.

A figure emerged from the veil of night haze, backlit from the searchlight, and ran in our direction.

"Halt!" repeated the threatening demand.

The figure didn't hesitate but accelerated by pumping his arms and legs with each stride. A blast echoed through the crisp air. The figure's arms flung out to the sides, sending his chest forward in a graceful arch, his legs folded beneath him, and he slammed facedown onto the pathway. The body skid and came to rest at our feet. The striped material turned red at the entry where the bullet drilled and filled the air with a mixture of burnt cotton and flesh.

Out of the haze appeared two other soldiers as if they were proud hunters gaming for deer.

"We almost lost him. He's a wild one," the older soldier announced. "Evening, Officer," he addressed me when he realized my rank.

"Evening, Private," I replied.

The private calmly boasted, "Won't they ever learn. When I say run, I mean run, run for your life." He chuckled. "I found this one stealing bread. He walked right up in front of me and belligerently stood there, reached his hand into the basket, grabbed the food, took a huge bite, and started to chew. I couldn't believe it. How blatant! I said, 'Run. Run, you slimy bastard, run.' Then off he went like a rabbit. I yelled, 'Halt!' He became insubordinate, refusing to follow orders, and ran toward the wire fence. I had to stop him."

I rolled the body over and discovered a pink triangle sewn to his shirt. His face was riddled with a mixture of fresh cuts from sliding against the earth and wounds that were scabbed over from prior physical beatings.

The private immediately added, "We've had trouble with this one, always trying to get things for free and not following orders. The dirty pig wasn't fit to grace this earth. These types are polluting our country and spreading filthiness and diseases. He deserved it."

I knelt and looked closer at the face of the sleeping boy with his eyes closed, his lower lip split, and his head full of brown hair. My stomach dropped, thinking that it could have been Paulik. "Who's the barrack's leader?" I demanded.

"Officer Waller, sir." Both privates nodded to each other. "Officer Waller made it clear that we should keep an eye on this one because of him being a *peilpel*."

"What's a *peilpel*?" I asked.

"You know, sir. A *peilpel*, a dolly boy."

I inquisitively looked at him.

"They're the ones that'll do whatever it takes to become the kapo. They don't like to have their hair cut so that they will bend over and part their cheeks for a favor or extra bread." The two privates laughed.

Other officers and privates mingle around the prisoner on the ground.

"He's still breathing," alerted Private Hemple. He placed a hand on my shoulder.

Air bubbles, tinted red, emerged from the prisoner's crusty nostrils.

"What's going on here?" demanded Officer Waller as he stepped into the pool of light next to his two privates.

"We had a deserter, sir," claimed the older private, standing at attention.

Officer Waller looked down at the struggling victim. "I see. It was just a matter of time for this one." He leaned down and brushed a strand of curly dark hair away from the prisoner's forehead. "It's a shame too. A real hard worker." Waller stood and closed his eyes, as if he was giving the last rites prayer.

"He's still breathing, sir," the younger private informed Officer Waller.

Waller peered through a slit in his eyes and raised one brow. He drew his pistol from the holster, aimed, and sent a bullet penetrating in the center of the prisoner's forehead. The unexpected impact sent particles flying in the bullet's wake and splattered my face with matter and dirt.

I quickly jerked back. "What the—"

"Jumpy, are we, Klein?" teased Waller.

I wiped my brow to remove the combination of plasma, matter, and dirt.

"That settles that. Privates, get some help to get this mess picked up," ordered Officer Waller. "I don't want any evidence that this took place. We must keep the camp as neat and orderly as possible. Evening, Klein, Private Hemple," he offhandedly mumbled under his breath. He turned on his heels and ceremoniously walked toward the watchtower, evaporating behind the wall of white light.

Compassion filled my body as I looked at the young corpse and watched blood trickle out of the bullet wound on his forehead and down along the side of his nose. I fought the urge to wipe the trail away with a handkerchief.

I shoved my hands into my pockets, trying to escape the overwhelming emotion, and reminded myself that what we were doing was for the betterment of Germany. The only way to bring our country back to its thriving and influential wholeness, the way it was before World War I and the Treaty of Versailles, was through sacrifices and deaths—this was inevitable. I understood and accepted on a certain level the theology that when two opposing forces collided, there would always be casualties. But it was the emotional level I was having difficulty divorcing from my soul and providing the proof that I wasn't cut out to be military. All I ever wanted to do was to play the piano all over the world.

Chapter 25

I positioned my hands on a piano's keyboard to begin a C major scale. However, there was no piano. A wall of darkness or void kept me from seeing my hands, although I knew they were just below chest level. I knew this because I could sense them. For some strange reason, this didn't matter or bother me. I knew as my fingers pressed down and engaged the hammers in striking the piano's internal strings, chords would ring out and fill the darkness. I proceeded as if everything was normal. The invisible notes vibrated against the void's barriers, causing the reverb to ricochet from all corners and echo deep inside my head. There was a slight moment when I wondered if anyone else could hear these chords or if it was just for my amusement.

I continued playing and decided to modulate, which widened and expanded the void as if the music was pushing the walls farther away from me. A cool brush of air wafted past me, filling my nostrils with the clean scent of vanilla. In the distance appeared a flicker of light.

I became transfixed that if I continued the basic C major scale, repeating notes in perfect meter, it would deter the void's desire to return. My prediction deemed correct, for the flicker of light in the distance grew and approached. The closer the orb came, the more I saw something bathing in its whiteness. It was some form, a dancing object that was flitting and spinning.

The light brought a sense of calm, a real sense of peace, as if the object performing within was a sort of spiritual dancer presenting a ritual for my benefit. It was a beautiful ballerina, dressed in white chiffon that floated and drifted behind as she turned and leaped. The spot of light became stationary about three feet away, and the dancer stopped and reached and beckoned me toward her.

A light flickered above me, shedding crisp crystals all around. That was when I discovered there was no piano before me and that I had been playing on an invisible keyboard. I also realized that I wasn't sitting on a bench, but perched on thin air. I looked back at the waiting ballerina, who was still extending her hand toward me.

Her face was aglow with the spirals of crystals from the showering of light above. Due to the brightness, her features appeared to be finely sculptured and dominated by large blue eyes outlined with the darkest and longest eyelashes. Her skin and cheekbones were translucent, blending into the whiteness that surrounded her. Her lips were the color of pink roses, and her blond hair was pulled tightly back in a bun with wisps of curls framing her face. She summoned me again.

Rushing fear filled me with worry that if I discontinued the scale, the darkness would return, extinguish our lights, and send me into loneliness again. I felt this responsibility to remain at my station and continue to produce the musical waves that were protecting our environment. The dancer's pull was stronger than I expected. I tried to communicate with the ballerina through my eyes that I couldn't cease playing. She gently nodded and motioned for me. I lifted my hands from the invisible piano's keys, and the music continued.

The spot of light showering down on me followed as I went to her. As we reached for the each other's hand, our columns of light intermingled and expanded to encompass us both. As our hands grasped, she twirled into me and pressed her other hand against my chest. A sharp pain shot through my cavity and pierced my heart, causing my body to stiffen. A violet ribbon attached to her palm extracted from within my chest as she pulled her hand away. She gently brushed her lip against my cheek and pirouetted, causing the violet ribbon to wrap around her waist. She pirouetted in the opposite direction to allow the ribbon to unwrap itself and flutter on the currents of air. She leaped, pulling my torso with her and lengthening the ribbon to its fullness, keeping a distance between us.

A strong scent of chlorine filled the air as another shaft of light appeared in the opposite direction, illuminating another figure. This image was thicker, stockier, taller, and more masculine. As the apparition solidified, the male form was wearing a wool swimming suit with the Wissler's Academy's crest embroidered in gold lettering on the chest panel. His face was opaque from the harshness of the white light, with a dazzling smile and dark brown hair. He beckoned me to come to him.

As I stepped toward the swimmer, the ballerina tugged on the ribbon, impeding my freedom to approach. The swimmer came to me as if he was stroking through the water. His shaft of light intermingled with mine and the ballerina's, creating an even larger and brighter pool of light. He took my hand and twirled into my arms, placing his free hand on my chest, and gently kissed my cheek. A horrific pain shot through my cavity, causing me to pull away from him. A golden ribbon was withdrawn from my heart and attached to his palm. He swam away, pulling the fabric taut.

The two figures continued to move in opposite directions, pulling their ribbons tighter and stabilizing me in a frozen position between them, not able to move one way or the other.

In my inflexible state, another shaft of light flickered in the distance, and a distinct hint of lilacs perfumed the air. This beam of light pulsated as it neared, revealing a female figure with brown hair cascading freely and casting her face in shadows. The bluish-gray taffeta material sloped down over her shoulders, scooped low in front to reveal enlarged breasts, and was stretched to cover her swollen stomach. Her movements were labored as she sauntered toward me. Without any invitation, she placed her hand on my chest and gently kissed my cheek. Before I could prepare myself for the inevitable flash of pain to shoot through my heart, she pulled back her hand, guiding an orange ribbon from deep within me. The edges of the fabric sliced through my aorta and chest cavity as she waddled backward until the ribbon expanded to its limit.

The three pulled in opposing directions, causing my body excruciating pain. Another shaft of light flickered. This beam of brightness approached swiftly and easily, as if it was as agile as a thoroughbred racehorse and accented with a musty aroma. This downward light employed a male figure with curly brown hair that flowed freely in the galloping breeze. This image wore a thin cotton two-toned striped pajama cinched at the waist with a rope. He galloped up to me, ducking under the ribbons to approach me from behind. He reached his hand through my back, gently kissed my earlobe, and grabbed ahold of my heart. The bolt of electricity thrust my chest forward and paralyzed my body, causing tears to stream from my eyes. He withdrew out a green ribbon and pulled it tight like the others.

I was immobile. My chest cavity was pulled in all different directions. My arms were useless as they dangled. My legs suspended below me, barely able to reach the ground from the intensity of the ribbons jetting out in all different directions.

The figures began to circle me, alternating two to the left and two to the right, weaving the ribbons under and over the others. As they continue the pattern, the ribbons laced themselves around me, encasing my arms against my body and sheathing me in a colorful lattice cocoon. The figures released the ribbons from their palms and knotted the ends together at my ankles, completing the mummification. Each character went to the far corners of the space.

A deafening and sharp crack ripped through the air and caused the ballerina to wince in pain as a red ribbon streamed from her abdomen, and the shaft of light flickered out. A second crack sounded as a red ribbon flung out of the swimmer's chest and wafted limply down, and the shaft of light dissipated. Another crisp pop followed, and a crimson ribbon ejected from the female's swollen stomach, and her light shaft blacked out. The final blast chucked the thoroughbred racehorse outside of his column of light with a red ribbon fluttering behind before floating to the ground and disappearing into the darkness.

There was a single stream of light bathing me, shrouding me with flecks of gold and white. I was enmeshed in a lattice of ribbons, alone and frightened as the flooring below me gave way and crumbled. I fell. I descended into a body of water. I sank as the walls of liquid swallowed me. I struggled to free my arms and legs but was unable move.

I submerged quickly like a weighted anchor, deeper into the abyss of wetness. Bubbles escaped through my mouth and nose and raced toward the surface, leaving me behind.

"Hans."

I wanted to speak, to scream out that I was down here in the water. I wanted to make sure that the person belonging to the voice could find me.

"Hans." The voice seemed to be closer. "That's it, open your eyes."

I wanted to shout but was afraid that the water would rush into my mouth, causing me to drown.

"That's it, open your eyes."

I forced them open, but all I could see were colors and forms melting together and creating a splotchy and mutant arrangement.

"There you are."

I blinked, and an image—a dark form—appeared. I blinked again, and colors scattered, spun, separated, and positioned themselves in perfect places, designing a familiar picture. I squeezed my eyelids tightly closed.

"Come on, you got to get up."

I forced my eyes open again.

Gunter Waller stared at me.

"What?" I struggled to ask.

"That must have been some dream. I've never seen anyone carry on so." He tossed my pants at me.

My head throbbed. "What are you talking about?"

"You were dreaming, I'd guess. You gurgled and gasped for breath, looked like a carp out of the water. You're wringing wet." He indicated that my undershirt was soaked and adhering to my chest.

A draft chilled me.

"Are you feeling all right?" He threw my shirt at me. "Get dressed."

"I'm all right, I guess." I flung off the blanket and found myself completely drenched. "What the …?"

"You better get it together. Get out of those wet things and get dressed. We have a meeting with the commander in about fifteen minutes." He shook his head. "Do you need me to help you?"

I felt exposed and vulnerable. "No, I'm okay."

"You don't look okay." He opened my trunk at the foot of the cot and pulled out an extra set of underclothing.

I staggered to stand and removed the wet articles, dropping them with a dull plop onto the floor next to the trunk. The morning's icy fingers caressed my nakedness, sending a shiver up my spine. I ran my hands through my damp hair, pulling at the roots to alleviate the throbbing.

"Are you sure you are feeling all right?"

I saw Waller standing there, holding my underwear, as a smirk skirted across his face.

"Yes, I am." It dawned on me that I was standing there totally exposed. "Just give me those."

"Sure." He handed the items to me, one at a time. He stepped back with his arms resting on his hips, watching.

I quickly pulled on the underclothing. "I'm good, thank you."

"You sure are." Waller walked away. "Hurry up! We have an important meeting with the commander. You don't want to be late."

I grabbed a towel and headed to the bathroom. As I pushed open the door, Waller was brushing his teeth.

"Aren't you ready yet?" He forced the toothbrush against the inside of his cheek to reach the back molars.

"I wanted to wash my face first."

He continued brushing. "You don't have much time. We have a mandatory meeting this morning about revamping the camp. The commander will not accept any tardiness." He spat a stream of sudsy residue into the basin. "What were you dreaming about?"

"I'm not sure." I set my towel on the sink next to him.

"It sounded interesting." Waller wiped his mouth with the back of his sleeve and smacked me on the buttock. "Don't be late, pretty boy."

He allowed the door to slam.

I look back at my reflection. My eyes were heavy with dark half moons residing under each. My skin was flushed and splotchy around my cheeks, causing me to appear much older than my eighteen years. There was an ashy tent around my temples, and my lips were dry. For a moment, I barely recognized the man looking back at me.

I filled my palms with water and dowsed my throbbing forehead. The water brought an urgent sense of life back into my skin, which seemed to quench its depravity. I glanced back up and began to search my reflection for answers.

*****

When I was about to turn twelve, I started this introspective search of myself. I realized things were changing everywhere, but I wasn't certain what the changes meant. I knew things were going to be different from that moment forward. I saw the evidence in my physical appearance, the sprouting of blond peach fuzz in certain areas, the painful hardening of my nipples, agonizing inability to coordinate my body's actions, and lowering tones of my voice. The area that I saw the most changes was in my face. The bone structure seemed to be in constant alteration. The round childish features began to become more defined with the cranium expanding to create a high forehead, thickening the bridge of my brows, and sending my eyes deeper in each socket. My chubby cheeks hollowed out as the cheekbones protruded and became angular. My jaw became sharper like the letter *L* as the hinges on both sides seemed to thicken and the mandible extended in length, causing my chin to protrude straight forward, then curved and collided together in a cleft. My nose lengthened. My lower lip became plumper and redder while the upper thinned out. My hair became coarser and wavier with a mixture of different hues of blond.

I became obsessed with discovering these alterations. Every day after showering, I would stare at myself for long times in the large mirror that resided inside the room that Father Michael had provided for me until they could find me a foster home. I studied my face, body, and my soul for hours. I took copious mental notes of the changes that were appearing. I became an explorer, discovering regions that had been mysteriously unexplored. I became an expert of myself and was aware of a new freckle on my shoulders or arms. I was in awe and yet somewhat embarrassed with the development between my legs. I watched as the blond peach fuzz thickened with darker curls and extended down and around my legs. I became pleased with the changes and admired the person's physique in the mirror.

Then the serious questions began to swirl through my mind. I searched within the reflection's image for unending answers belonging to questions that I never could ask, like from where did I come? Who my father could have been? Do I look like my mother? What would she look like today? Am I special? Am I attractive? I felt that if I looked hard and deep enough at the image in the glass, I would somehow discover the answers to these questions.

Sometimes during my exploration, I would fantasize that the reflection would be able to escape the confines of the mirror, wrap me in his strength, and take me away so we could live happily together. Someplace where there was no hatred or parentless children. The reflection would explain everything I needed to know about these changes and protected me from the things that would cause pain and loneliness. We would become one, united and safe.

During these explorations, I discovered the pleasure of touch. I found that by caressing specific areas resulted in varying degrees of responses. I became obsessed with these sensitive areas and enjoyed watching myself in the mirror. I found that if I lightly brushed my fingers over my nipples, they would grow more sensitive and harden. If I would gently pinch them, I would feel a spark in my penis, and it would pulse. I discovered that if I inserted my finger into my belly button, I would cause a similar reaction down below. It seemed that everything connected to my penis and caused it to come alive, like a snake, extending and hardening. By accident, I discovered that by tugging on my testicles, a pressure would build and send a rush to the tip of my penis. I also found that when my penis was erect, I could guide my foreskin back, revealing a sensitive head that would ooze a clear droplet. And if I continued to rub the head, it caused my legs to become weak, rapid breaths, and a burning sensation that was beyond anything I could describe. One day, I couldn't stop, and a convulsing milky liquid spurted out in long streams and landed on the mirror.

I thought that I had some infection. I stood there looking at the reflection, splattered with this substance, and not knowing what to do. As I pondered my options, I noticed Father Michael sharing my mirror. I had no idea how long or what he witnessed. He stood there a long time without words, just gazing at me. His brows met in the middle of his forehead, his lips were slightly apart, and his arms folded across his chest. We both didn't move. A sense of guilt or wrongdoing flooded me. I was exposed and forbidden, something like Adam and Eve after the fruit incident and banished out of Eden.

"Put your towel on," he calmly instructed. He looked away as if he was hiding his disappointment. "Or better yet, get dressed. We need to have a chat." He turned and walked out of the room.

*****

I run my wet hands through my hair, making sure that it was presentable, and blotted my face dry with the towel. As I passed my cot, I tossed the towel onto the pile of wet undergarments. I slipped into my holster, climbed into my overcoat, and grabbed my hat.

Chapter 26

The eastern sky was accentuated with a golden haze and laced with streaks of red clouds, which tapered into a mundane grayness as it reached toward the west. The air was thick with coldness and the ground dressed in snow. I followed the path to the administration building for the instructional session.

"Morning, sir," Hemple eagerly greeted me. He slipped his hand under my elbow.

I pulled my arm from his grip. "Morning, Hemple."

"Oh, I'm sorry, sir. I simply wasn't thinking." He forced a smile.

"You must—" I was interrupted by two officers merging into our pathway to reach the doorway. "Good morning, Officers."

They both nodded, pressed forward, and spoke in harmony, "Morning."

I halted Hemple from following. "You must be careful with how you conduct yourself in front of the other officers. Comradeship is one thing, but you must be aware of how things are misconstrued and misinterpreted."

Hemple looked at me with wide eyes.

I continued chiding, "I thought I made this clear to you the other day. Do we need to have another dissertation?"

"No, sir. It won't happen again," he stated.

"I hope not." I glanced away from him toward the entrance to the administration building.

He opened the door and glanced down as I passed.

The administration building was abuzz with commotion and urgency.

"Klein."

I halted at Commander Heiden's office doorway. Private Schwartz rushed from behind his desk and spoke rapidly like a machine gun. "Commander Heiden needs a word with you before the meeting. Would you please come in and go into his office?"

"Of course," I agreed.

Hemple moved to escort me into the commander's office.

I shook my head. "Go find us some seats in the conference room."

"It'll only be a few minutes," qualified Private Schwartz.

Hemple glanced from me to the receptionist and back to me. He forced a smile and disappeared down the hallway, which was like a school of trout swimming upstream.

"You know the way, Officer Klein?" asked Private Schwartz. He was already making his way back behind his desk.

"Yes, of course, I do."

"Commander Heiden will be in momentarily." He flipped open a file and lowered himself into his waiting chair.

As I walked toward the commander's office, I heard scuffling and scurrying noises behind the door. I listened to what sounded like a whimpering animal, struggling to free itself from some restraint. I slightly pushed open the door until it halted, and something darted to the far corner of the room.

I tried pushing the door further open; it still wouldn't budge. I peered around the jammed door and discovered Officer Waller adjusting his holster and blocking the door's swing with the toe of his boot.

"Klein, you gave me a scare with your sneaking up like that."

"I wasn't sneaking." I glanced over at the other person, who kept his head down and back toward me. "What's going on?"

"It's not what you're thinking," stammered Waller.

"How could you know what I'm thinking?" I qualified.

"I thought you might have been the commander," he continued.

"And what if I was?"

"But you weren't, so there's no need to worry about it," he joked. He removed his foot from blockading the door. "What brings you in here?" He changed the subject.

"I asked him to come in," a voice came from behind me.

I turned, saluted, and struck attention.

Commander Heiden and two other commanders were standing in the reception area. Commander Heiden placed a hand on my shoulder as he passed. "At ease, Klein. Please have a seat."

I nodded, removed my cap, and went to the seat that Office Waller was standing near.

Commander Heiden invited in the other two commanders. They walked in stiffly and made themselves comfortable next to Commander Heiden's desk.

The prisoner didn't move.

"Officer Waller, at ease," ordered Commander Heiden.

Waller placed his hands behind his back, feet shoulder width apart, and held his focus.

Commander Heiden leaned on his desk. "What brings you into my office uninvited, Waller?"

"I wanted to submit my barrack's report with you, sir," he replied.

"But the report isn't due until tomorrow, Waller," said the commander. He scanned his calendar on his desk.

"I wanted to be ahead of schedule."

"Fine, then. Hand it to me."

"I was only going to give an oral report, sir."

The commander peered over the rim of his glasses. "But I need the written as well. There isn't much I can do filing an oral report now, is there?"

"No, sir."

"So, what am I to do? Take notes as you orate the events?" The commander turned to the window.

"No, sir." Waller quickly added, "I can have it for you tomorrow, sir."

"When it's initially scheduled?"

"Yes, sir."

"Then what's this all about?" He didn't wait for Waller's response. "That will be all. Dismissed."

Waller snapped his heels together and raised a stiff right arm to salute.

The commander merely nodded.

Waller departed.

Without any indication, the prisoner faced the commander. His locks of chestnut curls cascaded down the nape of his neck, causing my heart to sink as if all the muscles in my chest have been cut loose. Paulik stood there with his face burning hot, refused to look at me, and waited for the commander to hand over the signed document.

"Klein, we've invited you here to ask you some questions about an acquaintance of yours." Commander Heiden motioned Paulik to leave.

I summoned all my strength not to watch him leave and focused past Commander Heiden's left ear, watching the snow filter down outside.

"I want to introduce you to our distinguished guests." Commander Heiden indicated the man to his right. "This is Chief of the German Police and National Commander Heinrich Himmler. He is the genius behind the conception of this and other campsites."

I offered my hand to the smallish man wearing pince-nez spectacles, which gave him more the appearance of an elementary school teacher than a Nazi leader. His elfish size was dominated by a large round head topped with brown turf, pallid skin, a tiny mouth that seemed pinched beneath a pencil mustache, and a shapeless chin.

"National Commander Himmler organized the SS in southern Bavaria, redesigned the SA, set up the Race and Resettlement Central Office, also known as RUSHA, and has dedicated his time promoting the Nordic race. He'll be addressing the meeting this morning," instructed Commander Heiden.

A moment of recognition rushed forth. Was this the man who informed the Führer of Ernst Röhm's speculative coup d'état that started the Night of the Long Knives and murdered Josef in the Hanselbauer Hotel in Munich? I slowly pulled back my offered hand.

Commander Heiden continued, "This is Colonel Reinhard Heydrich."

The slender commander towered over Himmler and Heiden in height. He offered a massive paw and shook my hand with the politeness of a gentleman. His face was long and thin with his nose occupying most of the façade. His smallish eyes appeared to be set too close due to the girth of his nose. His lips were full and positioned perfectly below the sharp curve of his prominent cheekbones and hovered above a masculine square chin.

"Colonel Heydrich is head of the counterintelligence branch of the SS and will be assisting Commander Himmler." Commander Heiden looked at everyone. "Why don't everyone sit down. This meeting will only be a few moments, Officer Klein." He indicated for me to sit.

"Thank you, sir," I said.

Meanwhile, Heiden sat in a seat next to mine, permitting Himmler to sit in his leather chair behind his desk. Heydrich positions himself to Himmler's right.

The uncomfortable silence in the room, the positioning of the interrogators, and my sweaty palms reminded me of Dean Meyer.

*****

"This will only take a few minutes." Dean Meyer smiled.

I felt the heaviness of the room as I sat there waiting for the interrogation to begin. I knew that what had transpired against me wasn't a malicious act of violence, but a prank that got out of hand. I hated sitting there, waiting. I hated that the people in charge were expecting me to point fingers. I hated that my reputation at Wissler's Academy would be measured by these next few minutes, depending on the answers to the same questions that I've already answered and re-answered. I even hated myself for allowing this to be found out.

"Hans, try and relax and explain to Dean Meyer exactly what happened," encouraged Professor Weinholtz as he placed a cold hand on top of mine folded in my lap.

I plead silently with the professor not to make me do this, but he encouraged by nodding his head to begin.

"Professor Weinholtz indicated that you might be able to identify the students who removed the frog parts from the science lab. Is this right?" Dean Meyer pried over the knuckles of his folded hands pressing against his lips. His bulging eyes were enlarged by the desire to settle this prank as soon as possible so that he could return to his common and mundane appearance of portraying the school's headmaster. I was sure he was not utterly interested in this so-called act of defiance more than he was interested in who was skipping physic class—if it didn't bother him directly. It was Professor Weinholtz who pushed this issue.

"Go on, Hans, it's all right. We need to address this," urged the professor. He leaned in toward me and squeezed my hands. "He's shy, Dean Meyer, but he's a good boy. Go on, tell what happened."

"What I was trying to tell the professor," I started with trepidation, "was that I had overheard some students thinking about doing a prank. It was only supposed to be a joke."

"But the prank was on you, wasn't it?" The dean flashed a smile, revealing his partial dentures, yellowing from the abundance of coffee and blueberry pie.

My palms were clammy, and my speech was nearly inarticulate. "Well, I guess so."

"It either was or wasn't, son." Dean Meyer impatiently fanned out his fingers to the side, resembling a peacock.

"They took certain parts of the dissected frog and strung them on a string and then hung them—"

"What parts?" inquired the Dean.

My lips tightened, and I released an audible sigh.

"It was the genitalia," piped in the professor. "They strung up the male frog's genitalia and hung them around Hans's neck after they pinned him down on the floor and dangled the parts above his face. I intervened as they were forcing his mouth open and …"

*****

"Klein," croaked Himmler with a throaty quality.

I snapped my attention toward him.

"We asked you here to gather some information. Information that's pertinent to an ongoing investigation, an investigation where your name was brought up," he politely informed.

I quickly glanced over to Commander Heiden for reassurance or more information, a look or a glance from him that would give me the confidence to divulge any information.

The commander adjusted in his seat. "It's not anything serious. They need to ask you some questions about a Father Michael from St. Emmanuel's."

"Sure, is everything all right?" I blurted out without thinking.

"That's no concern of yours," Himmler grumbled. His eyes studied me and my body language, trying to detect any unusual mannerisms to use against me in the future.

"Just answer the questions, Klein," encouraged Heiden.

"Yes, sir." I readjusted myself in the chair, making sure that my palms rested flat against my thighs, my feet were flat on the floor, and my spine erect and not resting on the back of the chair.

"So, you know Father Michael from St. Emmanuel's?" asked Himmler while lifting his shapeless chin and studying my reactions.

"Yes, sir, I know Father Michael."

Heydrich pulled out an overstuffed folder with color-coded file tabs. He opened it and sifted through several bundles of paper. He placed what he was looking for before Himmler. Himmler detached his studious eyes from me to glance down at the bundle attached with a pink cover page. Heydrich flipped through the pages, paused, and pointed to a typed paragraph. Himmler quickly removed the pince-nez spectacles and squinted his beady eyes to read the fine print.

"It says here that you were under the guidance of Father Michael for some time," Himmler read.

"Yes, sir. I lived at St. Emmanuel for a time after my mother died." I appeared calm while my palms sweated and shook.

Himmler looked up at me to study my face for an awkward moment. "Who was your mother?"

"She was a dancer, sir."

"Ballerina?" he crisply asked.

"Yes, sir," I replied, glancing down at my hands.

"Gerta Klein?"

"Yes."

"The Gerta Klein?" he inquired again.

"Yes, sir."

His face flushed pink, and his mouth pulled back into a slight smile. "Well, now. That's something." He leaned back, folding his arms across his chest and penetrating me with his eyes.

Heydrich took advantage of the awkward moment. "As you may be aware, Reichsführer SS Himmler and I designed this elite training camp for candidates like yourself. From my information, you're a prime example of the type of officer we desire to develop. I have encouraged Reichsführer SS Himmler to set up the Sicherheitsdient or SD, a highly developed intelligence network. This system has provided us with the needed and necessary background information on anyone working for, against, or outside the Nazi Party. We want to make sure that we have clear and concise information on members of our Party, and we have given extra attention to prominent persons in all fields of occupations. Since the beginning of this year, the enactment of the new anti-homosexual laws resulted in the discovery of several thousand sociosexual saboteurs. These so-called degenerates have been conducting regular business and infecting the moral and morale of our Germany."

Himmler leaned in, placing his hands on the desk. "It all falls under the jurisdiction of Federal Security Office for Combating Abortion and Homosexuality. The ombudsman, or homosexual, is a traitor to his people and must be rooted out." He nodded for Heyrich to continue.

"This condition is usually a medical problem, relating to glandular malfunction. The improper functioning of these glands doesn't produce the adequate amount of testosterone, preventing the individual a normal life. If treated, the sick person successfully may be cured and live a prosperous and fruitful life. If untreated, the disease will overtake the person, and then we must exterminate him so that he'll not influence or infect others. Imagine how many children haven't been born because of this evil plague. Lives that could help promote our cause. This is an act of treason toward the Führer and his ultimate plan. The disease will weaken our military strength and position against opposing forces. The Teutonic tradition was to drown all infected persons in bogs, but these wise ancestors let the Romans go unpunished for this degradation and even encouraged them. The results speak for themselves. The Romans lost their power due to this simple infringement, which weakened their forces," expressed Heydrich with a proud chest.

"What does all this have to do with Father Michael and me?" I asked with trepidation.

Himmler expelled a huge sigh.

Heiden shot a look to impede me from asking any further questions.

"We're getting to that." Heydrich jumped in to alleviate the tension. "In 1933, Pope Pius XI signed a concordat with the Führer. This agreement provided a guaranteed freedom to clergy, monasteries, nunneries, parochial schools and hospitals, and the Catholic laymen. Although this concordat was signed, it fed into the belief that these parties were havens for the breeding and spreading of this ungodly plague. Youth movements, Catholic Church, and even the military were investigated. Baldur von Schirach realized the infractions and decided to do something about the ongoing and unspoken problem. His devotion to the Führer and the purification of Germany made him hold firmly on the Hitler Youth Movement and declared to dissolve any competing youth organizations. So even though Pope Pius XI signed this freedom pact with Adolf Hitler, Schirach issued a decree that no young man could belong to a clerical group and the Hitler Youth Movement at the same time. No one could become a member of the Nazi Party if they didn't complete four years of service to the Youth Movement, eliminating people from being offered the better jobs in nearly all the fields of professions unless they were party members. Schirach encouraged juvenile gangs to invade Catholic youth centers, stealing role books, vandalizing buildings, and even setting them on fire. Even today, the Catholic Church is still harboring and protecting individuals that have practiced this abomination."

"We are in the process of cleaning out these unwanted areas so that we have a pure nation," Himmler said as he continued studying me.

"The Catholic Church has been charged with many violation and infringements, including assisting enemies of the state to escape to foreign countries. Illegally transferring funds to the Vatican and outside the providences. The Catholic Church committed homosexual offenses with minors and other clergy members, using pastoral letters and sermons to demoralize the military and inform their followers of biased information and lending and operating support to resistance within Germany and the in the occupied territories. Priests distributed food and clothing to enemies through the clerical disguise of helping people, counseling by spreading atrocious stories to outsiders and the Vatican, and attempting to deny all wrongdoings of aiding perpetrators," Heydrich reported.

"Has Father Michael ever presented to you any situation or opportunities of any gross indecencies?" asked Himmler.

"What?"

Heiden sat erect in his chair.

I quickly asked, "What, sir?"

Heydrich explained, "Paragraph 174, not to be confused with paragraph 175, prohibits sexual contact of any kind between older men and minors. Acts include putting an arm around a child, touching hands, hugging, and as simple as placing a hand on the youth's knee. Father Michael is being held and questioned about such involvements. Have you, at any time, while under the supervision of Father Michael, experienced any such advancement?"

My mind raced back to moments of tenderness with Father Michael at my going-away celebration when he handed me my mother's gift and hugged me goodbye. Could this be the kind advancements that they are alluding? But it was I who initiated the physical contact, not the father.

"No, he never made any advancement toward me. He was a complete and honorable gentleman the entire time I was under his supervision," I confessed, hiding any implications with my eyes.

"He never made you feel uncomfortable?" asked Heydrich.

"I was a child when I was in the care of Father Michael and Sister Margot at St. Emmanuel's."

"But you remained there until you were almost twelve, before you went to live with the Rhoden family, isn't that correct?" posed Himmler.

I slowly nodded.

"It's important that you try and remember anything that could've been an implication."

"Are you asking me to make things up?" I retorted defensively.

"No, we only want the truth. But we want to make sure that if anything questionable had been bestowed upon you and could affect your well-being, emotional, or mental status, it should be identified so that we get you the proper medical attention. That's the only way to weed yourself from this disease that may have been infected unknowingly upon you. This knowledge and the appropriate medical interventions will prepare you adequately to proceed to be beneficial to the Führer and your country."

"No, sir, nothing such as you are asking has ever happened to me, especially coming from Father Michael. He was like the father I never had."

Himmler emphatically stated, "I'm relieved to hear this. An officer of your caliber and potential to move high in the Party's status needs to be clean of all impurities. That'll be all." He stood.

I rose. "What will happen to Father Michael?"

Himmler glanced at me as if I offended his authority in some way. He walked toward the door without a word.

Heydrich gathered the color-coded bundles of paper and replied, "Father Michael is under serious investigation. There have been several counts against him under paragraph 174."

"Meaning?" I quickly asked.

"The matter will be properly handled."

"Klein?" Himmler faced me. "Do you still play the piano?"

I glanced at him.

"You were spectacular at the Hanselbauer Hotel," he stated with a knowing smile. "I had the rare opportunity to be there to hear your abilities."

"Thank you, sir."

"We must have the pleasure again sometime. Maybe I can put a good word in for you with the Führer so that you may have the opportunity to perform at the Olympics this summer."

"That would be an honor, sir."

"I thought so." He left the room followed by Heiden.

"He means it," Heydrich said with a big toothy smile as he tucked the bulging file under his arm. "It was a pleasure meeting you, Klein." He offered out his hand.

I wrapped my hand around the thickness of his. "Thank you."

"Klein?" called Himmler from the doorway. "Your mother, Greta Klein, was a truly magnificent performer. I had the pleasure of seeing her final performance of *Swan Lake*."

"You were there, sir?" I asked with astonishment.

"I stayed for all the curtain calls. Six, if I recall correctly. It would have been more, but the stage union wouldn't permit it. I never missed one of her performances. I followed her career very closely. She would have been very proud of you." He went into the reception area.

"We'll be in touch." Heydrick smiled and ducked through the doorway, leaving me alone in the office.

I took a moment trying to comprehend all the information thrown at me. *What can I do to help Father Michael?* I replaced my cap on my head when Paulik's face filled my mind. What was he doing in the commander's office with Officer Waller?

"They're about to start," Private Schwartz said, smiling as he leaned in the doorway.

"Thank you."

Chapter 27

I passed images of principal officers adorning the walls on my way to the conference room. As I entered, Private Himple waved both arms over his head, indicating that he had reserved a seat for me.

"Come in, Klein," encouraged Commander Heiden.

I quickly sat next to Himple.

Commander Heiden addressed the room. "Your presence here today represents something significant." He allowed his voice to pause and dramatically waited until all murmuring and shifting in seats quieted. "I want to address something that is beyond anything this country has ever seen before. You are chosen men—chosen to bring this country back to its greatness, chosen for your qualifications and abilities to be lucky enough to be a part of this encampment. However, we have become complacent and comfortable with our duties. That's why the Chief of the German Police and National Commander Heinrich Himmler and Colonel Reinhard Heydrich are here today."

Himmler interrupted, "Thank you, Commander Heiden." Himmler's sloping shoulders, thick waist, and short limbs accentuated his boxy appearance. His large head nodded for Commander Heiden to relinquish his position. Himmler scanned the audience, slowly shook his head, and snapped his tongue against the roof of his mouth, creating a clicking noise. "We're on the brink of the most powerful movement any country has ever seen. We're moving forward, and that begins with you here in this camp. By being here, you're showing that you're a committed member of the Nazi movement. Showing that you're ready to step up and proceed with any action that's needed. Showing that you're ready through your faith in the Führer and for the sake of the life of our blood and people to purify life for Germany as bravely as you know how to fight and die for Germany."

"What's he talking about?" whispered Hemple.

I shrugged and indicated that he needed to listen.

He readjusted in his seat and faced forward.

"What I want to present to you today is the next step in our Führer's plan for dominance, known as Order of the Death's Head. This order is to supervise the gassing and burning of unwanted inmates and the salvaging of gold fillings from teeth to be deposited in the federal bank in Berlin, so we're capable of building the needed equipment to move forward. We need you. What's happening in the surrounding countries are matters of utter indifference to me. Whether those people live in comfort or perish … interest me only insofar as we need them to work for us and our culture. Apart from that, it doesn't interest me. It isn't a question if women and degenerates collapse from exhaustion while digging tank ditches. What interests me is only insofar as completing the tank ditches for Germany."

He paused, looked around the room, removed his pince-nez spectacles, squeezed the bridge of his nose, replaced the glasses, and took a deep breath. "Most of you know what it means to see a hundred corpses lying together, five hundred or a thousand. To have gone through this and yet, apart from a few exceptions—examples of human weakness—to have remained decent, this has made us hard. Today, you'll reinstate your commitment, be given new orders to adhere to, and a new workout regimen to follow in the promotion of national health." He nodded toward Heydrich to proceed with the distribution of brown cylinder vials.

Heydrich towered over Himmler and motioned to several inmates that were waiting in the back of the room to start the distribution. Paulik moved along the far side of the room, passing vials to each man. He handed one to Waller, who grabbed hold of his hand. Paulik pulled his hand away.

A prisoner with a shaved head and blank stare presented me a vial.

Himmler proudly announced, "The bottles are Pervitin, or the wonder drug, under the code name OBM. This little pill will increase self-confidence, concentration, and the willingness to take risks, while at the same time reduce the sensitivity to pain, hunger, and thirst, as well as lessen the need for sleep. Pervitin will effectively help individuals to achieve above-average performance. Each tablet will eliminate the need to sleep for five to eight hours, and two doses are effective for twenty hours. And as the body becomes tolerant, the doses may be increased, but do not exceed six tablets in a twenty-four-hour period."

"We'd like you to take a dose now," instructed Heydrich.

Other men followed the order immediately, pulling the top off, emptying two tablets in their palms, and popping them into their mouths.

"What are you waiting for?" asked Hemple. "Just pop them in." He joked.

"What are they?"

"They wouldn't give you something that'll hurt you," he retorted.

"I'm not sure."

"Just do it."

I opened the vial and rolled out two tablets in my palm. I picked one up and dabbed it on my tongue. The bitterness was overpowering. I juggled them in my palm and contemplated the possible side effects.

"As this is only a means to be helpful, as is the use of schnapps or alcohol and shouldn't be abused," added Heydrich.

Abuse rang through my mind and was enough evidence that I wasn't about to venture on an addictive encounter with a substance that I had no understanding of its side effects.

"Hurry up and get it over with," encouraged Hemple.

I finally threw one pill back in my throat and swallowed without any water assistance. I shoved the other pill and the vial in my pocket.

Himmler cleared his voice. "There have been reports of the overexposure to alcohol. Intoxication is a matter that we must address correctly. The military command's understanding of your workload may lead to a need for unwinding, but as long as it doesn't result in public drunkenness. I expect severe punishment for those who allow themselves to be tempted to engage in criminal acts because of alcohol abuse. Those committing the most serious infractions of morality and discipline such as fights, accidents, mistreatment of subordinates, violence against a superior officer, and crimes involving unnatural sexual acts could expect a humiliating extermination."

I glanced at Hemple.

Hemple blushed and hung his head.

"Please rise," ordered Heydrich.

The room filled with screeching chairs pushed back and men standing.

"Raise your right hand." Heydrich demonstrated with the first two fingers extended as well as the thumb. "And repeat after me. I swear by God this sacred oath ..."

"I swear by God this sacred oath," the room echoed.

"I will render unconditional obedience to Adolf Hitler, the Führer of the German Reich and people, Supreme Commander of the Armed Forces ..."

"I will render unconditional obedience to Adolf Hitler, the Führer of the German Reich and people, Supreme Commander of the Armed Forces."

" ... and will be ready as a brave soldier to risk my life at any time for this oath."

" ... and will be ready as a brave soldier to risk my life at any time for this oath." Our choral unison ended as one.

My heart started racing as a thermal heat ran through my bloodstream. This must be the onset of the Pervitin. My fingers tingled, and my head pounded.

Chapter 28

My body woke me only after four hours of sleep, demanding the next Pervitin dose with a pounding headache. My fingers felt arthritic as they fumbled for the vial under my pillow, where I kept it hidden from others. A sharp pain radiated from under my shoulder blade as I sluggishly rotated onto my side to open the vial. I only had four tablets left, which meant that I'd have to get a refill after my platform duty this afternoon because I didn't want to try to face tomorrow without the miracle pills. I threw two tablets into my mouth, swallowed, and waited for the onset of numbness.

I laid on my cot, staring out the small square window above my station, waiting for the tablets' euphoric effects. I waited, watching the movement of clouds against the dark and dank early morning sky. I waited for the thermal heat to spread from my stomach, branch off in different directions through my veins, pump through the chambers of my heart, and pinpoint the most needed areas: my joints, my lower back, and my head. As I waited, my mind drifted to that moment right before night becomes morning when everything seemed so surreal and disconnected, and the dark shadows were about to be revealed and were on the verge of evaporation from the morning's glow. It was this exact moment when the newborn morning would kiss the night with its rose-pinkness, reach into every corner and crevice of the alley between the barracks, and present the surrounding area in a fresh new light. It was at this precise moment when I'd fantasize sneaking a long warm kiss from Paulik's lips as we hid behind a dumpster reeking of decay.

I was aware that this fantasy was just that, a fantasy. As the Pervitin tingled through my fingertips and attacked the dull pounding in my head, I knew we'd never have a moment to express ourselves, except for the stolen moments of glances, gentle touches, or a quick peck. The time always came too soon when we had to part and return to our pretense of not knowing each other. The reality of what our lives had become, a continuous mirage of secret meetings and growing passion. The illusion that our lives would somehow be removed from this existence and resume in a location that was far from the limitations of the barbed wire only existed in the crooks of my mind.

In this repeated fantasy, I would recognize Paulik's insatiable eyes and admire him as the rosy hue of the morning washed over his chocolate curls with hints of copper, highlighting his sharp cheekbones and accentuating the curves of his leanness. Enveloping him in my arms, I'd covered his beauty with kisses and run fingers through his hair. Although I knew that time was dangerously pressing for us to part, I'd engulf him tighter in my arms; he'd sigh with pleasure and nip at my neck.

There was always a fleeting moment of anxiety right before the Pervitin took full control of the body; the heart would pound with such velocity, it felt it would erupt. Paranoia invaded my fantasies as Paulik embraced someone else, another officer who was nestling against his long neck. Paulik's eyes would appear at half-mast with pleasure as I watched in pure shock as Gunter Waller revealed his face, cracked a smile, and he attacked Paulik's mouth with fervor.

But once the Pervitin encased me with its magical powers, I found the strength to push those thoughts out of my head, bound up out of bed, and enthusiastically start my day.

The days started with a rigorous weight training and calisthenics program. We were assigned workout partners, and I got the honor to pump iron with Private Hemple. Depending on the day, the training rotated to focus on different body parts: back and triceps, chest and biceps, but legs and abdomen every day.

The workouts became routine, the same type of weight-lifting exercises with increasing weight for each set. The problem with the regular lifting program was that the body became accustomed to the workout, and without changing programs, the muscles plateaued and refused to grow any larger. It had been two weeks of intense weight lifting, running, and war maneuvers, and Private Hemple hadn't developed the muscle tone like the rest of us; his frame still sported the childish-boy body that appeared on the verge of development no matter how hard Private Hemple worked out.

The afternoon train's whistle blared, indicating the new arrivals. Commander Heiden kept me on train patrol duty because I apparently was a welcoming sight for the people arriving. I positioned myself amid the harsh afternoon sun, feeling the platform's vibrations. My head was dull and cloudy, aching for the second dose of Pervitin even without a watch. I reached into my pocket and pulled out the vial, unscrewed the top, and emptied the contents into my palm. I tossed the last two tablets into the back of my mouth, tasting the bitterness on my tongue, forcing them down with my saliva. I waited, hoping the effects would be quick so that I could have a clear head before the train stopped.

The train slowed to a crawl, and I waited. Smoke billowed from the side of the train as it inched into the platform area. I waited. The train's metal brakes screeched to a halt. I waited. Two privates began to unfasten the cattle cars, and I was still waiting. Finally, with an internal explosion of heat, the magical elixir streamed through my body, forcing beads of sweat to sprout on my forehead, behind my ears, armpits, and between my legs. It also sent a cold shiver to quench the heat's path. My eyes pulsated and dilated with a dance of multiswirling colors, my temples throbbed as the blood rushed through the veins, and my hands tingled as the drug shot energy to each fingertip. I took a deep breath to ease the adrenaline and to allow the sensation to wash completely over me—a feeling of floating and invincibility.

My vision became acute, with the vibrancy and sharpness of each color of clothing the prisoners donned as they disembarked the train. Even though most of the hues were tans and browns, there was the occasional flash of blue, orange, yellow, or red that I craved to witness. The sea of confused and scared people swarmed the platform, causing chaos for the next few minutes, and it was the utmost importance to manage the situation as quickly as possible to maintain control and prevent any sense of rebellion.

I automatically started the selection process by separating the men from the women. "Men to the left, women to the right," I announced. I indicated the stairwells that led down to the camp yard below where they would be identified, recorded, and sent to their barracks. "Children will go into this shelter," I instructed behind me.

The shelter was a façade to mask a covered truck ready to pack the children in and take them to the far side of the camp. This tactic was designed to make the children feel calmer since they were expected to perceive the shelter as a safe place since it had been painted red and orange and looked like a gingerbread house.

My head started spinning, my hands shook, and it was harder to take a deep breath. The vibrant colors dimmed as if a dark cloud collected above. My heart pounded in my ears: *tha-thump, tha-thump, tha-thump*. But I managed to direct men to the left, women to the right, and the children to the area behind me. Every muscle in my stomach contracted and twisted as I saw a man with auburn curly hair and a large nose.

I grabbed his arm. "Stefan?" I called with excitement.

The man turned and stared at me with fright.

I immediately realized I mistook him for my Wissler Academy roommate, Stefan Joffe. I covered my error. "You need to go to the left." I forced his arm in the correct direction.

The bewildered man followed the instructions without any incidents and descended the stairs with the other men.

"Men to the left and women to the right. Keep moving." The momentary fever of the drug should level off soon, but I was overwhelmed by the increased pumping of blood through my veins, the pulsing behind my eyes, and the pounding in my temples. My vision became distorted, shaky, and blurry, with all the colors melding into one another.

An elderly man with wild unkempt gray hair stepped before me. His posture and gait seemed familiar; my heart stopped beating for a moment. I stepped in front of him, causing him to halt. "Professor Weinholtz?"

The man stood there, looking at me without any recognition. He slowly placed a hand on my chest and said, "I wish I were your

Professor Wienholtz. Then you could explain all this to me." He patted my chest three times and continued with the men down the staircase.

I watched until he disappeared.

A woman bumped into my back as she passed, carrying a newborn wrapped in a light blue blanket.

Without thinking, I pushed other disoriented prisoners aside to stop the woman.

The woman's hair cascaded over her shoulders like a chocolate waterfall. The way she walked with command and confidence was unsettlingly familiar.

The ocean of people pushed against me, creating distance between us. I forced myself forward; she was getting closer to the stairwell, and she must not descend.

As she reached for the railing, I grabbed her shoulder and stopped her. Her body became rigid.

"Inga?" I ask.

When she turned, she wasn't Inga. She didn't even look like Inga. The woman's round face was much older than Inga's.

I stared in disbelief. What would I have done if it was Inga? How would I have been able to help her?

The woman walked toward the stairs.

"Halt!" I commanded.

She hesitated.

I swung her around and looked at the blue bundle cradled in her arms.

She pleaded, "No."

I moved her to the side to allow the other women to continue down the stairs to the camp yard. I motioned for Private Hemple to assist me.

Private Hemple and another soldier quickly scampered over. I only had to indicate the blue bundle with my eyes, and Private Hemple knew what to do.

"Hand over the child," Hemple asked politely.

The woman instantly withdrew and pulled back. Hemple quickly moved in, and before the woman was aware, he had the blue bundle in his arms.

The woman screamed, "No, that's my baby!" She rushed Hemple, and the other soldier stepped in to intercede, forcing the woman back with a flick of his hand.

Hemple carried the child to the designated "gingerbread" location.

The woman pushed against the soldier with such strength, causing the soldier to lose his footing and fall. She pushed past another oncoming soldier and thrust herself onto Hemple's back, clawing at his ears.

The fallen soldier regained his footing, lifted his rifle, and slammed the butt against the back of the woman's skull. The first blow didn't seem to faze the woman as she pulled Hemple's cap off and grabbed fistfuls of hair. The soldier struck again and again until she limply crumbled to the platform. Hemple whirled around with his pistol drawn and sent a bullet, point-blank, into the woman's temple.

I looked at the dead mother, feeling nothing. I knew that I should have some feeling of humanity, but for some reason, no emotions registered.

Two guards came over. "Take her away. I do not want any evidence that this happened. We must keep the camp as neat and orderly as possible," I ordered.

"That was something else," Hemple said.

The guards removed the woman and carried her down the stairs to the wagon on the lawn.

"What happened to your ear, Hemple?" I asked.

"I think she bit me."

"You better get it looked at."

Chapter 29

The evening's chilly air filled my lungs as I lengthened my strides during my daily required five-mile run. The monochrome greyness of the trek soothed my eyes as I passed the silhouetted trees on both sides of the path.

I pushed myself to achieve the euphoric state of mind when the endorphins would release and take over my being. Tonight was a struggle as I tried to stop thinking about what happened on the platform and the woman's face. I shook my head to send it back in the depths of my mind. *Keep putting one foot in front of the other. Take it easy, this isn't a race.* It usually wasn't until the mile one marker, when my brain would release the tiny protein molecules into my nervous system and triggered the sedative receptors to provide the ever-awaiting pain-free state of mind. Once I achieved this desired state, I could run for long distances and maybe erase today's events.

As I passed the three-quarter-mile marker, the evening's dampness and chill added to the difficulty of finding a comfortable pace. *Don't give up. Just a little farther, and you will get through this wall. That is all you must do. Don't rush and focus on extending one leg in in front, push off the back leg, and repeat.*

The mile marker was up ahead, or I imagined that I could see it in the darkening light. Right on cue, warmth rushed through my veins as perspiration beaded beneath the sweat clothing and scarf that I had wrapped around my throat. I audibly sighed with relief as my body took over and slipped into the painless strides and relaxed breaths.

Paulik's face emerged as if he was running backward in front of me. His encouragement emitted from his intoxicating eyes and a slight hint of a smile. My cheeks reddened and my heart swelled as I wanted to hold him and express myself to him. I knew it was against the laws and could mean death by execution if discovered. There was something worthwhile in the act of allowing myself to follow my heart no matter what the cost.

Stumbling over a rock, I pitched forward and saw the snow-covered path dash toward my face, yet somehow, I avoided a collision with the ground, found my footing, and remained upright. The jarring disturbed the murky waters within me and woke the red-haired monster. He wasted no time and pushed off the bottom of the quagmire and streamed like a torpedo. He broke the surface with such force that sprayed green liquid in every direction. He roared and flung his head from side to side to rid his red mane from wetness, like a dog shaking itself dry. He grabbed my ribs, pulling his massive frame up with ease as if scaling a jungle gym, and clamped his claws around my throat.

He took over my senses and replayed the scene in Commander Heiden's office, where I interrupted Waller and Paulik. *What were they doing? Of all the officers in camp, why would Paulik associate with Gunter Waller?*

The red-haired monster roared a deep guttural cry, reached up through my throat, firmly placed a clawed hand on both sides of my jaw, and forced my head steady.

The silhouetted trees whizzed past as I increased my speed.

I squeezed my eyes shut, thinking that would rid myself of unwanted images, but I stumbled again. I somehow kept myself from splaying onto the ground and continued to speed up. I opened my eyes, and there amid the winding running path was Josef and Paulik before me. Both had their arms around the other.

The monster held my head and forced me to look. I denied any connection between the two. They were nothing alike. The beast jerked my jaw forward, causing me to run faster to keep from stumbling. The images started to spiral around each other and created a massive swirl of colors with a dark pinspot in the center. I watched the dizzying display and witnessed bolts of red flinging free like lightning bolts. The red flashes struck my chest and eyes with incredible pain. I ran faster.

My vision became a synergistic field of pulsating red lights as I discovered that Paulik was no different than Josef. They both used me to get further. How could I have been so stupid? Why did I not see this before? Am I so insecure that I am ignorant to the signs around me?

My legs pumped even faster as I tried to outrun the images and their meanings. The red-haired monster's grip slipped from my jaws and slid down. He grabbed a hold of a floating rib, causing a sharp pain to attack my right side. I lost my footing and sailed through the air. The whiteness of the snow-covered ground resting at the base of tree rushed into view. I closed my eyes and ducked my chin for the impact and hoped that I wouldn't collide with the tree's trunk.

The ground was hard. My breath was stolen from me as I tumbled and rolled several times. I came to a sliding stop on my back. The moon was partially shining through the clouds and bare tree branches. I remained there, feeling the blanket of snow melting under my fevered body.

*****

The spray from the shower doused me with a blanket of warmth, thawing my blood. I directed the stream to massage the isolated area of my solar plexus, which had become tight with the recent tumble. The pelting droplets rapidly tapped on my tense muscles, begging the release of the knots. The water rained down my body in rivulets and collected in a pool around my feet, before slowly ebbing and swirling through the drain in the middle of the floor.

I retrieved the bar of soap that was sitting on the ledge and rubbed the bar under the spewing water between my hands. I lathered my chest and alternately lifted each arm over my head to run the bar through the patches of dark blonde hairs. As I rinsed, the water pressure weakened as the shower next to me turned on.

Private Hemple's thin pale skin instantly turned pink from the water's warmth, giving him a healthy glow. His ear, bandaged from the attack on the train platform earlier, and cheeks were crimson as his sunken eyes peered from under the thick bridge of his brow to glance me up and down. He nodded and smirked, forecasting a predictable image running through his mind. He proudly stood with his hands anchoring his hip bones and swelled with pride from the effects my appearance evidently had on him.

I turned my back to him, explicitly dissuading him of any possible chance.

"How was your run?" he asked.

"Fine. It was fine," I flatly remarked.

"I'm starting my new position," he announced as he rinsed his head under the spigot.

"I'm sorry, what'd you say?" I shook my head free of water.

"That's why I wasn't able to run with you tonight. Not that it matters because you always leave me in the dust."

"Right."

"I'm going to be the SS Subaltern for the barrack's patrol," he gleefully responded.

The idea of Private Hemple becoming an SS Subaltern didn't make sense. He hadn't been in the camp long enough to be able to understand or handle the responsibilities that were required to accompany such a position. A subaltern position wasn't something to take lightly. "What about platform duty?" I asked with reservations.

"I'll continue that as well, like you do. This is an added responsibility." He smiled.

"When do you start?"

"I should be on the barrack's patrol by tomorrow. I'll be observing the barracks for the next couple of days before I get to perform my first arbitration. I should have ample time to get to know the prisoners."

I faced him.

He stood there smiling at me.

"Are you serious?"

"Yes, I'm the arbiter for the next several selections. I'll be working beside you when I come to barrack #265L. That's the barrack you are quartermaster for, isn't it?" he asked.

"You know it is."

"Isn't it terrific?"

"I haven't heard of any scheduled selection processes." I ignored celebrating his promotion.

He glanced down my torso and groped himself as nonchalantly as he possibly could, but hoping I'd notice. He offhandedly remarked, "We're over capacity now and are expecting to have more trains coming in. It's a way to free up space and remove the Musselman, myopes, and the sick prisoners that are of no use to the camp any longer."

"What do you mean Muselmann and myopes?"

"You know, the ones that aren't eating and the nearsighted ones," he proclaimed with self-righteousness. He turned his shower off, causing the pressure to surge through my spigot and sending me to step aside from the onset of warmth. He ran his hands over his body to remove the surfeit of water before grabbing a towel. "I'm meeting up with some of the other SS Subalterns right now, do you want to come?"

"No, that's all right. I think I'm going to stay here for a little longer." I turned back to the shower.

"Don't stay too long. You don't want to shrivel up and become a prune." He glanced at my lower body.

I closed my eyes, pretending he was no longer there, but still felt his lingering gaze. "Have a good night, Private Hemple." I glanced over my shoulder and caught him watching me as he dried off.

"Yes, sir, you too."

I closed my eyes again, letting the warm water continue its therapeutic massage on the back of my neck.

Hemple whistled while he dressed, a tune that was indistinguishable and uneven. He kept interrupting the melody with irregular rests as he donned on another article of clothing and then restarted at the same point of the music, which seemed to be a march of some type. His uninspiring arrangement didn't continue for long as he abruptly stopped in the middle of a musical phrase. The door opened and slammed closed, sending a rush of cold air to fill the shower room and a shiver up my spine. Hemple's insipid tune resounded as he passed by the window and dissipated into the chilly night air.

I soused my head under the hot water, thinking of Paulik and what it would be like if we weren't limited to sneaking around and parting glances.

I'd wake up in a big oak sleigh bed with white sheets and a down comforter. Paulik would be next to me, and a golden retriever curled at the foot. The sun would peek through the brown curtains, announcing the beginning of a new day. The golden stream of light would creep along the hardwood floor, scale the side of the comforter, and filter across his closed eyes, accenting the length of his lashes. His peaceful expression would be evident that he was dreaming of a place far away. I'd forgo the early chores, position myself next to him, and wrap his arms around my waist. I'd cradle his chocolate curls in the crook of my neck and kiss the crown of his head. He would slightly murmur as he nudged even closer to me, wrapping one of his legs over mine.

As I'd run my fingers through his curls, I'd realize the extent of my affection for him. He has become a part of my life as if he has grown and become an extended appendage of me. His breath was my breath. His pains were my pains. His joys were my joys. His life was my life.

The siren announced lights out and pulled my attention back to the bath house. I was alone with the shower raining down on me. The window darkened as the lights across the camp flickered out. This outage of artificial lighting allowed the fullness of the harvest moon to bathe me with its silvery glow and reflected off the water in a dazzling display of refractions.

The door opened and gently banged closed, followed by a current of cold air.

"Hello," I called out.

No answer.

I assumed that another officer was coming to take a late-night shower. But no one appeared. I stepped toward the dressing area to see if anyone was there. In the darkened corner, someone was squatting with their head in their hands.

I grabbed my towel and wrapped it around my waist as I walked to the cowering creature.

His knees were tucked up against his chest, face buried in his hands, and dark curls cascaded like waterfalls over his face. His slender shoulders were quivering from the chill. He must have come in here because the hot showers created warmth.

I gently touched his shoulder.

He scrambled to the far side of the room and crammed his face in the corner. Hunching his back forward, he wrapped his arms around his head for protection.

I cautiously approached, wondering if he injured himself in any way. I recognized his hands, those sleek and thin digits laced with black hair. I caressed his hands, leaning in and filling my senses with his familiar aroma. I wrapped myself around his shoulders and buried my face into the nape of his neck, filling my mouth full of his chocolate curls.

He shrugged his shoulders, slipped through my arms, and retreated to the area where he initially cowered. As I approached him, he confronted me with closed fists waving over his head, blindly striking my chest with the strength of a newborn, pounding with repetition.

"Paulik." I wrapped myself around his thin frame and pulled him into my chest so he couldn't hit me any longer.

He looked up at me with a glassy stare. His face was ashen, and his lips had a bluish tint to them. His dark eyes softened with recognition as he exhaustedly crumbled. He was suffering from hypothermia and was in dire need of attention.

I removed his worn boots as he leaned against the wall for support. His feet felt like ice and scabbed with sores. I rubbed his arches and toes to get the blood circulating again. He moaned. I removed his clothing and scooped him up into my arms. His body uncontrollably shivered as he pressed against my chest to absorb my body heat.

I carried him to the shower, stood him up with his back against my chest, my arms under his to support him, and I casually introduced him to the warm spray. He tried to immerse himself, but I held him back to keep him from going into shock or causing his heart to dive into dangerous rhythms. He reached like a child for the water, cupping handfuls to splash on his face and head. Gradually, he regained his senses and became himself again. He slithered around, reaching a hand around my head, leaned up on his toes, and kissed me. We stood there, considering each other's eyes, not saying a word, as the shower pulsated down. I guided us both into our baptism of warmth, where I began to bathe his body.

His energy revived, and his body temperature rose.

He held both sides of my face with his hands and stared into my eyes.

At that moment, I realized that what I harbored for him was real, and he shared the same feelings.

He inched closer and softly placed his lips on mine.

Chapter 30

The early December morning's sun slipped over the barracks' roofs and momentarily stole my sight as I exited the mess hall. I tilted my head and the brim of my cap down to shield my eyes from the onset of its orange-yellow brightness. The pathway was blanketed with new snow, giving the campsite a pristine appearance. I filled my lungs with the unsullied crisp air.

A low siren moaned mournfully and quickly raged into a full harsh and piercing wail. My curiosity scrambled to find the motive for this unscheduled alert. Could there have been a prisoner who escaped or some other infringement not adequately instructed to us during our intense training sessions? As the groaning siren moaned a second wail, I quickly stepped out of the path of several officers rushing out of the hall, stuffing the remnants of their eggs and bacon into their mouths.

I redirected my path toward the barrack # 267L with a newly intended importance to make observations on the cooperations of the prisoners during this unpredicted lockdown. I mitigated between people darting across my path.

As I enter the barrack, Private Hemple stood stiff-backed with a reddish face and straining his neck while trying to demand information from the inhabitants.

"Who is the Blockältester?" he barked, which produced no response. He grew agitated as he watched the prisoners milling about without paying him any heed. His jugular vein pulsed in his neck. "Where is the Blockältester?"

Still, there was no response.

The prisoners clamored down from the various leveled bunk beds and different areas from within the space to form controlled and yet chaotic clumps. They removed their clothing, piled them at their feet, and lined up in two straight lines down the length of the barrack, leaving an aisle down the center to pass. They stood shivering and exposed to the elements. Their bodies were representative of different degrees of malnutrition, disease, or brutal beatings. It was difficult to decipher what was dirt, bruises, scars, or fresh wounds that marred their flesh.

Hemple started pacing straight-legged with his hands firmly clasped behind his back down the middle of the aisle. He paused, turned his head, and furrowed his brow as he began interrogating an elderly inmate by pressing his face extremely close. "Are you the Blockältester?"

The prisoner didn't understand and blankly looked at Private Hemple, not even blinking an eyelid.

I whispered, "Private Hemple, what's the problem here?"

"These prisoners are being insubordinate and refusing to cooperate." He directed his answer to me but remained intimidating the prisoner.

"Hemple, they don't speak German," I calmly said. "They're mostly Polish and Yugoslavians."

He spun on his heels with bewilderment. "Why didn't you inform me?" He withdrew from the elderly prisoner and stepped into the middle of the aisle again, scanning the rows of naked men.

"You didn't ask." I tried not to sound smug.

"How do you keep records if you can't speak with them?" he demanded.

"I only observe, there's no need to communicate," I replied.

He glanced over the sea of men and then back at me. "They must have picked up some German since they've been here," he challenged. "They've been here long enough. They're just pretending not to understand."

"What are you trying to find out?" I asked.

He puffed up his chest and elongated his neck to appear taller and in control of the situation. "I'm trying to locate the Blockältester."

Paulik was in the back of the barrack, passing out cards to the prisoners.

With a nod of my head, I directed Hemple's attention toward Paulik. "Your Blockältester is doing his job. He's the one handing out the cards."

He studied Paulik intensely, watching him hand a card to each prisoner. "What are the cards for?" he quietly asked, proving he was unprepared.

"The cards have the prisoners' name, number, profession, age, and nationality," I whispered. "You'll be collecting them during the arbitration process."

"I see," he admitted while watching Paulik. His mouth tensed. "Why didn't he make himself known when I first came in?"

"I'm sure he wasn't immediately at your disposal because he was securing the entrances," I replied. "From what I'm informed, he must account for all the prisoners, lock the entrances, and prepare for your inspection."

"I'm aware of the proceedings, thank you," he defensively replied. "He's the Blockältester?"

I nodded.

"I thought the Blockältester was an elder prisoner?" He clicked his tongue on the roof of his mouth. "And isn't he the commander's assistant?" He glanced over at me with a knowing expression.

I met his challenge and looked deep into his eyes. Without as much as a flinch, I admitted, "Yes, he is."

He nervously studied Paulik.

"So, you see, he knows what he is doing," I added.

Once Paulik passed out all the cards to the prisoners, he approached Hemple and offered him a small stack of the ones that were unclaimed. As Private Hemple accepted the pile, Paulik retired to the far side and aligned himself with the prisoners on the left.

Hemple automatically fanned through the cards, not knowing what to do with them.

"Those are the cards of the prisoners that have passed away during the night, exercises, or other means. You'll want to file them with Commander Heiden," I advised.

"Yes. Of course," Private Hemple distractedly muttered. He continued looking at the lifeless placards and began to realize the importance of the responsibility of his new promotion. His face softened from the stony and pretentious adaptation he adopted from Commander Heiden's disposition. Private Hemple felt the weight of the lost lives represented on the 3×5 cardstock resting in his palms. He mindlessly shuffled through the cards, singling one out, read the stats for a long time, and flipped the card over to discover a pink triangle imprinted on the back. His eyes examined the marking, as if trying to memorize it: how the center extended to three points, the color had faded over time, the outline was a darker hue, and the far-left end seemed smeared, as if it had been bleeding across the surface. He immediately flipped it back and shoved it securely amid the other cards. He refocused on his duties by shaking his head with three quick ticks to the right and tucked the cards absently into his breast pocket. He returned to his sternly demeanor with a stone face, his arms behind his back and his chest puffed out.

Paulik opened a door and motioned the prisoners to file into the Tagesraum, located to the right of the front entrance. It was a small room about 7×4 square feet and used to hand out clothing and supplies to new prisoners. The room was apparently too little for all the inmates, but Paulik had been instructed to make sure that they all fit in, standing shoulder to shoulder, stomachs to backs, thighs to thighs. He continued leading them until the barrack was empty. The prisoners would remain in this holding room until the arbitration began, which could be up to several hours.

Private Hemple, Paulik, and I remained silent in the empty barrack, waiting for the signal. Occasionally, animalistic groans came from the men in the Tagesraum due to exhaustion, heat, and crammed like sardines. They started out like shallow and hollow moans that were almost inaudible, but grew into deep and gravely growls as they rose in volume and pitch. The sounds eerily resonated against the rafters.

Finally, there was a knock on the barrack's door. Paulik immediately turned the latch to permit another SS Subaltern to enter.

He approached Private Hemple. "Private, we're ready for the arbitration. Please assume your positions and have your Blockältester open the outside door leading from the Tagesraum into the courtyard."

"Yes, sir," replied Hemple and followed with a straight-arm salute.

The SS Subaltern marched out of the barrack.

Hemple looked at me with bewildered eyes, expecting guidance.

I indicated for him to follow Paulik.

Paulik led us out into the yard where a group of superior officers was waiting with clipboards. He indicated for Hemple to stand halfway between the barrack's entrance and the door leading to the Tagesraum.

I positioned myself to Hemple's left.

The afternoon's warmth caused the blanketed snow to puddle, creating patches of pools covered with a thin veil of ice throughout the yard. The clouds gathered and heavily hung with grayness, promising to unleash a new fury of coldness and precipitation.

Paulik gracefully leaped over a good-sized puddle to stand in the soft mud by the Tagesraum's door. He patiently waited for Private Hemple's orders to open the door.

Private Hemple teetered on his heels and blankly stared into space as his breath streamed white clouds from his nostrils.

"Start the proceedings," an official's deep voice beckoned from behind us, causing Hemple to stiffen with fear for his lack of knowledge of the proceedings.

"The Blockältester is waiting for your orders to open the door and begin the arbitration," I shared with Private Hemple.

He craned his head toward me with his brow crinkling together and looked at me as if I was speaking in tongues.

"Once he opens the door, the prisoners will come out, one at a time, and jog between the Tagesraum door and the main entrance to the barracks. During this time, you are to evaluate the prisoners' health and see if he is beneficial to the camp. You'll decide if the prisoner's card goes to the Blockältester or me. Then you, and only you, will decide which pile to exterminate."

"Exterminate?" he protested with an air of shock.

"Yes, exterminate," I reiterated. "That's arbitration. You're aware of this, aren't you?"

"Of course I'm aware. What do you think? That I'm not aware of my duties? I know that we're overpopulated, and this is the way to make room for other prisoners." He looked away defiantly.

"Start the arbitration!" commanded the voice from behind.

Hemple glanced back at me.

I nodded toward Paulik.

Hemple's beady eyes darted toward Paulik and motioned for him to open the door.

As Paulik opened the door, a wave of heat expelled and plastered our faces with the musty scent comprised of body odor, urine, feces, and infection that had been collecting and fermenting in the rafters of the tremendously warm and confined space. The opening of the door sent a moan of relief from the cramped prisoners as the cold air replaced the heat.

Paulik returned to stand at Private Hemple's right. He indicated for the prisoners to come out one at a time, by waving in the gray air.

The first prisoner came out and waded through puddles, breaking the thin layer of ice with his bare feet, and tried to hide the degree of coldness from registering on his face. He handed Private Hemple his card as he shifted his weight from foot to foot to acclimate the chill to his nakedness. The man appeared to be in his midthirties, which meant that he was more than likely in his mid to late twenties. His lean torso still had evidence of a once-muscular frame and tone. His skin was pinkish and covered with sufficient body hair, indicating his adequate health. If he weren't in average health, the hairs would have fallen out due to malnutrition or other possible diseases. His eyes were bright and clear, giving more evidence that this prisoner has not been here a long time.

Private Hemple looked him up and down for a period, glancing between the card in his hand and the naked man before him. He had the prisoner turn to observe the backside and motioned for him to jog from the Tagesraum door to the front entrance of the barrack and back. On the second pass, he handed the prisoner's card to Paulik and proudly puffed his chest out and bellowed, "Next!"

Paulik motioned for the first prisoner to return to the barrack and waved the next man out.

The prisoner that emerged was quite older with slumped, rounded shoulders. His excess and loose skin hung about him like an oversized wrinkled shirt. He sauntered toward Private Hemple, gingerly wading through the shards of ice-crusted mud to hand him his card. His skin was covered in lesions of raised purple and edged with midnight blue. His chest rattled from a deep cough that gurgled in his throat before escaping into the cold air. His skin was nearly hairless, except for the patch of curls reaching out from his groin. His eyes squinted to focus on the surroundings, giving evidence of his nearsightedness.

Hample cocked his head to the side in disgust and waved for the prisoner to jog.

The man attempted. The elements usurped his strength, and he crumbled upon his bony knees from his forward motion. He remained motionless and exhausted as he sank into the icy mud, covering his arms and legs. He tried to pull his hips up to stand, but slipped, falling face-first into the mud and caking his entire front side. He idly remained there as if he were dead. When it seemed like he was about to give up, he arched his spine with such determination, pulled himself to his feet, and proceeded to trollop through the muck.

Hemple handed the card to Paulik, who accepted it with reservation and glanced over to me.

"Next!" called Private Hemple.

Chapter 31

The holiday season's staples of holly and ivy, Tannenbaum, gingerbread, and presents seemed different during this year's December celebrations. Beside the nonappearance of these colorful and fragrant adornments, there was a sense that something was missing, not quite right. Maybe the campsite wasn't donned with lights shooting their hues into the night sky, or candlelit trees framed by window sills, wreaths hanging on every door, the hustle and bustle of last-minute shopping, the absence of Saint Nicholas peering around each corner, and the nutcrackers. The omission of the Christmas spirit loomed and hung heavily in each corner and crevice of the barracks and barbed wire fences.

I roamed the campgrounds hoping to bump into Paulik on his way to or from the barrack, the latrine, or Commander Heiden's office. I wanted to see his kind coffee-colored eyes, full lips, and inhale his unique scent. I craved to touch him.

A dampness crept through my overcoat, causing me to clutch the front of my collar tighter around my neck. I forged forward against the gusts of wind whipping around the barracks and sending me staggering backward. The drab evening tried mustering up snowflakes but could only produce drizzles of sleet. I anchored myself around a wooden pole as another harsh artic wind ambushed me, trying to protect my facial skin from the stinging ice pellets.

I quietly start humming a melodic version of "Stille Nacht."

*****

The festoons of green garland comprised of branches of pine and fir needles accented with roses, apples, wafers, and red berries draped between the high wooden beams ran the length of the church. The organ's pipes filled the rafters with the procession of music. The stained-glass window above the altar, lit by the full moon in the midnight sky, cast its colorful image of the Christ Child in Mary's arms throughout the chamber with reds, oranges, yellows, and blues.

Sister Margot guided me to a pew, where I sat on the edge of the hard wooden bench and focused on the crucifixion of the near-naked Jesus floating above the burning candles. The flickering of the wicks caused the ivory Jesus to appear as if he was breathing. I imagined his diaphragm expanding and deflating from the depth of his breath. His beautiful lean body glistened with yellow and outlined with the blueness from the flames and transmitted an elegance that caused my breathing to labor. I followed the lines of his extended arm, down the roundness of his shoulder, over the curve of his elbow, narrowed to the wrist, and expanded out to the delicate hand. I took in the way each digit gracefully curved caused by the pinch from the spike that was driven into the fleshiness of his palm and anchored him to the wooden cross. I scaled down the right side of his lean torso, where the fatal wound was inflicted below his rib cage and just above the small cloth that loosely draped around his slender hips. My desire to see beyond the provocative drapery caused warmth to ignite behind my cheeks and set them ablaze with red. I couldn't look away. I stopped breathing. I was hypnotized with this image of the celestial being. An image I have seen many times before. But tonight, for some reason, it had cast a spell upon me as if I was seeing it for the first time. My fascination fixated on the curvature of his ankles as one foot placed upon the other. His heels resembled broken wings folded to the sides as his toes aligned into oneness. I was intrigued by the way the third and final skewer held both feet securely to a small triangular platform that was attached to the wooden beam.

The enchantment was interrupted by a little doll of fruit placed in my upturned and empty palms resting on my lap. I had received this Christmas toy from the letter I left for the Christkind, who was the Christ Child's messenger. I took such care to decorate the note by sprinkling sugar on the letters to make them look like twinkling stars. I placed the message on the windowsill so the beautiful fair-haired imp with golden wings dressed in a long white robe and a glistening crown of candles would have no trouble finding it. I was in such awe that she had left me this doll of fruit that I dared not taste its sweetness. I coveted it as close to my side as I could and carried it with me everywhere. I must have dropped it during the magical charm that bestowed upon me by the Jesus figure. I immediately secured my Christmas toy between my hands and pulled it to my chest. I looked up at the woman sitting next to me, who smiled.

Sister Margot was the mother figure that I became very much enamored, and Father Michael became the father figure. I liked the family we created at St. Emmanuel's, just the three of us.

*****

A hand touched my shoulder. Warmth immediately flushed throughout my being as Paulik smiled. His face blotched with an edge of blueness from the frigid air, and ice speckled his hair.

He looked at me with kind brown eyes as he took hold of my hand. He opened my fingers and placed a tiny package in my palm. The gift's wrapping was the same material of his shirt and the ends were knotted to keep the enclosure secure. He closed my fingers tightly around the present.

I opened my hand, and I untied the knots to reveal an angel carved out of a small piece of wood. Her wings were delicately hand-painted with white swirls and accented with flecks of blue. Her face was without any details, leaving the head to be blank and expressionless. Her triangular gown was smoothed down by filing.

Paulik lifted my hand, with the angel encased within it, and grazed my knuckles with the softness of his lips.

"Klein? Is everything all right?" A voice slipped through the roar of the wind to reach my ears.

Hemple braced himself against gale and sleet, smiling.

Paulik dropped my hand and scampered away, teetering and sidestepping as the wind tried to lift him off his feet.

"I'm fine," I stated.

"What are you doing out here?" He leaned against the opposite side, resting his head against the pole. "What was that all about?"

I chose not to reply. I slid the carved angel into my coat pocket.

Hemple pressed his shoulder against me.

For some reason, I didn't back away.

He tilted his head and arched his brows high on his forehead. "I'm going to the mess hall for some dinner. Would you like to join me?"

I shrugged and braced myself against another upsurge of icy wind.

"You're shivering," Hemple stated. He placed a caring hand on my shoulder.

"I'm fine," I protested.

"How long have you been out here?"

"Not too long." The coldness was settling in my throat, causing me to cough.

"It's freezing out here. Come with me to the mess hall and have a Christmas meal." He encouraged with a crooked smile that made his eyes twinkle. "They're serving a traditional holiday meal of liver dumpling soup, fish, pork roast, goose, even wiener schnitzel." He laughed, causing me to join in. "I heard there's red and white sauerkraut, beer, Glühwein, and mulled cider. They also have Christstollen, Lebkuchen, marzipan, Dresden Stollen, and—"

"Okay, okay, enough. You've convinced me, all right?"

"Great." He offered his arm.

I hesitated a moment before refusing to take his arm. Instead, I gently pushed his shoulder, guiding him toward the well-lit mess hall. As I was leading him, I looked back toward the barrack, shoving my hand in my coat pocket to hold the angel in my palm.

Chapter 32

"Thanks for inviting me to dinner." I smiled at Private Hemple as he leaned against the mess hall door, leading to a dark and frigid night. The searchlight swept around, exposing harsh angles of the snow-covered grounds.

"My pleasure." He smiled as he waited for me to exit and followed me out. "I'm meeting with some of the other officers. We're going to have some cocktails and look for Saint Nic's reindeer. Would you like to join us?"

"As appealing as that sounds, I have to do my last barrack check."

Hemple scratched the back of his neck. "I can go with you if you like the company."

I glanced toward the barracks and shook my head. "You go ahead, and I'll catch up with you later."

"You sure?"

"Yes."

"Promise?" He reminded me of a child.

"Promise, and even cross my heart."

He pranced in a circle. "All right. Don't take too long. We'll be in the privates' quarters." He started to rush off but turned toward me again. "You'll come, right?"

"I'll be there. I can be there sooner if you let me get my duties done for the night."

"Yes, yes." His excitement was refreshing. "I'll see you momentarily." He darted off toward the privates' quarters. As he ran down the cleared path, he leaped in the air. "Yahoo!"

I made my way to the barracks, thinking of the times I spent Christmas with Inga and her family—the traditional celebration, the elaborate meal, and the presentations of presents. I remembered the sitting room filled with people: Mr. and Mrs. Rhoden, Father Michael, Sister Margot, Professor Weinholtz, friends and relatives, Inga (and her latest boyfriend), and myself. Inevitably, the celebration would always end up around the piano with me playing Christmas carols while everyone sang, especially "Stille Nacht."

A hand grabbed my arm and led me past the barrack.

Paulik, drenched and shaking, apparently had been waiting for me to come out of the mess hall. He guided me. He pressed me against the side of the barrack as the searchlight swept past. Before I could speak, he pulled me behind him through a snowdrift around the back of the other barracks. His breathing labored from the cold, and his hands shook.

I followed him past the administration building, the train depot, through the lines of people walking down the stairs to the yards to be checked in. He guided me through a covered archway leading to the far end of camp, through a wooden door, to the back of the dark and odorous boiler house.

In the corner was a makeshift bed of rumpled wool blankets and a small pillow that he presented as if it was a present. The look of expectation filled his eyes.

I could only look at him, speechless.

He smiled, slowly walked toward me, and pressed his small frame against my chest. He extended up on his toes and guided my overcoat from my shoulders, folding it in half and placing it on a crate. He circled me several times, studying me, before stopping and unknotting my necktie. With flare, he pulled the tie through the collar and dropped it on the cement flooring. He walked behind me, caressing the nape of my neck with the bridge of his nose, reached around, unbuttoned my shirt, and peeled it back, trapping my arms to my side. He playfully bit my earlobe and nestled his head against mine, working his way back in front of me. He glanced up with a mischievous smile before pulling up the undershirt and traveling his lips across my breasts. He rested his head on my chest, and his hands fumbled with my belt as he attempted to free the passion. He masterfully unclasped the buckle, opened the fly, peeled away the wool pants, and buried himself in my loins, swallowing me deep. Artfully, he worked my shaft, causing me to lose the only chance of inhalation, instigating my body to react with a flood of tremors and triggering every muscle to clench. His eagerness and my cravings became one.

I managed to free my arms from my shirt sleeves and pulled him off my saliva-soaked hardness before guiding him onto his back. I admired the perfection of his nakedness, the display and patterns of hair covering his thighs, chest, and arms.

He coyly lay there, beckoning me to join him.

I lowered myself, first tasting his lips and feeling his fur-covered chest caress mine. Last to come in contact were our hips and thighs as our firmness pressed against each other. Once our bodies were completely in contact, we explored each other's faces with kisses. His body writhed beneath me, sending electrical shock waves through my being and driving me to the edge. I rose up on my knees, gasping for deep breaths to keep from exploding, for I knew I wanted this to last longer.

His devilish grin made me chuckle.

His fingertips sent nettles through my skin as he traced my abdomen and reached around to grasp my buttocks. He pulled himself up and placed his warm lips on my navel, causing me to shiver. He leaned back, guiding me back down on top of him and offering himself fully to me.

I hesitated and looked at his face with concern.

Without a word, he invited me by tilting his hips and wrapping his legs around my back.

I blindly aligned myself while staring into his dark brown eyes burning with desire.

He held me at bay for a moment while he took a deep breath and adjusted to my girth, which sent a shiver of cold sweat to escape throughout every pore in my body. He opened his eyes and looked at me, taking a stream of air deeply into his diaphragm, causing himself to relax and allowing me to reach the deepest point of entry.

We began to pulse to our interruption of an allegro, creating slow and long rhythms from our execution of giving and taking. I spread Paulik's hairy legs farther apart, and I leaned in and started kissing his mouth as I rode him.

His kisses reflected the pressure that was building as he gently bit my lower lip.

My hips continued to pump, gathering speed and causing sweat to cover our bodies.

Each thrust caused him to thrive and whimper between kisses.

We continued tasting each other's lips and tongues as our bodies trembled, shuddered, and quaked.

I paused and looked down at his face contorted with pleasure.

His eyes closed, forehead wrinkled, and his mouth gaped open with his tongue begging for more. In this one instance, I was again overwhelmed by his beauty, his coloring, his desire. I was emotionally connected with this man in a way I never knew was possible. A pleasure beyond the physicality of being with him was empowering, enlightening, and even spiritual.

An amber glow radiated off him and spilled all around us, engulfing us in a blanket of admiration. Our entanglement was symbiotic, where we had entirely come together as one, breathed as one, and moved as one. I debated if I should continue or extend this moment, delaying the ultimate zenith of release.

Paulik swiveled his hips ever so slightly, sending me to the point of no return. I couldn't withhold the floodgates any longer. This little pivot from his passion-filled muscles liberated me with an explosion of agony and bliss, filling him with my devotion.

The convulsions of my ecstasy triggered his eruption, showering ribbons of milky liquid all over his chest and stomach in various sizes of splattering pools.

We remained stiff as if we had just experienced a near death of some kind, unable to move as our hearts skipped several beats. We both gasped for air like a fish out of water. Sweat dripped off my forehead and nose and cascaded onto Paulik as he glistened from his perspiration. Exhaustedly, I lowered myself onto his sticky chest, and we kissed once more before ceding to complete fatigue, intertwined within each other's arms.

I rolled off and positioned myself alongside him. My fingers and toes tingled.

We watched the shadows dance across the ceiling as he rested his damp forehead amid the curve of my shoulder, and he played with the sprout of blond hair running down my abdomen. We said nothing. We listened to our breath, in unison, accompanied by the harsh hissing from the machinery that surrounded us.

Paulik lifted his head and searched the darkened space with darting eyes.

My palm caressed the side of his face, trying to reassure him of our safety.

He withdrew from my touch as his head snapped toward the back of the room.

"What is it?" I searched the blackness of the far corner.

"Shhhh!" He covered my mouth with his hand.

I strained to listen and distinguish between the hissing of the machines and any other strange noise.

"Did you hear something?" I quietly asked.

His smile tried to reassure me that it was nothing, but his eyes were almost black.

I sat up with my back leaning against the cold brick wall. I scanned the darkness to see if I could see what Paulik was sensing. All I saw were black piping connecting the machinery to the vents in the ceiling, like rows and rows of arms supporting the roof overhead, reminding me of the Royal Ballet Corps's performance of *Swan Lake*. Each ballerina's arms were in perfect unison with the girl before her, dancing as one.

He wrapped himself around me and shuddered.

I encased my arms around his frail frame, running my fingers through his dark curls, down his bony spine, and came to rest on the curve of his hip. His fear seeped into me, migrating throughout my being, and attacked my soul. What if I never see him again? What if something takes us away from each other?

He grabbed my face with clenched fists, stared deep into my eyes, and kissed me hard and passionately.

From the far corner came a hollow sound.

I scampered up, grabbed my trousers and pistol, and quickly made my way through the maze of pipes and furnaces. I came to a corner bathed in a bluish hue from the moonlight sneaking through the cracked window. I discovered an empty pint bottle of scotch, a cigarette balancing on the ledge of the windowsill, and a milky white splatter dripping down the side of the wall.

Chapter 33

"What is this, Kommandant Schultz?"

"Don't ask questions. Follow the commands!" barked Commanding Officer Schultz, standing two inches from my face. He peered through his wire-rim glasses, daring me to flinch or question his authority.

I had been standing at attention and listening to his demands for the past twenty minutes in this subzero temperature of February.

The clouds hung very low over the campsite like a gray wool blanket resting atop the tall smokestacks, littering the ground with ashen flakes. The thick sulfurous smoke poured out of the dank silos, causing the snow to gray as it settled into mounds, hiding the factory-like buildings. I wasn't familiar with this locale of the camp; I had always been on the lower east side. Here, it seemed lifeless, a place no one would expect a second promotion would take him.

"Do you understand the instructions?"

"Yes. I count the people, then close and lock the door," I said.

"Gut!" He inched closer to my face and stared at me with his ice-cold blue eyes.

"But what is this place?"

"Silence!" Our noses touched.

"But my promotion, Commander …" I was still trying to understand.

"*Don't ask questions!*" He spat onto my face with the punctuation of each word. "*You understand?*"

I understood that I wasn't supposed to ask questions, just follow orders. But I was confused about where we were and why we were here. I uttered, "Ja, Commandant Schultz."

"Gut!" He turned on his heels and snapped them together, sending a sharp crack into the cold, stale air. Militantly, he marched straight-legged across the grounds to slip into a small wooden shed. He sat at a control panel behind a dusty pane of glass collecting dirty snow on the outside windowsill. From the belly of the hut, Private Hemple appeared and sat next to Commander Heiden and Commander Schultz, looking up under his brows with a pained expression.

The cold bit at my toes through the thick leather boots and the two pairs of woolen stockings. I shifted my weight from one foot to the other, ever so carefully, so I wouldn't attract attention. All I must do was stand here and count the people as they entered through the small doorway and then latch the lock behind them. But something didn't feel right.

Singing rang over the mounds of dirty snow, emanating from the direction of the barracks on the east side. People were skipping, jumping, and winding along the worn path, their arms praising and rejoicing toward the heaven of grayness and singing to their God in full harmonic tones.

Their song warmed and revived me. I unlatched the door as they approached and opened it for them.

They saw the exit and quieted to silence.

Heavy flakes of snow landed on my shoulders and the brim of my cap.

All at once, they began to rush for the door, smiling and laughing.

I smiled in return.

They blew kisses and thanked me, while some even threw themselves to my feet for rewarding them with freedom.

The joyous revelers continued to enter through the opening as I mentally took note of how many had passed. "Eleven, twelve, thirteen …"

A single person wasn't celebrating. He walked tranquilly with his eyes fixated on the beaten path, his shaved head hung down, concealing his identity, and his shoulders were rounded forward as if he was being pulled toward the core of the earth.

The loneliness of this figure against the background of glorification brought a revelation to my eyes—this wasn't a doorway to the outside world, and these people weren't being freed to return to their homes and families.

The lone figure stopped in front of me, and his face was drawn and beaten, lips cracked and swollen, and eyes sunken and dark. He looked at me for a long moment before his tired eyes lit up and revealed their almond color.

My heart sank, recognizing these eyes belonged to Paulik, the man I made love to in the broiler house, the man I kissed in the mess hall, Commander Heiden's office, and in the latrine. This man and I created a secret language by communicating through our eyes. Someone must have found out—that's why I was ordered to perform different and odd jobs before reporting here and lost track of him. A month and a half of wondering where he was and how he was doing. A long month of trying to relocate him—they must have transferred him to another barrack.

Our eyes stay locked.

I tried to console him with our secret language.

He came closer, searching my face with those fantastic almond eyes, tilted his head to the side, reached up, and wrapped his arms around my neck. He whispered, "Goodbye, Hans." He kissed my lips lightly and walked through the doorway without looking back.

I was unable to move. I didn't hear Commander Schultz screaming at me; I was deaf. I didn't feel the sharp blow to the back of my neck; I was numb. I didn't notice my face lying in the snow; I was blind. I didn't feel them lift me up and toss me through the door; I was senseless.

Once inside, Paulik scooped me up into his arms and kissed my mouth.

His smell brought back all those moments we spent together.

He pulled me closer to his chest.

I heard the thumps of his heart beating and felt the love he harbored for me as he caressed my throbbing head.

The door latched, sending an echo throughout the metal chamber. A hissing sounded as the heat began to invade the occupants with waves of oranges, reds, and yellows. The heat's waves caused people's limbs to waver and contort in an odd form of ballet.

My legs took on a mind of their own, lifting gently off the floor.

Paulik tried desperately to keep my legs down. He knew what was happening from all those days in Commander Heiden's office. Paulik knew. His arms began to perform their graceful moves—he fought hard against the lure of the waves and guided me to my feet. He wrapped one of his legs around my waist, an arm around my shoulder, and buried his face in the arch of my neck.

Our fingers intertwined as our kissing palms lifted into the fifth position above our heads and slipped apart to float down next to our sides.

Paulik arched his back, revealing his tender neck, which I wasted no time in caressing with my lips.

Others vacillated, with their arms and legs fluttering in unnatural adagios. One performer demonstrated several pirouettes before a demi-plié with his arms pulsating to his side. Another performed a high third arabesque, before lifting himself and floating on an invisible orange wave. A man stood with his right arm in the second position, allongéd his hand, and reached outward, combrés en round en dedans, and lowered his head toward his knees in complete exhaustion and enveloped himself elegantly over a person curled into a ball below him. An older man brushed his foot through the first position into arabesque for an extended moment before offering his hands to an imaginary yellow partner and grand jetéd to the far corner.

Paulik pulled my face to his and tried to say something, but his sound was swallowed by the growing humming noise.

I looked deeply into his brown eyes and saw the feelings that he held for me. I tried to relay the same feelings I had for him.

Our bodies began to glisten with perspiration as we continued to meld together, draining ourselves with the endless contortions of this ballet.

It didn't take long before I realized how lethargic and languid our steps became.

Paulik tried to fight the temptations of the heat and begged for me to continue the tondu en ronde.

My arms and legs became heavy, and I fell out of timing with him as my strikes on the floor with my toes became delayed. It became hard to catch my breath. My eyes fluttered.

Paulik wrapped himself tighter around me and guided me to the center of the stage. He bowed to me as he held my hand.

I bowed to him in return.

He positioned himself in front of me, placing my hands on his slim hips. He extended his right leg and arched his back so his head rested on my shoulder. He développed his right leg to a full extension. I placed my hand under the extended leg and lifted him into the air. His body extended out from my chest at a forty-five-degree angle. He split his legs again as he alit on the floor. I lifted our clasped hands, and he pirouetted under my arm and wound into my chest. He placed his hand on my shoulder, and he looked deep into my eyes. Without a word, I read his thoughts, and we waltzed the entire stage. Everyone else had ceased their movements as we continued. Our spinning slowed until we came to a halt.

The audience stood on their feet. The professor applauded vigorously with a cigarette between his lips, Ian and Walter with their arms around each other's shoulder. Josef, looking as beautiful as ever, pressed his fingertips to his lips and blew us a kiss. I scanned the entire audience, and I couldn't find Stefan or Inga. Out from back emerged my mother. Her petite body was draped in a pale blue chiffon dress that ethereally billowed as she walked toward us. She beamed with pride, and her eyes expressed their approval of Paulik.

Paulik pressed my face to his. "Kiss me," he urgently demanded.

Mother took our hands and led us offstage.

Epilogue

The moon provided the only light as I ran through the tall grass leading to the lake. If I could get on to the other side of the lake, there was a path that led to the river, and I could run all night.

"Halt!"

I dared not look; I ran. I ran as hard and as fast I could as I rounded the oak tree leading to the lake's clearing.

A crack sounded through the night as the trunk of the tree barred the bullet's penetration, sending bark flying into my face.

I crouched but kept running. The lake's clearing provided many options. I went left, hoping the Nazi would go right. I rounded the lake, past the towering rock that people liked to jump from, and curved with the bend.

"Halt!"

A soldier posed on the opposite side of the lake, bent over from exhaustion of trying to keep up with me. He stood and lifted the rifle to eye level.

A flash of light coincided with a pop, sending a speeding bullet to whiz past my ear like a gnat.

I ran. I accelerated and darted into the thick trees leading to the river.

Panting filled my head as I continued running. I ran and ran and lost track of time. I ran along the thickets, tearing my flesh with thorns and thistles. I ran.

The sky began to pale as the morning sun rose. I ran. I continued running, ignoring the pain in my legs and lungs. I ran.

A barn appeared in the clearing ahead, and I ran for it. I ran faster in case the Nazi was still behind me. The opening would give him a clear shot. I ran.

I reached the barn and slid in through the door. I scaled the ladder to the hay loft and peeked out. Nothing. The Nazi must have given up. My legs vibrated from the exertion, and I dry-heaved. Exhaustion overpowered me, and I crawled in the hay and rolled on my back.

I dreamt that I was still running. There was no place to go. I just kept running.

"Wake up!"

I lifted my heavy eyelids. A pitchfork was inches from my face.

"Who are you?" a voice demanded.

I cleared my eyes. A young woman poised with the pitchfork ready to stab me if needed.

I tried to sit up.

"Stay down."

I fell back down.

"Who are you? What do you want?"

I lifted my hand to gently push the pitchfork to the side.

"Don't move."

I gave up and lay there.

"Tell me, who you are!"

"My name is Stefan Joffe, and I am a student."

To be continued.

About the Author

John-Michael Lander's first novel, *Surface Tension*, relied on his experiences as a competitive diver and traveling the world. He has had a diverse life that includes acting (theater, film, and television), teaching, drawing, and writing. He was accepted in the Institute of Children's Literature and Long Ridge Writers Group and is currently pursuing a PhD in education in Curriculum, Instruction, and Assessment. He taught for seven years at Stivers High School for the Arts in downtown Dayton, Ohio. *Saving Balleria* is in the editing process, and *Surface Tension: The Hollywood Years*, David Matthew's continuing story, is in development. By day he is an independent consultant for Arbonne, a health and wellness business.